The WRIGHT SECRET

Also by K.A. Linde

AVOIDING SERIES

Avoiding Commitment
Avoiding Responsibility
Avoiding Intimacy
Avoiding Decisions
Avoiding Temptation

RECORD SERIES

Off the Record
On the Record
For the Record
Struck from the Record

ALL THAT GLITTERS SERIES

Diamonds
Gold
Emeralds
Platinum
Silver

TAKE ME SERIES

Take Me for Granted
Take Me with You

STAND-ALONE

Following Me
The Wright Brother
The Wright Boss
The Wright Mistake

ASCENSION SERIES

The Affiliate
The Bound
The Consort

The WRIGHT SECRET

K.A. LINDE

To every woman who kicked, scratched, bit, and clawed her way to the top. Who refused to smile when it was demanded of her. Who wouldn't back down and "act like a lady." Who ignored the critics who said women were too emotional and that it couldn't be done.

We are doing it.

One

Morgan

I was going to do it.

I was going to ask out my brother's best friend.

Patrick and I had known each other since we were kids. But I was far from the doe-eyed fifteen-year-old who had fallen head over heels for him all those years ago. I was the CEO of Wright Construction. It was a position I had been working toward my entire life. Now that I was here, I wanted the other thing I'd been waiting for.

"Paging Morgan," David said, waving a hand in my face. "You in there?"

I cleared my head. "Yes, I'm here."

He cocked a half-smile in my direction, dropped the pen in his hand, and leaned back in the plush leather conference chair. Everyone else had already disappeared for the afternoon. Even my brother and the former CEO, Jensen, had left a half hour ago. Only me, the workaholic, and my new CFO, David Calloway, were still hard at work.

"I think we should call it a day," David said.

"You go ahead. I'm going to stick around for a couple more hours to look this over." I gestured at the stack of paperwork in front of me.

"And I thought I worked too much."

"You do."

"What does that say about you?"

"I work an obscene amount."

David laughed. "I'm not used to having a boss who works more than me."

"Well, get used to it. Expect early mornings and late, late nights."

"My favorite." He shoved his laptop into his messenger bag and straightened out his suit.

David had recently moved from Silicon Valley to our humble town in Lubbock, Texas, for the job. He was still adjusting to the flat, dusty, and dry place I called home. I loved the idea of trees and hills and oceans but maybe for vacation. David would come to love Lubbock, too. It just usually took a year.

"Don't work yourself to death," he said.

"Can't make any promises."

David waved as he breezed out of the conference room. I liked him. He was funny and charming and easy to work with. I couldn't imagine walking this new road with anyone else.

I was in a transitional period, moving into CEO, while Jensen started his new architecture company. Since I had moved up from CFO, I was working with David to get him acquainted with the company. He had been here a couple of months now, and we were both ready for the training wheels to come off. I knew Jensen was gun shy by nature about these sorts of things, but I was ready. I was so fucking ready. A fact I'd relayed to him more than once this week. I wasn't going to sit on my hands much longer, and he knew it.

I turned back to the paperwork, trying to return to the right headspace to work again, but it was impossible to focus. My anticipation over what was to come with Patrick kept slipping into my mind.

I was going to ask him out.

I'd put it off long enough. He couldn't possibly see me as the baby I'd been when I first crushed on him. A four-year age difference had been a lifetime in high school, but it was next to nothing at twenty-seven and thirty-one.

A knock on the door pulled me out of my thoughts. I pushed the papers away from me again with a huff. This was hopeless.

"Come in."

I whirled my seat around and watched in a daze as my daydreams were conjured from thin air.

"Patrick," I muttered. My mind went blank for a split second before recovering. I crossed my arms over my chest and eyed him skeptically.

"Hey, Mor."

I liked the way the nickname only my family used sounded on his tongue and the shape of his perfect lips when he said it. It was way better than the other nickname he liked to use—Mini Wright. I might still be small, but I was a force to be reckoned with. There was nothing mini about my personality.

"To what do I owe the pleasure?"

"Came to give you this." He handed me a piece of paper.

I took it from him but kept my eyes on him for a second longer, admiring his crooked smile and the baby blues that were my undoing.

"What's this?"

It took me a full minute to process what I saw on the top of the document. Then, my head snapped up at him. I jumped out of my chair.

"You're quitting?" I gasped.

"Nah. I just handed you my two-week notice for no reason."

"Don't be a shit."

"Me?"

I rolled my eyes at him and glanced back down at the paperwork. I straightened my shoulders and tried to relax. God, Patrick was the only person who could get me to lose my composure. But Patrick quitting Wright Construction could be a blessing in disguise. Not that I was going to let him know I thought so.

"Outside offer?" I guessed.

He shrugged. "Yeah."

"And you're not even going to let me counter?" I asked with an arched eyebrow. I tossed the paperwork back at him. "How much?"

He caught it and then set it on top of the paperwork I'd been ignoring. Then, he placed his hand on my shoulder and looked down into my dark brown eyes. It was *that* look. That one I couldn't shake. I swore he saw me in those moments. When it was just me and him and not my family or friends. Definitely not his best friend, my brother Austin. But then the moment broke, like it always did, and I was just his best friend's little sister again.

"I brought this to you before I told everyone else, Mor, because I know you don't like to let people go."

My mouth popped open, and I quickly recovered. "Well, I've let enough people go in my life."

Both of my parents had died before my sixteenth birthday. Two out of three of my brothers had moved out of state at one point. I didn't like change. Not like that.

"I know." He ruffled my hair.

I ducked out from under his touch.

"You've always been like that. Loyal. I like it."

I swallowed. "Well, I'm a Wright through and through."

"Most of the time, I feel that way, too. But Tech made me an offer I couldn't refuse, and it's not about the money."

I exhaled in relief. Okay, so he wasn't *leaving,* leaving. Just working at Texas Tech, which was near the Wright building.

"And I can't change your mind?"

"You know I'd do anything for you," he said with that same grin.

My heart skipped a beat. "Anything, huh?"

"Oh God, what have I promised?" He laughed. "Come on, Mor. Let's get out of here. I'll drop the paperwork off at Julia's office on the way out."

Julia was the head of HR and also Austin's girlfriend. I adored her and everything she had done to help my brother.

"I can't," I said reluctantly. I glanced at the hours of work I still had ahead of me.

"You work too much."

"You're not the first person to say that today."

"Oh?" he asked.

"David says it all the time actually."

"David," Patrick said, his voice flat.

"Yeah. He's a great guy. I'm glad we hired him," I rambled on. "But I'm behind because of all the training. So, I can't really leave."

Patrick's eyes slid to the paperwork. "It's Friday. This will all be here on Monday morning."

"Monday," I scoffed. "I'll be working from home all weekend."

"You give me a headache."

I laughed. "No, I don't. I'm awesome, obviously."

"Obviously."

I took a deep breath and debated on what I should do. I knew this was my chance. We were alone. We were bantering. All I had to do was open my mouth and ask him to go out with me.

What's the worst that could happen?

He could say no.

Yeah, that was the worst, most humiliating thing I could imagine.

I hated to think that things would get awkward between us because I loved what we had. But, at the same time, could I continue pretending like I didn't have feelings for him? I'd been doing it long enough. And I was pretty sure he was the only one who didn't see it.

I opened my mouth to finally do it. I looked up into his bright blue eyes and conjured all the confidence I had in my work. He looked at me, as if waiting for me to complete the thought written on my face.

But nothing came out.

I glanced away from him, and my cheeks heated.

Fuck, I'd choked.

What the hell? Why couldn't I go after him?

"You forgot, didn't you?" Patrick asked.

"Forgot?" I asked in confusion.

"Steph's party tonight."

My eyes cut to my computer. "Fuck."

"I thought so."

"I didn't exactly forget. I just had my dates mixed up." I tried to cover. I cringed. "Don't tell Steph."

Patrick laughed and nudged me. "My sister comes in from San Francisco for her birthday, and you forgot? No way you're ever living this down."

"Ugh! She'll skin me alive if she finds out," I said with a laugh.

"That sounds like Steph. Why don't you come over early with me and get some food?"

I inhaled sharply at the casualness of the conversation.

Of course, Stephanie and I had been friends since we were toddlers. We'd cheered together in high school back when I had real friends. She'd gone off to Berkeley for music while I'd stayed in town and gotten my business degree at Texas Tech. We still saw each other whenever she was in town and chatted and liked each other's statuses. So, it was perfectly normal that Patrick had invited me to hang out before Steph's party, but somehow, my mind strayed right to being with Patrick and how I'd totally choked.

"Oh...I couldn't impose."

"You'd hardly be imposing," he said. "And, really...when was the last time you ate?"

"I ate...today," I muttered defensively.

"What? Kale and Skittles?"

"Don't act like you know me!"

Because, yes...that was what I'd had. A kale smoothie of some variety and a bag of Skittles to get me through the following couple of hours. Food was kind of lost on me when I got into a project.

"Psh. I do know you." Patrick reached for my arm to guide me out of the conference room. "That's why I am making you leave work. You're a human, not a robot. Someone needs to remind you of that."

"I know I'm not a robot," I said with an exaggerated eye roll. I gestured to the conference table and shuffled all the paperwork together. I stuffed it into a folder and carried it with me out of the conference room.

"I haven't seen proof of that. We'll feed you and see how it goes from there."

"What if robots could eat regular food?" I countered. "I could be a very advanced robot."

"Of course you would be an advanced robot," he drawled. "What other kind of robot would we hire as our CEO?"

I guffawed. "Nothing less than the best for Wright Construction."

"Basically." From the conference room, Patrick veered me toward my office down the hall. "Now, let's head to my parents' house. They'll feed you. If you're lucky, I might even whip up those mashed potatoes I know you love."

"All right." A pang hit my chest at the thought that he remembered I loved his mashed potatoes. I was such an idiot.

I snatched my purse out of my office, stuffed the leather folder into my purse, and then followed him toward the elevator.

Patrick got off on Julia's floor and placed his two-week notice on her desk. Then, we took the elevator down to the bottom floor. My black Mercedes was parked in its designated spot. I could see Patrick's Lexus SUV three rows behind mine.

"I'll follow you," I told him.

"Let's take mine. There's not much parking, you know."

"True."

I hopped into the passenger side of his SUV and took a quick glance over at him. It seemed my luck had held out for the day. I hadn't worked up to the nerve to ask Patrick out, but we were still together. Not that it was a date or anything.

My eyes shifted back up to his, and I licked my lips. His eyes flickered to my lips for a split second before facing forward. It was so fast that I swore I had imagined it. Patrick had never looked at me like that before. My hope for our future was just that—hope.

But, tonight, I was determined for him to see *me*.

Not just his best friend's little sister.

Two

Patrick

"I still can't believe you forgot. Don't you have a secretary?" I teased.

"I have an assistant. Not a secretary," Morgan snapped.

"My bad."

"You know who would be the perfect assistant though?"

I arched an eyebrow. "By your tone of voice, I'm not going to like it."

"A straight white male."

"You'd do it, too."

"I mean, what could be better than to have a man at my beck and call? Bet no one would call him a fucking secretary."

"They would if you told them to," I suggested.

She laughed. Her eyes crinkling and her teeth showing. That was her best laugh. It meant she really meant it. "Thanks for feeding into my wild plans."

"Anytime."

"So, this new job. Are you sure Tech really needs you?"

"Well, I've already accepted."

Morgan looped a strand of her dark hair behind her ear. "I don't know. I still think I could make you a better offer."

My eyes darted from the steering wheel to her face. The way she'd said *better offer* was super suggestive, but, damn, by the look on her face, she had no clue. Morgan did that all the time. She had no idea that half of the things that came out of her mouth had double meanings.

"And what's that?"

"I need a new secretary."

She held on to a straight face for a full three seconds before bursting out laughing. I followed along with her and shook my head.

"Good try."

"I think you'd be perfect for the job."

"Just for that, I'm going to tell Steph."

Morgan rolled her eyes and turned up the radio as we drove the rest of the way to my parents' house.

I pulled onto the street for my parents' house. They'd been living in the same house for as long as I could remember. Even longer than that. It was home even though it wasn't anything as extravagant as the Wrights'. I'd grown up securely in the upper-middle class, but my parents prioritized vacations and activities over fancy houses or cars. Family was always more important than things. It was probably why I owned a home that was almost paid off and an SUV I'd had since I graduated college.

"Tell me about the new job. What are you doing?" Morgan asked.

"A lot of the same that I've been doing at Wright— managing big contacts." I grinned wolfishly at her. "Speaking of…have you made your donation to Texas Tech this fiscal year? I can just see it now—Morgan

Wright Library, the Wright wing of the Rawls College of Business, Wright something wing of another building. That would look very impressive."

"Oh, boy," she grumbled. "This is going to cost me a pretty penny, isn't it?"

"Probably."

I parked in the driveway and was glad that we had gotten here early. The street was going to be jam-packed here soon. We hopped out of my truck, and Morgan came around to my side.

"So, that's what you want to do? Schmooze people for donations?"

"I'm pretty good at schmoozing."

"You've never schmoozed me," she accused. She batted her pretty little eyelashes up at me.

"Is anyone able to schmooze Morgan Wright?"

She giggled. "Depends on who it is."

I liked her giggle, too. It was even rarer than her real laugh. I'd gotten both in one night. I guessed she really needed to get out of that office. I wondered when the last time she had gone out was or if she socialized outside of work at all. She'd even stayed in on Halloween to work. I knew because I'd invited her to the party my friend was throwing. Admittedly, none of us had really been in the partying mood around Halloween after Austin returned from rehab. I'd only gone because I'd promised the girl I was seeing that I'd make an appearance. I'd broken up with her that night. Another one bit the dust.

"And, anyway, it's more than that. Donations isn't the only thing we do. It's how we stay in contact with businesses and alumni. We also negotiate contracts and make sure the university continues running."

"Sounds like a big job."

"A little bigger than being your secretary."

She rolled her eyes. "If you say so."

I knocked twice before walking into the house with Morgan on my heels. "Knock, knock," I called out. "I'm home!"

"Well, look who decided to show his face," Stephanie said.

"Hey, sis," I said, dragging her in for a hug.

She squeezed me extra tight and then punched me in my kidney as she screamed, "Ha! Gotcha!"

I coughed at the sudden jab and then darted for her. I grabbed her around the middle and picked her up off her feet before dropping her onto the carpet. She gasped as she hit the ground and tried to kick me.

"Wow, things really haven't changed," Morgan said behind me.

"Mor!" Steph cried from the floor. "Let me handle my dipshit brother, and then I'll come snuggle you."

A tall man with ginger-red hair walked into the living room at that moment and stared down at the display with wide eyes. Morgan stepped over me and Stephanie.

"Hi, I'm Morgan Wright," she said, extending her hand.

"Thomas Cooper. I'm Steph's boyfriend."

"He's in real estate," Steph volunteered from the floor.

"Nice to meet you."

"How do you know Steph?" he asked.

"We grew up together. Toddlers to high school."

"She's the bitch who took the valedictorian spot from me!" Steph told him.

I guffawed and pushed Steph back down to the floor.

"Guilty," Morgan said without a trace of guilt.

I got up off the floor and brushed off my suit pants. I shook Thomas's hand. "Good to see you again, man."

"You, too, Patrick."

Steph jumped up and adjusted the long front-angled blonde bob she was sporting. "Pleasantries over. Let's drink."

"Party hasn't even started," I said. I'd been much more conscious of how much I drank and for what reasons ever since my best friend had gone to rehab.

"I'm the party," Steph said, as if it were obvious.

Morgan and I shared a look. I could see the same thoughts flitting through her mind. We were eerily in sync today.

Thomas followed Steph into the kitchen, and Morgan nodded her head, as if to ask if we should follow.

"Feels kind of weird, doesn't it?" I asked.

She nodded. "Casually drinking feels like it has consequences now. Even more than it did after my dad died."

Her dad, the infamous Ethan Wright, had died of an alcohol overdose. I'd been in college at the time with Austin, who had dealt with the death by drinking heavily. Morgan had only been sixteen, and I couldn't imagine how hard it had been for her.

"I know what you mean." I put my hand on the small of her back and guided her toward the kitchen.

"It'll probably be okay."

I nodded. "I think so."

She took a deep breath and then let it out. A smile returned to her face, and my eyes darted to her lips again.

Why the hell am I noticing her lips today?

Normally, she wore lipstick. That had to be it. Today, she didn't have any lipstick on, and I could see that they were chapped from her worrying away at them with her teeth.

"Where's Mom and Dad?" I asked as Thomas passed me a beer.

Morgan took one, too. I loved when girls drank beer. Or hard whiskey.

"Out back, being ridiculously cute," Steph said with a sigh.

"So, Dad's grilling, and Mom is trying to tell him how to do it better even though we both know he's the only one who has ever touched that grill?"

"Pretty much."

Morgan took a long swig of her beer. All fears of alcoholism running in her family forgotten. I had two healthy, well-balanced, and adjusted parents...and Morgan had zero. She had four amazing siblings, but it wasn't the same thing.

Steph slung her arm around Morgan and urged her out to the backyard. Thomas watched them with curious eyes.

"Your girlfriend seems really nice," Thomas said.

I sputtered, spewing beer all over the kitchen. "She's...she's not my girlfriend."

Thomas backed away with a laugh as I grabbed a towel to mop up my mess. "Sorry. I just thought...you know, you showed up together and all."

I saw the entire encounter through Thomas's eyes in that moment. Morgan and I showing up together, joking and having a good time. My baby sister's friend from high school. Our knowing eye contact. My hand on her back. Fuck, we must actually look like a couple.

"She's, uh, she's my best friend's little sister. She's way too young for me."

Thomas laughed. "You and I are the same age, man, and I'm dating your sister."

That realization slapped me in the face. It wasn't like I hadn't dated someone younger than Morgan before. We were only four years apart. But, with Mor, it felt like such a bigger age gap.

"Her brothers would kill me for even having that thought."

Thomas held up his hands. "Well, don't kill me for having that thought about your sister."

"Treat her right, and I won't have to."

"Done."

We shook hands like gentlemen and followed the ladies out the back door. My mind was still on the observation Thomas had made about me and Morgan. My eyes found her as soon as we walked into the backyard. She was standing with Steph, laughing uproariously at whatever outrageous story my sister had been regaling her with. Color had come back into her cheeks, and her long brown hair swayed around her face. The slacks and blue silk blouse that had seemed so ordinary when I stumbled into the conference room earlier hugged every feature. Every. Single. Curve.

Her eyes locked on mine for a second, and I realized, in the waning light, they weren't solely dark brown. They had flecks of gold around the irises. And they were emotive. So was her mouth. And quite literally everything about her.

She tilted her head when I didn't turn away. *What the hell did she think was running through my head?* She couldn't know. She'd think I was a total creep. There was no way that she would be interested in me. *Fuck, I cannot believe I'm having these thoughts.*

She was so hot. Like stunningly hot. *Why had I never noticed before? Had I just tried not to look? Just seen her as young as Steph?* I didn't even know. Because, now that I was seeing her...I couldn't stop looking.

And I was pretty sure her three older brothers were going to murder me for thinking about their little sister like this.

Three

Morgan

"So, are you and Patrick finally...you know?" Steph asked me.

I laughed. "Yeah, right."

"In high school, the puppy-dog eyes were annoying, but now, he's just an idiot if he doesn't see it."

"He's not an idiot. He just has no interest in me. I'm fine with it."

Steph snorted. "Yeah. Uh-huh. I'll believe that when pigs fly. You can't fool me. I knew you long before you were CEO of Wright Construction. Which, by the way, congratulations!" Steph squeezed my hand and did a little jig.

"Thank you." I was glad that we were moving the conversation away from Patrick. It was hard enough, being stuck in my head with the constant loop that he didn't want me. It was another thing to talk to another person about it and realize how lame I sounded, still pining for him.

I took another long drink from the beer in my hand and turned my attention back to Patrick. He was talking to his parents and Thomas by the grill. Other people had shown up for Steph's party a while ago, but it was still pretty small. I was glad it wasn't a huge event.

As if he could feel me looking at him, Patrick glanced in my direction. Our eyes met, and I waited for him to make some stupid face or nod in my direction or just plain ignore my gaze. That was the norm after all.

But he didn't do any of those things. In fact, he stared back at me. My body heated at that look. His eyes were saying a hell of a lot more than I'd ever seen there before. He swallowed hard as his eyes swept my body from top to bottom. And I wasn't fucking imagining it. When he had first come out of the house, I'd thought that look was a mistake maybe. But there it was again. Something had changed...and I didn't know what it was. Or if I was reading into things.

When he hastily turned away, I tried to clear my head. This was Patrick. He didn't see me that way. Though I'd always wanted for things to move forward, I never really believed I had a chance. Even when I was going to ask him out earlier, it had been more to put a final nail in the coffin. I'd assumed he'd turn me down, and then maybe I could move forward.

Now, I didn't know what to think.

Patrick and Steph's parents served burgers on paper plates with sides on a foldout table in the back. I mingled with some of the girls I'd gone to high school with. Even though many of them still lived in town, I never saw anyone. I didn't really have time, and we didn't have a ton in common. My life was work, and theirs were their families.

I picked up my fourth beer from a cooler when I felt Patrick's presence at my side.

"Hey, lightweight. Are you going to be okay with that?"

I sent him a dazzling smile as I popped the top. "I don't think I've had a drink since that night we got smashed at Louie Louie's this summer. I forgot how good it felt to relax."

"Good thing you're not driving."

"Oh God, you know I'd never."

"I know. That's why I'm sober as fuck."

I laughed and nudged him. My buzz had loosened everything up.

Good-bye, inhibitions.

Patrick steadied us both by placing his hand on the small of my back. Something ignited inside me. All I could think about was kissing him. His lips weren't far from mine. I just had to stand up on my tiptoes. I leaned forward into him until our sides were nearly pressed together.

"Patrick?"

"Yeah?" he said, his voice coming out strained.

"I'm glad I came with you."

He released a strangled cough and then pulled back from me. He became suddenly infatuated with the shirtsleeves he'd rolled up on his button-down earlier.

"I'm glad you decided to come to the party. Maybe we should lay off the beer," he suggested. He snagged a water from the cooler and passed it to me.

My cheeks heated when I took it from him, avoiding eye contact.

What the hell is wrong with me? I'd made that sound so freaking sexual. *Why did I think he'd want to kiss me? God, I really need this water.*

I started downing the bottle just as Thomas cleared his throat and drew everyone's attention to him.

"Hey, everyone. I'm so glad that all of you could be here today for my lovely Steph's birthday. Steph, could you come over here?"

Steph ran up to where he was standing with her arms raised high like she was Rocky. She winked at him, and he laughed.

"I know most of you don't know me, but we both wanted to thank you for being here on this special day. And I'm especially glad that all of her friends and family are here in one place today."

Then, he faced Steph and dropped to one knee. Steph gasped, her hand flying to her mouth as he produced a black velvet box.

"Oh my God," I whispered.

"Smooth," Patrick said.

"Stephanie Tara Young, will you marry me?" Thomas asked with a smile.

Tears ran down Steph's cheeks as she nodded. "Yes! Yes, yes, yes."

She pulled Thomas up to her and thoroughly kissed him. When she finally released him, he took the diamond out of the box and slid it onto her ring finger. Everyone cheered in celebration. Her dad popped open a bottle of champagne, and soon, we were all toasting the couple.

"Did you know about this?" I asked, sipping on the champagne.

Patrick shook his head. "I heard him talking to Dad earlier, so I guessed. But no one told me."

"Pretty romantic of him to get everyone together like this for her."

"Oh, yeah?" He shot me a questioning look. "Aren't you normally president of Club Cynical?"

"Still am. Most of the people here I judged pretty hard when they got married and had kids. Hell, I felt that way about both Jensen and Landon."

"But?"

"Well…since Sutton…"

"Right," Patrick said.

I didn't have to explain it to him.

My younger sister's husband had died this summer. It was a tragedy like nothing else. They were young and hadn't been married long. He'd left behind my now broken sister and their eighteen-month-old son, Jason. Sutton colored everything that I'd once found cynical with a new outlook.

"But I'm happy for Steph. Thomas seems like a great guy."

"He is."

Patrick nodded his head toward his sister, and I followed in tow. He picked Steph up when we approached and twirled her in a circle.

"Congrats, sis. I knew, someday, someone would love you," Patrick said.

Steph smacked him. "Jackass."

I cracked up and pulled Steph into a hug. "I'm so happy for you."

"I can't believe it!" she cried, thrusting her hand out toward me. The diamond was pretty massive with a halo around it. It fit Steph perfectly.

"It's beautiful!"

I moved over to congratulate Thomas as well. We spent the rest of the party talking about all the plans that would have to go into the extravagant wedding that Steph clearly wanted. I even got wrapped up in the wedding talk. I'd had to help Sutton with her wedding after all.

But, by the end of the night, I was tipsy and exhausted. I hadn't had this much people time outside of work in a while. It was nice and made me want to go home and crawl into a ball to recharge.

"You ready to head out?" Patrick sidled up to me and seemed to know exactly what I was thinking.

"Yeah, but I have a question."

"What's that?"

"I thought I was promised mashed potatoes."

Patrick shot me an incredulous look. "I didn't promise them. I said, if you were lucky."

I batted my eyelashes at him, hoping I looked innocent. "Are you sure I'm not lucky?"

He searched my face for a second before answering calmly, "Maybe you are. I guess I could make you some mashed potatoes at my place."

I tried to mask my shock when I gripped the empty beer I'd been nursing for a while now. "That'd be good. You clearly owe me."

"Clearly," Patrick easily agreed.

We said good-bye to Patrick's family. I got a knowing look from Steph that I chose to ignore, and then we were bundled back up in his SUV. Patrick tapped out a rhythm on the steering wheel to the song on the radio, and I tried not to glance over at him.

This was friendly.

Just a friend offering to hang out.

There was nothing different.

Except…there was.

I couldn't put my finger on it. Maybe the flirting. Maybe the looks. Maybe the ease in which he'd invited me over to his place.

I knew that I shouldn't question when something this unbelievable happened to me, but, well, this was me. If something seemed too good to be true, it usually was. I followed my gut in business. My gut was telling me that something was happening with me and Patrick.

My heart might be singing a happy tune. My brain might be telling me I was an idiot. But I was following my gut. I hoped that this wouldn't all blow up in my face.

Patrick parked his car in the garage at his house, and I followed him inside. I'd been to his place before a couple of times with Austin or for some kind of party. I'd never been here with only Patrick. The house felt empty with just the two of us in it even though it wasn't that big of a house. I'd always liked that it was a modest size and cozy with furniture you were meant to relax in rather than for decoration. It was too homey to be a typical bachelor's pad, like Austin's house had been before he sold it. Everything about it screamed Patrick.

"Make yourself at home," he said, pulling off his jacket and tossing it onto the back of a chair at the breakfast nook. "Want a drink? I have all of that top-shelf bourbon that Austin got rid of when he stopped drinking."

"Uh, sure. I didn't realize he'd given that to you."

"Most of it he got rid of." He pulled down a fancy bottle with a long, skinny funnel top. "But some of this stuff can only be purchased through the company, so he gave it to me. I keep it all put away when he's over, and he doesn't ask about it."

"Smart."

Patrick poured us each a glass and passed one to me. I took a tentative sip of mine and cringed. I liked bourbon, and this stuff was smooth, but, damn, was it potent. Patrick tipped his back like a shot and poured himself another.

Guess he's not leaving anytime soon.

I kicked off the heels I'd been wearing all day and sighed in pleasure. "Oh my God, I've been waiting to get out of those torture devices."

"I like them."

"Yes, well, that's one of the reasons women wear them." I took a steadying sip of bourbon. "Also, I'm short."

"You're not that short."

"I totally am. And, in this business, I get looked down upon enough for being a woman. I couldn't imagine if I didn't wear heels. I literally wouldn't be able to look anyone in the eye."

Patrick stepped toward me. He was over six feet tall and towering over my small frame. He was close enough that I could feel the heat coming from his body. My face flushed, and I was pretty sure it wasn't from the alcohol.

"How the hell could anyone look down upon you for being a woman, let alone for being short?"

I shrugged helplessly. "I don't know, but it happens constantly."

"Those people are idiots. Height doesn't mean anything about how capable you are. And being a woman doesn't change the fact that you can run this company better than anyone else. If anyone says or acts differently because of that, it's their problem. Not yours."

"I know," I said. "I try not to let it bother me. I'm here because I earned it. I'm here because I fucking deserve it. The rest can go shove it."

Patrick smirked, a quick, flirtatious thing. "Fuck."

"What?" I asked, trying to decipher what was going on behind his tumultuous blue eyes.

He shook his head, as if he couldn't decide what the hell he was doing. He looked so torn. I couldn't even imagine that everything I had ever wanted was staring me right in the face. I willed my hand to move, willed it to reach out for him.

Why is that so difficult?

With a short breath, I set my drink down, leaned forward, and placed my hand against his forearm. His eyes snapped back to mine. I wasn't mistaking his look now. Patrick wanted me.

My heart fluttered. My stomach catapulted. My mind buzzed.

This was real.

This moment was real.

"Morgan," he said, his voice strained.

His hand moved down my arm and to my waist. My breath caught on contact.

"Yeah?"

He didn't say anything else. Just slipped his other hand into my dark hair and tilted my face up toward him. Our mouths were an inch apart. I could taste the liquor on his breath and feel the heat from him. We were barely even breathing as we stood frozen in that moment for a second.

Both of us desperate to move forward and also terrified to break that barrier between us.

Desperate and frantic and excited and petrified and delirious.

His nose brushed against my own, soft and gentle. A question. As if he couldn't believe any more than I could that we were standing here, on the precipice. That all we had to do was lean, and we'd free fall right off the cliff.

Four

Patrick

Fuck, *I'm going to hell for this.*

Morgan moved forward until our bodies fit together like a seam. Soft and supple met hard and solid. It was temptation at its finest. The serpent's apple dangling from a thread.

And I didn't think I could turn back. Something had come over me. The thought of Morgan had never crossed my mind. Then, Thomas had put that thought in my head, and everything had shifted. Once it was there, I couldn't stop thinking about it. I couldn't stop seeing her as this gorgeous, restrained woman who had literally been standing right there all this time.

I wanted to lean in. I wanted to give in to this. I wanted it fucking desperately.

She was here. I'd invited her over. She was offering herself to me. It would be so easy. So goddamn easy. I just had to close that distance. To take what I definitely fucking wanted.

But, fuck, I shouldn't. I shouldn't fucking do it.

This was *Morgan*.

She was my best friend's little sister. She was still my boss for the next two weeks. And I couldn't take advantage of her like this.

God, this sucked. If she were anyone else, I would do it. I would go through with it. But other girls had never really mattered to me. Other girls didn't have consequences.

Morgan was much more than that. We'd known each other our whole lives.

And, if I do this, will it fuck everything up?

My dick was saying to fucking forget all of that and enjoy this moment. But I couldn't do it.

It went against my nature, but I pulled back. Our bodies peeled apart. I dropped my hands to my sides. I felt the heat dissipate from between us. It felt empty and awful.

"Morgan, we…we shouldn't do this."

Her eyes opened, wide with confusion. And hurt. I'd rejected her, and I could see that in her eyes.

"You're…you're drunk," I added as an afterthought.

She instantly snapped back to the person she'd been before the fatal almost kiss. She straightened and pushed her shoulders back, and all that pain was tucked away and hidden. Damn, I never wanted to play poker against her.

"Okay," she said softly.

"I could, uh…how about those mashed potatoes?"

She pursed her lips and glanced away from me. "Maybe I should just go."

"Nah, don't go," I insisted. I knew it would probably be better if she did go, but I wasn't ready for her to leave.

"I think I'll grab an Uber or something. I'm tired."

I could see the lie on her.

"Just crash here."

"Patrick," she said with a sigh.

"Morgan."

"Is that a good idea?"

"It's fine. I'll get you some clothes, and you can take my room. I'll take the couch."

I disappeared before she could disagree. I didn't know why I was pressing this. For all intents and purposes, her leaving was the smart move. I wasn't usually the gentleman. I'd dated a lot of girls. I'd pushed my luck and gone home with many girls who had had more to drink than Morgan. The only reason I was saying no was because this was Morgan.

Yet I couldn't let her leave. I didn't want her to leave. I wanted her in my bed. I wanted to taste that kiss. I wanted to taste a hell of a lot more than that.

Fuck, I hated being conflicted. And I was conflicted.

I changed into lounge clothes, grabbed Morgan a Texas Tech T-shirt and some basketball shorts, and brought them out to her. "They're both going to be huge on you, but hopefully, you can roll the shorts until they fit."

Morgan took the clothes in her hands. She stared down at them in disbelief. I didn't know what she was thinking.

Is she thinking that she's insane for ever thinking about kissing me? Or is she ready to bolt?

She waffled for a second before turning and disappearing into the bathroom. I blew out a breath of relief. I was being a fucking idiot either way. But I wanted her here.

While she was gone, I got out the supplies for mashed potatoes. I didn't know why I was even making this right now. We could do a million other things to get back into our easy rhythm that we'd had forever. Yet here I was, peeling potatoes over the trash can and setting a giant pot of water to boil.

"I didn't think you'd make the mashed potatoes," she said, appearing in the kitchen.

I turned around to look at her and nearly dropped the potato in the trash. I couldn't mask my expression fast enough. My T-shirt brushed her mid thigh, and she'd hiked the shorts up so high that I could barely even see them. I'd seen Morgan in skimpy bikinis for over a decade, and nothing was as hot as seeing her in my clothes.

She plucked at the shorts. "They really don't fit."

I cleared my throat and turned away. My dick twitched, just thinking about getting under those shorts. And I couldn't do a damn thing about it. Or at least...I wouldn't.

"They're fine," I said, my voice strained.

I heard her pick up the drink she'd left on the counter and down it. She poured herself another without comment. I didn't blame her. I actually couldn't handle the heat in the kitchen.

She hoisted herself up onto the counter and watched me work. I was deft in the kitchen. I'd learned from my parents who were both excellent cooks in their own right. It made me feel in control when I was here.

"Maybe we should talk about this," she finally worked up the courage to say.

"The mashed potatoes? Don't worry; I know you like them with sour cheese."

She huffed. "You know I don't mean the potatoes."

"Is that a euphemism?" I joked.

"Patrick..."

"There's nothing to discuss. We're friends."

"Friends," she said hollowly.

"Yeah."

I couldn't believe I'd just friend-zoned Morgan Wright.

She paused and seemed to consider my words before letting out a breath. "These had better be the best fucking mashed potatoes I've ever had."

I laughed and went back to work. Morgan wandered into the living room and turned on some horrid reality TV show. She watched them all whenever she could. I really didn't understand it, but she always said it made her feel smart. It made me feel like I was losing brain cells.

When the potatoes were finally done, I brought out the entire container and two spoons.

Morgan laughed when she saw the giant bowl. "You're a dork."

"Thanks." I handed her a spoon. "What are we watching?"

"*Hell's Kitchen.* I like when he yells at people."

"Oh, you've stepped your game up with cooking shows."

"I still like *Keeping Up with the Kardashians.*"

I shook my head. "You're an enigma."

She dipped her spoon in and took a huge mouthful of mashed potatoes. "Holy fuck, these are amazing."

I nodded through a mouthful of my own.

"You should cook more often," she told me.

"Probably."

We fell into a companionable silence as we ate through more than half of the bowl of mashed potatoes. When Morgan's eyes started drooping, I ordered her to bed. I was sure it was the first time in a while that she'd given herself permission to sleep before midnight. She would work herself to death if she didn't watch out.

I stripped out of my T-shirt and settled onto the couch, cursing myself for this situation. Mostly that I wasn't in my bed with Morgan right now. That we had spent the night watching cooking shows and hanging out like normal. But also pissed I'd never gotten into setting up a guest bedroom. Then, I wouldn't have to sleep on the couch. There were worse things…like screwing up a lifetime friendship with one drunken mistake.

I cushioned my head against the pillow and tried to get the image of Morgan in my T-shirt out of my head. Not that I was having much luck. I couldn't stop thinking about what she looked like in those shorts. I was going to have to go to the bathroom and take care of this. *Christ!*

This was *Morgan*. Morgan fucking Wright. I didn't need to be jacking off to the thought of her in an oversize T-shirt and basketball shorts. I'd seen her practically naked at the lake. I'd seen her in a cheerleading uniform. I'd seen her in skimpy dresses.

What the hell is wrong with me?

A voice cleared from the hallway, and I looked over to see her tiny figure standing there, watching me.

"Hey," she whispered.

"Do you need something?"

She nodded her head.

I couldn't get up right now to help her. Not without it being completely clear exactly what I was thinking.

"How can I help?"

She took a deep breath and then straightened her shoulders. "Come to bed."

"Morgan."

"Patrick, get in bed," she said in that voice that didn't broker argument. And she punctuated the entire thing by turning around and walking away.

I was not going to sleep with her.

Christ, I am not going to sleep with her.

I went to the bathroom and paced, thinking about a cold shower and ice water and anything to make my erection less obvious. I couldn't believe I was going to get into that bed to begin with, but to get in there hard as a rock was out of the question. I could do this. I could sleep next to Morgan. She was just Morgan after all.

My pep talk didn't do much to help me, but I walked across the hall and into my bedroom anyway. She was on the right side of the king-size bed. The covers were nearly up to her chin. She startled when she saw me in the doorway. Maybe she hadn't thought I'd show.

I shut the door behind me and got into bed on the other side. My bed was a thousand times more comfortable than the couch, but with Morgan so close, I felt like I was sleeping on hot coals.

"I didn't think you deserved to be kicked out of your own bed." She turned onto her side and faced me.

My eyes caught hers in the darkness. The streetlight was the only illumination that cast across her sharp features.

Without a second thought, I brushed her dark hair off her face. "Get some sleep."

She scooted forward until we were nearly as close as we'd been in the kitchen. "You're not going to kiss me?"

I swallowed down a lump in my throat. Her asking that made me want to maul her like a wild animal. To kiss her breathlessly until she had to surface for air.

"No," I struggled to get out.

"You should."

"That's not going to happen."

She reached out and put her hand on my bare chest. She dragged her nails down my abs, past my belly button, and then thumbed the front of my boxers. I stifled a groan and then grabbed her hand.

"You don't want to do this, Morgan."

She blinked twice. "How do you know what I want?"

"You're not the kind of girl who deserves a quick fuck when she's drunk. And you're definitely not the kind of girl who should get that from me."

"What does that mean?" she said, her voice dangerously quiet.

"You're Morgan Wright," I said, as if that explained everything.

"Thanks for reminding me." She glanced down to where I still held her hand. "You haven't let me go."

"I know." I hastily released her.

"Sometimes, I don't want to be Morgan Wright," she said so quietly that I almost didn't hear her.

"Come here," I said with a sigh.

I couldn't have what I wanted. I really wanted to give in, and she was making it so difficult, but I didn't want it to feel like it was her fault. This was my fault. I should have known better.

"What?" she asked warily.

I grabbed her hip and turned her, so she was facing away from me. Then, I tugged her snug against my chest and wrapped an arm around her waist. It wasn't enough. It wasn't even close to enough. With her ass against my crotch, I could feel every tiny movement that she made. I could feel as her muscles finally relaxed into me. I could even feel when her breathing evened out, and she succumbed to sleep.

With a sigh, I placed a kiss on her shoulder. A kiss I never would have given her if she'd been awake, and I tried not to notice how she fit perfectly against me.

Five

Morgan

I woke up, wrapped around Patrick. The T-shirt I'd borrowed had snaked up to under my breasts, and he had his arm wrapped across the bare skin. Our legs were locked, and he was breathing gently. My eyes darted to his clock. It was already ten o'clock.

Fuck! I couldn't remember the last time I'd slept that long. Probably not since college. And what a crazy fucking night.

I reluctantly slipped out from Patrick's arms. Everything that had happened the night before came back to me. I couldn't believe that we'd almost kissed. That I'd asked him to sleep with me. I hadn't been *that* drunk!

Embarrassment hit me fresh. I grabbed my clothes and called an Uber. I needed to get out of there. I didn't know why I felt like I was making a walk of shame when nothing had even happened between us. I thought he'd kissed me as I was falling asleep, but my delusions had probably invented that. Patrick had made it clear that I wasn't the type of girl he was interested in. He'd always liked crazy bartenders, easy one-night stands, and uncomplicated flings he never had to commit to. I was obviously none of those things.

I was Morgan Wright.

As he had so eloquently reminded me of last night.

When I got home, I buried myself in work and ignored my phone the rest of the day. I didn't want to answer if he called. And I didn't want to be disappointed if he didn't.

By the time I finally went to sleep later that day, I'd managed to go a full fifteen hours without looking at my phone. I wasn't caught up by any stretch of the imagination, but I felt like I'd accomplished something.

The next morning, my alarm buzzed at some ungodly hour. I slammed my hand on my phone several times, trying to get it to turn off before I realized that it was for church. I grumbled and finally switched it off.

When I woke again, it was with a jolt.

"Shit!" I cried.

I threw the covers off me and rushed through my morning ritual. I was going to be late for church. Jensen was going to kill me.

It was a Wright family tradition to go to church every Sunday morning. Our mom had gone every week, even when she'd had cancer. If Evelyn Wright could get out of bed, then she was there. Skipping wasn't an option. Not for me.

I sped all the way there. The cops were on my side, and I didn't get pulled over. Though that really would have been my luck at this point.

My entire family was already seated in the front row when I burst in through the front doors. I cringed as I heard the music that signaled the beginning of the service.

"Sorry, sorry, sorry," I muttered to Jensen as I passed him.

He raised his hands, as if to ask me, *Where the hell were you?*

I waved him off and kept walking. Landon and Austin were laughing at me behind their hands. While my brothers' significant others—Emery, Heidi, and Julia respectively—all sent me big smiles and waved. It looked like my younger sister, Sutton, and her son, Jason, hadn't made it. That was becoming increasingly more common. And I didn't have words for her as to why she should find solace here when she was grieving and angry at the entire universe.

I reached the end of the aisle and stumbled over my high heels when I saw the face staring back at me.

"Patrick," I muttered.

"Hey, Morgan." He slyly smiled up at me and then scooted down further away from Austin to give me room to take a seat between them.

I stared at the space for a second longer than I should have before unceremoniously plopping down.

"Why were you late?" Austin asked me.

"Slept through my alarm."

"Way to go. You're making me look good."

I rolled my eyes at him. "It was an accident."

"Uh-huh. Does that accident have a name?"

"What?" I snapped. Okay, maybe I was still on edge from the stuff with Patrick.

"I'm not judging," Austin said with a laugh. "You have a stressful job. What you do in your free time is up to you."

"Austin, leave Morgan alone," Julia said. She swatted him and flicked her rose-gold hair off her shoulder.

"She's my little sister. I'm supposed to mess with her."

"Aren't you also supposed to keep her from dating other guys?"

"Right. Forgoing my sacred duty." Austin turned back to me. "No boys!"

I rolled my eyes. "You're ridiculous. Listen to the sermon."

Austin laughed and turned back to face the front. But I felt like I had a laser pointed straight at my head. Patrick's eyes were drilled into the side of my head. I knew then that this wasn't going to be a thoroughly enjoyable church service.

The heat from Patrick's body was noticeable. Our legs almost brushed. I could sense every movement he made next to me. I could feel him shift and rearrange and fidget through the entire thing. While I ignored him. Or tried to ignore him the best I could.

All I wanted to do was turn and look at him. This, this right here, was the reason I hadn't ever made my move on Patrick. I was remembering quite clearly why. I'd never wanted it to ruin our friendship and the easy way we coexisted together. I just wanted him to see me for me.

Now, I'd been rejected. I understood that I wasn't what Patrick wanted. Or at least...if he did want me, it was just physical, and he wouldn't even act on the physical. I didn't want to deal with that. And I wouldn't.

So, we both just sat there. Neither of us acknowledging the other since I'd sat down, and I listened to the sermon.

Which turned out to be a huge mistake.

I'd been to services before where I felt like the thing the pastor was saying was directed at me. But, today...the service was *about* me. Like, he might as well have plucked the story of this weekend right out of my life and put it on display in front of the entire congregation.

That heat I'd been feeling turned me crimson. I was a cigarette destined to start a forest fire.

It couldn't end soon enough. By the time the last song was over and we were dismissed, I actually felt faint. I made some excuse to Austin about having to use the restroom and then disappeared. I needed to find a quiet place to breathe.

I pushed through the crowds, down the hallway that led to the back side of the church, and burst outside. I ground my teeth together and paced the sidewalk. *What the hell is wrong with me?* Yes, this was Patrick. Of course, that made it different. But I needed to get a grip.

I might have told him that I didn't want to be Morgan Wright sometimes. But I *was* Morgan Wright. And I was a badass. I took no shit. I fought for my place and worked my ass off and charged into things headfirst. This running and hiding and fear didn't suit me. I fucking hated it.

The door crashed open behind me, and I whipped around. Patrick walked outside, hastily shutting the door behind him.

"What are you doing out here?" he asked.

"I needed to get some air. Now, I'm going back."

Patrick put his hand on the door to keep me from leaving. "Why didn't you answer any of my calls yesterday?"

"I was working."

"And you what? Didn't check your phone?"

"No, I didn't."

He breathed out heavily. "Why did you leave?"

"When?"

"Don't play stupid, Morgan. I know you're brilliant."

"I figured you were used to girls sneaking out."

He didn't wince, but I could see the fire in his eyes. "Don't pull that shit with me."

"We're at church."

"You ran out without even a good-bye and then ignored me for twenty-four hours," he said, not even stopping to acknowledge my comment.

"What does it matter, Patrick? You made your intentions clear. I don't want to deal with this right now."

Patrick released his hold on the door. "You're right. I just don't want you to think that you needed to leave."

"You think I didn't need to leave?" A hysterical, short laugh escaped my lips. "I should have left right away. In fact, I should never have even gone over to your place."

The words hung heavy between us like a dense fog. Neither of us said a word. I didn't know what he was thinking. Whether he regretted our interactions from Friday night. Whether he wished, as I suspected he did, that they had never happened. And I couldn't ask.

Just as he opened his mouth again, the door opened, and Jensen exited the building.

He arched an eyebrow at the two of us standing out here alone. "Am I interrupting something?"

"No," Patrick and I said at the exact same time.

Smooth.

"All right," Jensen said disbelievingly. "Can I have a minute, Morgan?"

"Sure."

Patrick nodded his head at Jensen and then disappeared back into the church without another word to me. My heart panged in his absence.

Fuck, why couldn't I act like a normal human being about this? Why does it have to be so complicated with Patrick?

"Is something going on between you two?" Jensen asked once Patrick was gone.

"No. He was making sure I was okay. I wasn't feeling too great during the service."

"I know you've liked him for a long time."

"Don't," I said.

"Okay," he said, holding up his hands. "Not why I came out here anyway."

"Why did you come out here?"

"Did you miss the dozen text messages I sent you yesterday?"

I was really kicking myself for not checking my phone. "I kind of got sidetracked in my office at home. I didn't look at anything but the work I had."

Jensen sighed. "I know what that's like. Especially on the weekends, it's nice to just dig into work. Nothing else distracts you."

"Exactly."

"Unfortunately, you can't have many more days like that. It's one of the hardest parts of the job. When you take over tomorrow, you'll have to be more responsive."

I froze. "Did you just say…"

Jensen laughed. "Yes. No more temporary status. You and David are going to do great. I don't need to be looking over your shoulder the whole time. I know you've been annoyed with me, but I just worry."

"I know."

"But Jensen Wright Architecture is in production. The company is yours."

"I can't believe this day is finally here."

"You've earned it."

My love life might be in shambles, but at least, professionally, everything was falling into place. It would have been nice for the CEO position to come with some romantic benefits. Women had flocked to Jensen once he got the position. All I seemed to do was intimidate men. Even Patrick.

Well, fuck it.

I wasn't going to let that hold me back any longer.

Gone was the girl who had been pining for Patrick Young for twelve *long* years. I'd made my move. He'd rejected me. The entire thing had crashed and burned. I wasn't some simpering high school cheerleader anymore. I was the CEO of a Fortune 500 company. I didn't need to wait around for a guy who clearly wasn't interested in me.

There were plenty of guys I could date if I wanted to. I'd just held out hope. Young, desperate, irritating hope that Patrick would come around. But he wasn't going to come around.

I'd thrown myself at him, and he'd done nothing. Twice!

The man who was known for dating around and sleeping around wouldn't even *kiss* me. If that didn't send a clear message, I didn't know what did.

I'd get over him.

I would.

I'd force myself to move on.

And I'd start this week.

I pulled out the phone I'd neglected all day yesterday and found a number I'd ignored over and over again. Travis Jones. A very cute and flirtatious childhood friend who I wasn't just picking because Patrick hated him.

Six

Morgan

The next morning, I rose bright and early. I wasn't going to let the events of this past weekend affect me any longer. Today was my first official day as CEO. Today, I was out of the transitional period. Today, I would rule the world.

I put on my power black high heels and grabbed a black suit jacket on the way out the door. Only a handful of other people were already at Wright Construction when my heels clicked across the tiled floor. I'd seen David's car in the parking lot. He was an early bird rather than a night owl like me. He was probably settling into my office by now.

As the elevator dinged on the top floor of the office space, my heart started racing. Up until this point, it had all been just a dream. I mean…there had been the transitional period to prepare me for this. I *was* prepared for this.

At the same time, fear hit me fresh and new. I'd worked my whole life for this, and I suddenly felt sick to my stomach. I'd earned this. I deserved this. And yet...did I?

Of course I did. *Christ.* My brain was a hamster's wheel of insecurities.

I was never good enough. I never worked hard enough. I never put in as much as I could. There was always more that could be done. No matter what. No matter that I worked hours and hours longer than anyone else or that I dedicated my life to this company. No matter that my brothers hadn't put in half as much as I had. It still felt like I wasn't right. Like I was stealing. Like I was cheating.

But I couldn't show that on the outside. My exterior said Morgan Wright was ready to take on the world. My insides squirmed and shifted and wondered if this was all a prank.

I took a deep breath and forced myself forward. There was no going back. There never had been. I wouldn't give this up for the world. I'd clawed my way to the top. Past the blatant sexism and around the disdain. I'd won their hearts with charm and magnetism. I'd won their loyalty with endless hard work.

This day meant more than I could possibly put into words. And I didn't think a single person in my life had a clue of the enormity of the moment...or how terrified I was that I'd fuck up.

"Morgan!" David called, pulling me from my sobering thoughts.

I popped my head into his office. "Morning."

"How does it feel?"

"Like everything I imagined," I lied.

"I thought so. How did this weekend go?"

"Ugh! I barely got anything done this weekend. But today is a new day, right?"

"Right!"

"Feel free to move into my old office whenever you're ready."

"Will you be in Jensen's?"

"Yep. It's in need of some serious redecorating."

David laughed. "Sounds good."

I waved before continuing down the hallway. The door to my new office was ajar. I pushed it open and startled when I found someone already inside.

"Can I help you?" I asked the man standing by my desk.

"Yes, can you tell Jensen to hurry up? Also, I'd like a coffee with cream and two sugars," the man said impatiently.

I took a step back at the audacity. I'd just been having an inspirational pep talk with myself about my new CEO position. I had been overcoming my own fears and taking on the challenge I knew I had earned.

Then, here comes this douche bag who thinks I'm an assistant?

There was nothing wrong with being an assistant. But considering the man wasn't even looking at me, acknowledging me, or respecting me...I could tell it was an insult. He was in my fucking office and treating me like shit. *What an awesome start to my day.*

"Did you say cream and one sugar or two?" I drawled sarcastically. "I can't seem to remember."

The man whirled around in anger, as if he couldn't believe I'd used that tone with him. Then, his jaw dropped open. "Morgan?"

"Ah, you've heard of me." I stepped forward and came around to the back of the desk.

"I didn't realize it was you."

"Obviously."

"But you don't recognize me?"

"Should I?" I asked, finally taking a closer look at the man.

He was in his fifties with light-brown hair and a gut that he couldn't hide in his black suit. He did sort of look familiar, like I'd seen him somewhere before but I couldn't place where.

"We've never met. I'm your uncle Owen," he said, holding out his hand.

A shiver ran through me in disgust. Uncle Owen. So, *this* was the man my father had hated so much that he basically sent him into exile. I didn't know what the beef was between my father and his brother, but it'd had to be *bad* for that sort of reaction. Not that my dad had been known for his even temper or anything. He was an alcoholic after all. But my uncle's disappearance to Vancouver with his wife and two sons was legendary. My father had burned all of the pictures of them together, and his name had only been used as a swear word.

Owen dropped his hand when I didn't shake it. "Ah, so you have heard of me."

"What are you doing here?"

I knew that he worked for the Canadian branch of Wright Construction in Vancouver. When I was a kid, I'd always assumed that it was some kind of peace terms between kingdoms. Like sending a British monarch to Scotland or Brittany or Calais while their rival was on the throne. I'd been pretty obsessed with European history at the time. It started my love for celebrity gossip.

"I had an appointment with Jensen. What exactly are you doing in his office?"

"Jensen isn't with the company anymore. This is my office. Surely, you got the company-wide memo about me becoming CEO."

I didn't know why I was egging him on. Perhaps deeply ingrained prejudices were working against me, but I couldn't like this man. Blood didn't always equal family. This man was a stranger.

"I read that the company was in a transitional period, and you would eventually move into CEO. But my meeting today was with Jensen, and I wasn't informed that it would now be with you."

"I'll take that up with my brother."

Conciliatory. That was the word screaming in my head. I should make this right. I should make him comfortable. I should pacify his apparent aggression. But I didn't.

"See that you do." Owen straightened out his already impeccable suit. "It seems that you're not prepared for our meeting today. I'll have to reschedule for later this week. Maybe bring Jensen back in to hold your hand."

I clenched my jaw and didn't spit out the first thing that came to mind. *Fuck you, you fucking fuck.*

"Buh-bye," I said, sending him a wave that might as well have been flipping him off. When he left the office, I slumped back into my seat. "Fuck."

I snatched up my phone and immediately dialed Jensen's number.

He answered on the third ring. "Hey, how's the first day?"

"You scheduled a meeting with Uncle Owen and didn't warn me that it was happening on my first day? What the hell, Jensen?"

"Shit. Was that today?"

"Who are you, and what have you done with my brother? Shouldn't you have warned me about this? I didn't even know you had ever met him before. Let alone that you were having some meeting with him this week! He's creepy!"

"Yeah, yeah. Sorry. I should have double-checked the schedule for you. I would have postponed the talk until later in the week. But, yes, unfortunately, Owen is a pest that you have to deal with as CEO."

"He thought I was your secretary."

"His people skills are lacking. When I first got the job, he tried to stake his claim on it, as if he somehow deserved it since Dad was gone."

"God, he really does think we're royalty."

Jensen chuckled. "Don't worry about him. You'll have a meeting about the new environmental changes we're making, moving forward, and look over updating the contracts to bring them to code. He's usually a nuisance for a week or two, and then he's gone."

"How often do you meet with him?"

"Rarely. I try to do as much as I can through email. He likes to assert himself upon Lubbock like a long-lost hero. I think his version of history is different than the one Dad told us."

"Well, first impressions make me believe Dad."

"Just try not to antagonize him."

"It's hard not to."

"Morgan," Jensen said in that voice that only my brother could pull on me.

"All right. I'll do what I can."

"Just another day in the office. See you, Mor."

"Bye."

I hung up the phone and slouched in my chair. *What a fucking start to my day.* Somehow, a man I'd never met had just confirmed all the fears I'd had about starting the job. The positive energy I'd been searching for had been sucked right out of the room with his departure.

Seven

Patrick

"Are you going to explain this?" Austin asked, breezing into my office and slamming down a piece of paper onto my desk.

"Good morning to you, too."

"You're quitting?"

"I did plan to tell you."

"When, dipshit? You told my girlfriend first."

I grinned up at my best friend. "To be fair, your girlfriend is the head of HR."

"And?"

"Legally, she has to know that I'm quitting. She's kind of in charge of that."

"She's going to lord this over me forever now. You do know that, right?"

I smirked. "I might have guessed."

"You're an asshole."

"Learned from the best."

"Fuck you," Austin said. Then, he sank into the chair in front of my desk. "So…tell me what's going on."

"I got offered a cushy job at Tech."

"Nice!" Austin fist-bumped me. "But I meant…what's going on? I didn't see you all weekend. You were totally weird at church. Now, you're quitting without even a heads-up. New girl?"

"No, I think you're imagining things."

Of course, there was no *new* girl. There was just Morgan. Not new to my life, but certainly new to the way I was thinking about her. And I had been reevaluating every interaction I'd had with her in the last decade. Not that I could say that to Austin. He'd likely beat the shit out of me for even thinking about his sister this way. It wouldn't matter that nothing had happened. He wouldn't believe that from me even if I did tell him.

I wasn't known for my patience or discretion. I definitely wasn't known for missed opportunities. Austin knew enough of my exploits to find this thing with Morgan unsatisfactory, to say the least.

Even if I was never going to make that move.

"I'm not imagining things. I've known you long enough. I know when there's a new girl. You always disappear like this."

"I didn't disappear. Steph was in town. She got engaged this weekend. I was home."

"Whoa, baby sister engaged. How does it feel?"

"Weird," I admitted. "I like Thomas, but still…it's my little sister. How did you feel when Sutton…"

The words hung between us. Sutton's wedding had been a big event. It was still hard to believe that her husband had died less than two years later.

"I thought she was an idiot, but Maverick turned out to be a good guy. And, now, I feel sick to my stomach when I think about what happened to her."

"I know."

It was this cloud over the entire Wright family. It was inescapable. Sutton wasn't even around that much anymore, but her presence was felt everywhere.

"Fine," Austin said after a minute. "Don't tell me who she is. But if I find out it's butcher-knife-wielding Mindi again—"

"It's not."

"So, there is someone."

I blew out an exasperated breath. "No."

Austin laughed as he stood and headed for the door. "You're acting really weird, dude. It's not like you're trying to date my sister or something."

I choked on the next inhalation and tried to cover it up with a cough that turned into some stupid laugh.

Fuck, just give yourself away.

"Right," I managed to get out.

With relief, I watched him walk out. I needed to get my shit together. Mostly, I needed to stop thinking about Morgan Wright. I had one week left at Wright Construction, a week of paid leave, and then I was out of here. I needed to keep my head down and focus on work.

———

I spent the next two days doing exactly that. By the time Wednesday rolled around, I was feeling slightly less shitty about what had happened this weekend. It helped that I'd been actively avoiding Morgan, so I hadn't seen or heard from her since we talked at church.

I still didn't know what to make of that conversation. She'd left because she thought I expected that. She'd seemed ashamed to have even stayed the night. Part of me hated that, and part of me was pissed that she'd even insinuated that I'd have made her get a cab home. We'd been friends long enough for her to know better.

Or, at least, I thought we had. Then, she'd gone and ignored all my text messages about the situation and blown up on me when I confronted her.

Fuck.

Okay, so I was still thinking about it. After today, I'd only have to come into work two more days. I needed to stop jumping every time I left the office, like I was about to run into her. Morgan was a professional anyway. She wouldn't do anything if I did see her. Not that I'd likely see her. She lived in her office on a regular week. Considering she was the CEO and taking over the Tech negotiations on top of that, it seemed unlikely that she'd surface.

We didn't even work on the same floor. She worked up with Austin and the new CFO David Calloway. There would be no reason for me to be up there either. Except to see Austin.

I shook my head. Bad idea.

I needed to avoid her. To keep avoiding her.

Nothing good could come from this. From whatever this was.

The smart thing to do would be to find someone else. Call up one of my flings, like Mindi. Austin thought it was ridiculous that we were on again, off again, depending on my mood, because one of those times, she'd chased me out of her apartment with a butcher knife. She was nuts, but she kept my mind off things. There was nothing serious about a girl like Mindi.

I had a penchant for slightly dumb, super hot, and extremely crazy women. They found me. It happened without fail.

No one like Morgan had ever been interested in me. And I'd never been interested in anyone like her. Not on purpose or anything. It just happened that a guy who didn't want a relationship didn't end up dating girls who were relationship material.

"Ugh!" I said, pushing back from my computer.

My mind was on anything but the document I was filling out. In two days, it wouldn't even matter. They'd put someone else in my job and that person would handle my issues. I'd be free, working at Tech and working on a university schedule, which was probably the most advantageous part of the job.

With a frustrated sigh, I left my office and took the elevator up to the top floor. I knew that I shouldn't be doing this. It was stupid. I probably wouldn't even see her.

Fuck, do I want to see her?

What the hell is happening to me?

This was not me. Since when did I even think about a girl, let alone obsess over whether or not I was going to see her? I'd known Morgan my whole life. Things would be back to normal. There'd be no tension. There'd be no interest. We'd just be friends again.

"Knock, knock," I said into Austin's open office.

"What's up, dude?" he asked.

"Bored out of my mind, and ready to get out of here."

Austin rolled his eyes at me. "You're the dick who's leaving."

"I'm basically moving across the street."

Austin shrugged. "Right now, you work two floors down."

"You'll get over it."

"Probably." Austin glanced back up. "Hey, dude, while you're here, what are you doing this weekend?"

"Nothing."

"Tech is away. I thought we could grab lunch and watch the game."

I nodded. "Yeah. Sounds good. Anyone else coming?"

Austin frowned. I'd come to realize what that look meant. He was worried that, if we invited other guys out, they'd be drinking around him. I didn't do it anymore. I'd seen the consequences of that at my own birthday party earlier this year. I wouldn't put that temptation in his path.

"If you want," he said, as if he wasn't worried.

"Nah. Just you and me."

He smiled up at me and then groaned. "Oh God, please tell me that you're not bringing me more work."

I whipped around and found Morgan standing in the doorway. She arched an eyebrow at me before directing her attention back to Austin.

"Am I interrupting something?"

"It's just Patrick," Austin said with a dismissive wave.

"Right," she said. Her eyes slid to mine and then back to Austin. It was a dismissal. "I want you and David in on the next conference call I have."

Austin slammed his hands onto his desk. "Another conference call?"

"Don't act like you hate it."

"I love the job. I hate conference calls. Everyone hates conference calls."

Morgan gave him the stink eye. "I don't hate conference calls."

"Well, you're superhuman."

"Obviously." She grinned. "Ten minutes, Austin."

"Yeah, yeah."

"I guess that's my cue," I said to Austin.

He gave me a two-finger salute, and I followed Morgan out of the office. She glanced back at me. Any hope that things would be normal was dashed in that look. The tension between us felt like a living thing. Like a real barrier separated us. I wasn't her brother's best friend right now. I wasn't the guy she always joked with. I certainly wasn't the guy that she'd hung out with so casually for so many years.

I was the guy who had rejected her.

As much as that *wasn't* the case, she clearly saw it that way. It was written in her dark brown eyes.

I hadn't wanted to take advantage of her, and in the process, I'd ruined our friendship. On her end and mine. Because I couldn't help noticing how good she'd looked in her blue dress and jacket. The way her brown hair rippled past her shoulders like a waterfall. The hint of lipstick on her lips. The added couple of inches in her high heels.

Fuck, I needed to *stop*.

"Did you need something, Patrick?"

"I…no. I was just leaving."

She sighed. "All right."

"Did you need something?"

"Me? You're the one on my floor."

"Oh, right." I took a step back. "Right."

"Patrick, what's going on?"

Man, I was right. I should have stayed away. I shouldn't have come up here and talked to Austin. I had known I would run into Morgan. And that was a mistake.

"Nothing. Just came to talk to Austin. Forgot you were even up here," I lied.

She pursed her lips. "Uh-huh. Maybe you should get back to work."

"Probably so."

She took a step forward, like she was going to stop me or say something but then she didn't. I didn't know what was going through her head. She probably thought I was out of it.

And I was. Even though I knew I should stay away from Morgan for her own good, I couldn't seem to do it. I'd wanted her Friday night, and I wanted her now. But it hadn't been fair to her then, and I knew she wasn't really interested in me now. I just needed to get through the rest of the week, and then it'd be better. Everything would go back to normal.

Eight

Morgan

Who thought dating was a good idea?

It was awkward and stressful and nerve-racking. I mean, I could just be at home, not interacting with any more people again ever. Crawling into my introverted bubble for a few minutes longer.

I used up all my extrovertedness every day in meetings and on an outrageous number of freaking conference calls. Not to even mention, that weird interaction with Patrick yesterday.

As if it wasn't bad enough that he'd been avoiding me like the plague since church on Sunday, now, he was showing up on the top floor and acting like a crazy person. What the hell was that even about?

I didn't even want to think about it. Because the more I thought about it, the more confused I got.

Was it always going to be like this? It was one night. We could get past it. Maybe. At least, I hoped it wouldn't always be this awkward.

I really needed to stop thinking about it. Especially while I waited for my date to show up.

"I'll take another beer," I said to Peter, the bartender.

"Sure thing, Wright," he said with a head nod as he slid a bottle toward me.

I'd decided to go really casual with the date and meet at Flips, the local bar. I didn't want an awkward dinner or movies or something like that. I didn't really want any kind of expectations. I wanted a few drinks and maybe some heavy making out. That might make me feel better about the madness of my life.

Truly, I couldn't even believe I'd left the office for this. I'd almost canceled a couple of times, but that awkward conversation with Patrick had kept me from doing it. I needed to move on. I couldn't keep running into him at family events and have everything feel uncomfortable. I needed a hot new boyfriend who would make me forget all about Patrick.

I tipped my beer back and waited in my sky-high heels. I'd gone all out in a dress that Julia had insisted I get the last time I went shopping. It was skintight and left little to the imagination. At the time, I'd had no idea where I'd wear it.

The door opened then, and Travis Jones walked into the bar. He was as cute as I remembered. He'd been a senior when I was a freshman, and he'd gone to a rival high school. Landon had punched him in the face when Travis asked me to prom. He had taken it back after that and gone with someone else. But, for a few awesome days, I'd been the only freshman in the school going to senior prom.

"Morgan," he said with that confidence he'd always had. He pulled me into a hug and kissed my cheek. "This is a surprise."

"I'm full of surprises," I said, stepping out of his embrace.

"How many times have I asked you out, and you've never said yes?"

I shrugged. "You were always joking. Trying to make up for that time you ditched me and went to prom with someone else."

"To be fair, your brother did break my nose."

"I suppose Landon was a bit intimidating as the starting quarterback."

"No intimidating brothers tonight. I'm glad you texted," he said. His eyes swept me up and down with acute interest.

"Me, too." It was still up to debate whether or not that was true.

Travis ordered himself a beer, and then we took our beers over to a booth and cozied up in the corner. I hadn't seen him in a while, and we played catch-up. He congratulated me on becoming CEO, but the way he said it made it seem like maybe he wasn't really congratulating me. Travis was a pharmacist at the medical center. He worked long hours and made good money, but it was still as if he were wary of my success.

Two drinks later, and I decided I didn't care. I wanted to have a fun time. The way to do that was to not talk about work.

"Do you ever just...miss high school?" he asked with a laugh.

I balked. "No."

"What? Why not? You were a hot cheerleader. Everyone threw themselves at you."

I didn't like to talk about high school that much. Most people closest to me remembered that my father had died my sophomore year, right after my birthday. I might have been both popular and a cheerleader. But I'd also been a wreck, and boys both hadn't mattered and filled the time. If Landon had punched every guy I'd fooled around with in high school after dad died, then he wouldn't have been able to throw a football.

"High school wasn't for me," I said instead. "Do you miss it?"

"Sometimes, but sometimes, I'm surprised I'm still stuck in Lubbock."

"Don't you love Lubbock?"

"It's home," he said with a shrug. "I just always thought I'd get out. Hard to meet new people here."

"Now, that is true."

Though I'd never wanted to leave. Lubbock wasn't for everybody. It was big enough to have everything you needed but not big enough to have everything you really wanted. It'd grown exponentially in the last decade. I loved the small-town vibe in the bigger city. The college town always kept it fresh. The high schools were amazing. It was a great place to raise a family. There was too much to love to want to leave. I couldn't imagine being offered something better than this place.

"And shit like this happens here," Travis muttered.

"Like what?" I asked. I turned around and tried to figure out what he was talking about.

"Sorry. I know you're friends with the guy, but he starts shit every time we're in the same building."

Then, my eyes caught him, striding into the bar and up to the pool tables where a group of his friends from the gym were playing.

Patrick.

Fuck. I hadn't expected that to happen. *What are the chances?*

"Why do y'all not get along?" I asked.

"High school bullshit. His girlfriend dumped him, and then I took her to homecoming. He acted like it was the end of the world. It's been long over."

Yeah. That wasn't the way Patrick had told that story. Or, to be more specific, the way Austin had made fun of him about it. Patrick always said that Travis had stolen his girlfriend and taken her to homecoming while they were still dating. Then, when Patrick had decided to ask

60

someone else out, she'd come back running. He'd taken her to homecoming anyway, and then after homecoming, she'd dumped him *again* for Travis. I still thought that she'd only done it for the mums.

"Fuck, and now, he's coming over here," Travis grumbled.

I froze. I'd known when I picked Flips as our date location that it was because it was so visible. But I'd thought the date would get back to someone and then to Patrick. I hadn't anticipated him actually *being* here.

Fuck. Shit. Damn.

What the hell am I supposed to do? Act cool. This is normal.

Patrick didn't want me. *Who cared that I'd just spent twelve years obsessing over him?* I was determined to move forward, and if that meant Travis Jones and some very fine making out, then I'd go for it.

Patrick approached the table, and I plastered a fake smile on my face.

"Hey," Patrick said. His eyes glanced to me and then Travis.

"Young," Travis said in greeting.

"Jones," he said coolly. Then, he just glared at the pair of us.

"What are you up to tonight?" I said when I realized he wasn't going to say anything else.

"Just hanging with the guys."

"No Austin, right?" I asked quickly. The last thing I wanted was for my brother to be at a bar right after rehab.

"Of course not."

"What's up with Austin?" Travis asked.

"Nothing," Patrick and I said at the exact same time.

I bit my lip and glanced down at my empty beer. *Smooth.*

"Morgan, can I talk to you for a minute?" Patrick asked. "Alone."

"We're kind of on a date right now," Travis told him.

"I noticed that. Thank you for stating the obvious."

I sighed heavily through my nose. *Jesus, these boys.* They were going to come to blows in the middle of the bar over something that had happened in high school. And I'd be stuck in the middle as some damn catalyst that really made zero sense. This was *not* what I'd signed up for.

"Sure. Just for a minute," I said to Patrick. Then, I turned to Travis. "I'll be right back. Could you get me another beer?"

Travis looked pissed about the interruption, but the fact that I'd asked for another beer showed I was coming back. He couldn't be that upset.

I hopped out of the booth and onto wobbly legs. *Whoa.* I hadn't stood up for a while. I stumbled a few steps, and Patrick caught me around the waist. I hastily retreated and leaned against the side of the booth until I got my bearings.

"How much have you had to drink?" he asked.

"I don't know. A couple of beers. Why?" I said as I followed him down a few more booths until we found an empty one for me to lean on.

"You look drunk."

I rolled my eyes. "What do you *want*, Patrick? Can't you see that I'm on a date?"

"Yeah, I see that. But what the fuck are you doing with Travis Jones?"

"I asked him out."

"Why?" he asked, baffled.

Because you blew me off!

That was what I wanted to shout in his face. But I didn't.

"He's cute," I said instead.

"You know he's a douche bag."

So are you!

I ground my teeth together to keep from saying what I wanted. *I couldn't be that drunk!*

"That was in high school. People change. I've changed."

"I think this is a bad idea."

"Thanks for letting me know," I said with a pointed eye roll. "Next time, I'll definitely care about your opinion."

"Morgan," he muttered.

"What? You're *not* one of my brothers. I have three of them, and they're annoying and nosy enough. I don't need you to come in here and act like one of them, too. As if you have any right to know or care who I'm dating. So, back off."

He took a step back at my forcefulness and then shook his head. "I'm just looking out for you."

"Well, look out for someone else. I'm a big girl. I can do what I want."

I turned and took a step away from him, but he grabbed my elbow and stopped me.

"I don't want you to do something that you'll regret."

I stared up into his big baby-blue eyes full of concern for me and didn't hold back the angry voice in my head. "Too late," I spat.

Nine

Patrick

I saw red.

What the fuck am I supposed to say to that? I'm the person she regrets? Me?

Fucking fuck fuck!

I looked at her hurt expression and then watched her walk away, back to that douche bag.

Fuck! This is ridiculous.

Everything she'd said was true. Completely true. A hundred fifty percent true. But also false. It made me want to rage.

I'd walked into the bar and seen her sitting there with Travis fucking Jones of all people, and something had changed. I didn't even know what it was. My stomach was in knots. My hands curled into fists. I felt like beating the shit out of this dude. The same dude I'd wanted to beat the shit out of in high school. And, this time, there was no explanation.

I had no claim on Morgan. I'd been purposefully avoiding her all week. There was no reason for me to feel this amount of anger. And yet...I did.

Christ, what the fuck did it even mean?

All I'd known was that I had to get her alone. I'd had to change her mind. I'd had to say something.

And then the whole thing had backfired in my face.

I didn't stick around to see what was going to happen. I didn't want to know. Morgan clearly liked to come on to guys when she was drunk. I hadn't been anything special at the time. I'd made the right move, turning her down last week.

But, still...this twisted, tainted feeling kept swirling through me. It'd been a long time since I felt it. Something I didn't even like to acknowledge.

Jealousy.

I was jealous of Travis Jones.

I didn't want him near her. And I couldn't even put into words why that was. I was going insane, and it was all her fault. No...all my fault. I could have had her. But I'd been the gentleman. I hadn't wanted her to wake up in the morning and not want what we'd done. Even if my body had said that it very much wanted her.

And, now, I was going crazy.

I needed to calm down and get over it.

It wasn't like a girl like Morgan Wright would ever actually be interested in me anyway.

―――――――

The next day was my last at Wright Construction. Steph and Thomas had stayed the week, and I'd promised that I would come over to see them before they left for San Francisco. I slipped out of the office on my last day with a round of congratulations and then left the place behind forever.

When I showed up at my parents' house, my mom and dad had gone to Market Street to pick up some groceries for dinner. Steph was in the shower, and I knew that it could be an event. Thomas greeted me at the door and offered me a beer.

"Just water is fine with me," I told him and took one out of the fridge. I leaned back against the counter. "How much has Steph already planned with this wedding?"

Thomas's eyes rounded. "I'd guess everything."

"Did you decide on a date yet?"

"She said she needed at least six months to plan this thing, which means May. I'm okay with whatever she chooses. Like today, when she decided she wanted to have it in Lubbock instead of San Francisco."

"Really? She wants it *here*? She hasn't lived here in like a decade."

Thomas shrugged. "Don't argue with a woman in wedding-planning mode."

"Sound advice."

"Speaking of, would you like to be a groomsman?"

"I'd be honored," I said, holding my hand out for us to shake.

"Great. Thanks. I think Steph is going to have a bunch of bridesmaids, so I'll have to find some other friends."

"That sounds like Steph."

"What sounds like me?" Stephanie asked, stepping into the kitchen. She was in sweats and had her hair up in a baby-pink towel.

"I heard you're having a ton of bridesmaids."

"Whatever. I don't have a firm head count," Steph said. "But I am asking Morgan."

"Really?"

"Yeah, she was, like, my bestie in high school."

"She seemed surprised that you even invited her to your birthday party."

"Yeah, well, that's Morgan. She's cynical, and she's always thought that people don't really like her. But I love her to pieces, and I want her there for my big day. Plus, I can rely on Morgan to crack the whip and get everyone in line."

I shook my head. "You're using her to keep anyone from becoming a diva?"

"No, I'm using her because she'll look pretty in a dress," Steph drawled sarcastically. Then, she gasped. "What if we had a New Year's Eve wedding? Then, I could make everyone wear sequins and glitter!"

Thomas's groan was audible. "What happened to six months?"

"But…glitter!"

"I'm not touching that one with a ten-foot pole," I said, backing away.

"Oh, yeah? Are you going to finally tell me what happened with Morgan last week?" Steph pushed.

"Nothing."

"Psh…I wasn't born yesterday." She poked me in my ribs. Hard. "Did you two hook up?"

"No, we didn't."

Steph dramatically blew out her breath. "Well, why the fuck not?"

"Because she's…Morgan."

"So?"

"So what?" I snapped.

I was still pissed about last night. I didn't know what had ended up happening with Morgan and Travis. I didn't really want to think about it. Add it to a long list of things I didn't want to think about. Like how badly I'd fucked up.

"She's a successful woman who is into you. I don't know why because she's way too hot for you and way too smart for you and totally out of your league. But you're telling me that you had someone like that at your place, and you never made a move?"

"For one, it's Morgan!" I insisted. "Two, she had been drinking. And, anyway, she's not into me. She's already dating someone else."

"Who is she dating?"

"Do you remember Travis Jones?"

Steph laughed. "Of course I remember Travis. You hated him, and he asked Morgan to prom that one time."

"Yeah. That guy. She's dating that guy."

"You're an idiot. Morgan is not interested in Travis Jones."

"Well then, explain to me how I saw her on a date with him last night at Flips."

"If nothing happened last weekend, then I'd guess she's probably trying to get over you rejecting her."

I sputtered at the accusation. Of course, I had rejected her in so many words, and Morgan had looked upset about it, but I had never thought that Morgan would date someone else because of that.

"You need to fix this."

"Fix what?" I asked. "Morgan isn't into me."

Steph stopped and stared at me. Then, she burst out laughing and doubled over. She couldn't seem to get air in.

"What the fuck, Steph?"

She held up her hand, as if to tell me to wait until she could catch her breath. She beat her chest twice and coughed. "You're so oblivious."

"To what?"

"Morgan. God, you just need to talk to her. Go make this right with her. If you don't, you'll end up regretting it."

"Steph…"

"I don't know how much longer she'll wait for you to wake up, Patrick. If she's already trying to date someone else, then the clock is ticking. As your sister and her friend, go," she said, shoving me toward the door. "And tell her about the bridesmaid thing, too."

I shook my head. I couldn't comprehend what had just happened. "You think she likes me?"

"I think you should ask her yourself, dummy."

Steph didn't have to tell me twice. I was out of the house and on my way back to the office in a heartbeat. She was right. I needed to talk this out with Morgan. I didn't even know what I was fucking feeling, but trying to ignore it obviously wasn't solving anything.

I parked up front as the five o'clock crowd was leaving the building. Heidi and Julia waved at me as I passed. I cracked a smile and hurried inside.

Most of the building was empty when I took the elevator up to Morgan's office. I knew she'd still be there. She stayed all night when she could.

I rounded the corner for her office and frowned when I saw it was empty. There was no way she had gone home. I glanced into the conference room where I'd found her last week. Empty.

Well…shit.

I heard voices down the hall. They were coming from Jensen's office. A lightbulb switched on in my mind. Right. With Jensen gone, she would have moved down the hall.

I walked toward her new office but stalled when I heard her giggle. I knew that giggle. I didn't really know when I'd become an expert on all of Morgan's different laughs, but the only time I'd heard that was either when she was drunk or flirting. I'd always thought her flirting with me was her normal goofing off. Wasn't so sure anymore. And, after what had happened with Austin, I didn't think that she'd be drunk at work, so…who exactly was she flirting with?

If this was fucking Travis Jones, I was going to lose it. Between last night at Flips and now in her office, I felt like I was losing my mind.

"You're going to have to tell me about that meeting at least a dozen more times. It gets funnier every time."

David Calloway.

I clenched my hands into fists. I liked the guy just fine. He made a good CFO. He fit into the Wright family like he'd been there all along. A bit too well honestly.

Morgan giggled again. "I mean, you should have seen the look on his face when he stormed out."

I didn't like that he was making Morgan giggle.

"Seriously, Morgan, I'm starving. Let's go get dinner. We can talk about that issue I have over Thai food."

Or that he was asking Morgan out for dinner.

"I do love Thai."

Fuck.

It had only been a few days since we were together, only a night since she'd done who knew what with Travis fucking Jones, and now, she was into David?

This is a mistake.

A huge fucking mistake.

Yet I couldn't let it go. This uncomfortable feeling settled in my chest, and I knew I was about to make an idiot out of myself. Again.

I stepped forward into the doorway. Morgan's eyes rounded when she saw me there. David whirled around and grinned.

"Patrick"—he walked over, sticking his hand out, and I shook a little harder than was necessary—"good to see you."

"Yeah," I said unconvincingly.

Morgan stood from behind Jensen's desk. She looked tiny behind the giant thing. But I knew her appearance was deceiving. She was a force to be reckoned with.

"You're here late," Morgan said. It came out like an accusation. "Isn't it your last day?"

"Yeah...it was."

"Were you looking for Austin?" David asked. "He already left."

"No, I wanted a word with Morgan."

"Of course. We're sorry to see you go."

I met Morgan's dark eyes. She seemed confused and guarded. As if she didn't know what I was going to say. *After this past week, how could I blame her?*

"Yeah. Tech made me an offer I couldn't refuse," I said to David.

"I definitely know what that's like. Wright Construction was that offer for me," David said. "Should I give you two a minute?"

"Just wait outside, David. We can go get Thai after this," Morgan said.

And standing there, between Morgan and her dinner date, I felt like as stupid as I was. Morgan was moving on. She already had two dates this week. Whatever had almost happened last week was like a dream from another lifetime.

"You know what? Never mind," I said, taking a step backward. "We can do this another time. I'm just going to head out."

"You sure?" David said. "I really don't mind."

"It's cool," I said before turning and walking out of the office.

It was official. Morgan Wright made me act like a fool.

Ten

Morgan

I stood, frozen in place, as Patrick walked out of my office. David was giving me a questioning look that I couldn't answer. I didn't know why Patrick was here, what he'd come for, or why he'd refused to talk to me when he was the one who asked.

Honestly, I couldn't even believe he was *here*. After seeing me last night at Flips, he'd stormed out of the bar, leaving me alone with Travis. I'd felt so twisted up about the exchange that I ended the night shortly after that. After Patrick's apparent jealousy, I hadn't had the same gusto that I'd felt when I first started the date. Travis had done his job...maybe a little too well and made me realize that dating wasn't really for me right now.

"You think he's okay? He looked kind of pale," David said.

"I have no idea."

"Maybe I should check on him?"

I shook my head. "No, let me do it. I'll be right back. Just...wait here."

Without waiting for his reply, I hurried down the hallway to the elevator and found Patrick standing there with his arms crossed over his chest. He whirled around as I approached. And seeing his uncertainty infuriated me. I didn't even know why.

All this time, I'd wanted him to see me...to chase me down...to want me. Now, I'd finally tried to let him go, and he was giving me all the signs that we should be together. And, also, acting so strange—arguing at church, randomly showing up to talk to Austin, blowing up on me at the bar—and, now, this? *What the hell?*

"What's your problem?" I snapped.

"My problem?" he demanded.

"Yeah! What are you doing here? Last night might have been an accident, but this isn't. And, when you came up to see Austin earlier this week...that wasn't either. So, if you have something to say, why don't you just spit it out?"

"Yeah, I came here on purpose. I came to see you. I came to talk to you."

"Then, why did you run out so fast?" I asked in frustration.

"Do you really have to ask that?" He shot me an incredulous look.

"I don't want to play games, Patrick."

"You think *I'm* playing games?" he asked in exasperation. "Two guys in two days, Mor, and I'm the one playing games?"

"Two guys?" I asked, brows furrowed.

"Sorry, don't let me keep you from your dinner date tonight."

I shook my head. "I don't have a date tonight. And, not that it's any of your business, my date last night basically ended after you left."

Something like relief crossed his face and then disappeared. "What about David?"

"What *about* David?"

"Thai. Dinner. Tonight," he ground out.

"Oh my God," I gasped out with a light laugh. "It's not a date. It's David. I'm his boss. He's my CFO."

"As if that has ever stopped anyone."

"It's not like that," I reassured him. Then, I sighed. "I don't even know why we're having this conversation. Why do you even care who I date?"

"Come here," he said, his voice low, soft, and seductive.

It was a tone I'd definitely never heard from him before.

"Why?" I asked, guarded.

He reached out and pulled me closer to him. I stumbled forward on my high heels and nearly fell into his arms. His hands ran down my suit jacket, across my open palms, and then back up. I shivered.

What was happening? Oh my God, was this happening? Was this even real?

"I made a mistake," he told me.

"You did?"

He leaned forward and ran his jaw across my cheek. His five o'clock shadow scratched me. I had to close my eyes to keep from groaning. His lips moved to my ear, and he grazed the sensitive shell. My whole body came alive.

"Yes. Last week, you thought I rejected you."

"You did," I whispered. The hurt unmistakable in my voice.

"I thought I was saving you from yourself. But that wasn't the case, was it?" he asked, his eyes moving back to mine. Our mouths only inches apart.

All I could do was shake my head. I'd absolutely wanted him. In every way.

"You wanted to kiss me then, right?"

"Yes," I admitted.

"And you want to kiss me now."

I swallowed. "Yes."

"Good. I can work with that."

I laughed a breathy little thing that made his eyes crinkle in satisfaction. "I thought that we couldn't do this and that I deserved someone else and all that."

"Still true." His thumb dragged across my bottom lip.

"What's changed then?"

"I thought you were making a drunken mistake. And then I spent a week without you. A week where you were my every thought. Where I had to watch your indifference. Where I had to watch you with some other guy. And I decided...I didn't like that, and I didn't want that. We still probably shouldn't do this...but I want to."

A chill ran through me at his words. Goose bumps erupted on my bare arms. I was putty in his hands. I'd thought that last week was my last chance. That Patrick would never be interested in me. *Who knew that a week apart was all he needed to see the light?*

"Are you going to kiss me then?" I asked.

He leaned forward until our lips were almost touching. I held my breath and waited. I was anxious with anticipation and desperate for that moment I'd been waiting for, for so long.

I felt the lightest touch of his lips on mine before he said, "No."

"Oh my God, you're killing me." I pushed him away from me.

"You know what you're going to do?"

"Tell you to shove it?" I joked.

He grinned. "You're going to cancel your dinner plans with David."

"Patrick."

"And then you're going to come over to my house, and I'm going to cook you dinner."

"You are?"

He nodded. "You probably haven't eaten all day anyway."

"I've eaten! And more than kale and Skittles."

"Mor?"

I laughed. "All right, all right. Dinner it is. Let me tell David."

I walked back to my office, silently pleading with myself not to freak out. I didn't know what was going on with me and Patrick, but I needed some serious chill if I was going to find out.

"Everything all right?" David asked.

"Yeah, it's fine, but I'm going to need a rain check on dinner."

David raised his eyebrows. I could see him piecing together everything that had happened.

"I see. Okay."

"Sorry that we never got to what you wanted to talk to me about. Did you want to talk now?"

He shook his head. "Rain check. Go have fun. You've earned it."

"All right. Are you sure? I feel bad about canceling."

"It's all right. Maybe I'll see if Sutton wants to get dinner."

"Sutton?" I asked curiously.

"Yeah. We've been hanging out some…when I can coax her out of the house."

"I didn't realize that."

"I remember that day as clearly as anyone else. I didn't even know her then, but now that I do," he said with a dreamy look in his eye, one I'd seen many a guy have about Sutton, "I want to make this time as easy as possible for her."

"That's really nice of you, David. I'm sure she and Jason appreciate it."

He frowned. "I don't need appreciation. She has enough to worry about, and that little boy needs all the love he can get."

"I know. I worry about her."

"Well, hey, don't worry about her tonight. Go have fun with Patrick," he said with a wink.

I blushed. "Mind not mentioning this to my brothers?"

"My lips are sealed."

"Thanks. I'm not ready to have three overbearing alpha men looking over my shoulder before I'm ready. Trust me."

"I could see that. Have a good time."

"Thanks. Night!"

I waved good-bye and then headed downstairs. Patrick was waiting for me at my car.

"I thought I was meeting you at your place," I told him.

"I decided to kidnap you."

"Isn't that illegal?"

"You're consenting to it."

"Am I?"

"Just get in the car, Morgan," he said with a laugh.

His eyes were bright, and I actually swooned at the sight. *How did he do this to me? How had he always done this to me?*

"Fine. But under protest."

"Liar," he muttered as he hopped into the driver's side.

He was right. I didn't protest a single thing about this. Not a single thing.

We made it across town in record time, and Patrick jogged around the truck to help me out. I couldn't believe that I was back here. I'd basically thought that last week was the end of this. Dreams dashed and all.

As I crossed the threshold into his house, everything felt totally different. Last time, I'd been excited to finally make my move. That I could finally make this happen.

Now, I was out of my element. I hadn't seriously dated since college. And, even then, three guys in four years hadn't been much to write home about. Actually, none of them had met my brothers. So, I literally hadn't written home about them.

"What are you thinking for dinner?" he asked as he peeled his suit jacket off.

"I...have no idea. What can you make?"

He laughed. "Everything. Why don't I just put something together? You don't like mushrooms or olives, right?"

I startled and froze in the middle of the kitchen. "Yeah. How do you know that?"

He seemed to think for a minute. "I don't know. I pay attention."

My heart melted. I'd never realized that Patrick had paid that much attention to me. *How had I thought that I could move on from him?*

"You can change into my clothes again if you want," he added with a grin.

"Are you trying to get me out of my clothes?" I teased.

"Not yet."

I gulped. "Awfully confident, aren't you?"

"Weren't you throwing yourself at me the last time you were here? Something about *get in bed* right now?"

I smacked his arm as my face flamed red. "God, try to embarrass a girl, why don't you? Is this how you treat all your dates?"

"Yeah, no," he said, setting a pot on the stove and adding water and a hefty dose of salt. "I've never cooked for a date before."

"Ever?" I gasped in disbelief.

He shot me another grin. "Ever."

"Is this a date? I mean, did I just make an ass of myself?"

"Morgan, relax."

He grabbed my arm and pulled me over to him. I moved into his arms and tried to do what he'd said. He pressed my back against his chest, skimming his hands over my hips. My breathing hitched at the movement. So intimate. Then, his lips brushed against my shoulder, and my whole body shuddered. I melted back into him.

"That's better," he said with a breathy laugh. "You were so tense."

"Well, I have a tendency to overthink things."

"You?" he gasped in mock horror.

"Oh, shut up."

He laughed. "Stop overthinking. Yes, of course, this is a date."

The rest of the tension left my body at that comment.

"But maybe you should change out of that dress." His hands slipped over the form-fitting plum dress I'd put on this morning.

"What's wrong with my dress?"

"It's very distracting."

"Oh, yeah?" I asked, spinning in place to face him.

"Yeah. I'm trying to cook for you here, and all I want to do is this."

He grabbed me by the backs of my thighs, hoisting my legs up and around his waist. I gasped and slid my arms around his neck to steady myself. My body was pressed tightly against him, exposing ample thighs for his viewing pleasure. I stared into his baby blues and saw the desire mirroring mine. It was intoxicating.

Feeling the part of the seductress, I flicked my tongue out across my bottom lip. Then, I dragged my bottom lip into my mouth. His eyes followed every movement. His body was hard and strong beneath mine as his hands slipped up my thighs to my ass and held me firmly in place.

All I wanted in that moment was him. All of him.

This was our choice.

This was our desire.

This was everything.

Patrick eased me back onto the counter to free up his hands. I groaned as he grazed my breasts on his ascent. He pushed harder against me, as if his own body couldn't hold back, even as his hands worked their way up to my face.

He cupped my cheek with one hand and dragged the other to the back of my head before pulling me toward him.

All of this anticipation, all the need, and all the innumerable times I'd imagined this moment happening…it was nothing compared to reality. To the way our bodies twined together and our heat mingled. To my racing heartbeat and his steady confidence. To the desire that snaked through my core and enveloped us both.

His lips touched mine, tentative at first. Tender as he explored me. His tongue darted out and ran across my lips until I opened for him. We met in the middle—tasting, touching, learning. He nibbled gently on my bottom lip, and I was a goner. I moaned at the caress, and the dam broke. He tugged me tighter against him and kissed me, like it was the last thing he would ever do. And, when I succumbed, drowning in him, I knew then that the wait had been worth it.

Eleven

Patrick

Fuck, *Morgan feels good.*

Her lips were soft and supple. The way she worked her tongue…fuck. I couldn't even begin to describe it. *How could I have known her so long and never done this? Not even thought about it?*

Of course, I knew why. Same reason I probably shouldn't have my tongue down her throat right now. But, shit, I'd tried to be a gentleman. I'd thought I was making the right decision before. And I knew there would be hell to pay for this later. My past had made sure of that. Didn't mean I had any intention of stopping this. Not a chance.

Not with her tight little body pressed against me and her hands shaking but clinging to my shirt and her toned legs wrapped around me in the most compromising of positions. I could think of something else I'd like to be doing between her legs. At least a couple of other things.

But Morgan wasn't any girl. As much as I wanted to dive right between her legs and make her come for days, I knew to take it slow. I didn't want to overwhelm her. In some ways, she still felt so innocent in my hands. As if all of this was so new for her.

When she was with me, she wasn't the proud, sarcastic, cynical workaholic that I'd known my whole life. She was this sensual, eager, beautiful woman. Maybe even a little, dare I say it, scared. I'd never seen Morgan scared a day in her life. All I wanted to do was prove to her that she had no reason to fear any of this. And pray that I could keep my word.

Morgan gently pushed me back. "Wait…"

"Are you serious?"

She grinned and hauled herself off the counter top. "Serious. Not that I don't want to keep kissing you."

"Yeah, because…I kind of thought that's what you wanted."

"Yeah. I mean, I do. I just…" She sighed and glanced away. "Is that what you want?"

"Morgan, are you overthinking this again?"

"Yes," she said with a shy laugh. "I don't want a repeat of last weekend, and I don't want to be jerked around."

"I'll admit, I've been acting erratic."

I had never been the guy to talk about my feelings or discuss this sort of thing with…well, anyone. Let alone right after the first time I kissed someone. I wasn't much of a talker in general unless it was joking around. But I could see that Morgan was legitimately afraid to take another step forward.

"A little?" she asked.

"Okay, a lot, but I talked to Steph."

"Oh God," Morgan said, going pale. "What did she say?"

"What do you think she said?" My curiosity was piqued.

"No idea."

There was definitely something she wasn't telling me.

"She laughed when I told her that I saved you from making a drunken mistake and that you weren't interested in me because you were already dating. She told me I needed to fix this. I just couldn't figure that you actually liked me."

"I do," she whispered.

I put my hand under her chin and made her look up at me again. "I think we're both on uneven ground here. This is new to me. Being here with you like this kind of terrifies me."

"Why? It's just me."

"I know that, but you have three older brothers who are my closest friends. And I don't want them to beat the shit out of me."

"They're not going to. When we're ready, we'll tell them like adults. Because we're fucking adults."

"Yeah. I'm sure that'll go over great," I said with a shake of my head.

"I mean, I think they might be macho idiots, like they always were when I was dating, but it's you. They know you."

I blew out a heavy breath. "Didn't stop me."

She paused and gave me a weighted, curious look. "What does that mean?"

"Our senior year of college, Steph and Austin hooked up."

Her jaw dropped. "What?"

"Yeah."

"She never told me!"

"Well, I found out and blew up. It was the only argument Austin and I ever had that I thought would end our friendship. She was only eighteen at the time and still in high school. I accused him of taking advantage of her. So, when you and I were together, I kept thinking about what had happened with Steph and what Austin's reaction would be."

"Wow," she muttered.

"I know."

"Well, I don't think that's going to happen, but I understand why you would be worried. It's not like we have to tell anyone what's going on yet. It's our first date, and I don't particularly want their nosy noses up in our business anyway. Why don't we just go back to dinner and making out?"

I breathed a sigh of relief. I'd been holding that in for a long time. It was probably the main reason I'd never even looked at Morgan. After that shit with Steph, it had taken a long time for me and Austin to get back on solid footing. I never wanted to go back to that. But, if there was something here with Morgan, I didn't want to stand on the sidelines, wondering when I was going to get into the game.

"Maybe I should get started on the spaghetti sauce then," I said.

She stood on her tiptoes and brought her lips to mine once more. I pressed her into my body, enjoying the feel of every inch of her against me. Already, my mind was drifting into the gutter. I opened her mouth and teased my tongue against hers. I was ready to say, *Fuck it*, when Morgan's stomach grumbled.

I broke away. "I thought you said you'd eaten."

"Um…well, I did. This morning. At, like, eight o'clock?"

I shook my head. "Get out of my kitchen, so I can feed you."

"Fine."

She scrunched up her nose at me as she walked out of the kitchen. I swatted at her ass with a wooden spoon, and she laughed before scurrying away. When she was gone, I finally got to work.

Cooking was an art form. Probably the only one I'd ever excelled at. Once I got into it, it was my Zen. Everything else would drift away, and it was just the ingredients and my masterpiece.

I didn't know how long I'd been working when Morgan peeked her head into the kitchen again.

"Something smells amazing in here."

"Here. Try."

I took the wooden spoon out of the sauce and offered it to her. She leaned into me and licked some of the sauce off the spoon. My eyes were glued to the way her body reacted to my cooking. She groaned and closed her eyes, and her face turned into pure ecstasy.

"That is incredible," she moaned. "How are you so good at this?"

"Lots of practice and patience."

"I wish I could cook," she said. She leaned her hip into the counter as I poured our pasta into bowls. She glanced down at the ground and frowned. "Jensen says Mom was a good cook, too."

"Your mom was an extraordinary woman."

"It seems unfair that you remember her more than I do."

"I know. I'm sorry."

She waved me off. "Nothing to be sorry for. It's not your fault she died of cancer when I was five and never taught me to cook."

"I could teach you," I offered. "But I think it's probably more enjoyable if I keep doing what I'm good at and you do what you're good at."

"So, you think I'd suck?"

"Definitely."

"Jerk."

I grinned as I placed both of the plates on the table and grabbed a bottle of red wine. I poured each of us a glass. Morgan sniffed it before taking a sip. She made a horrible face and then had another sip.

I tried to hide my laugh. "You're, uh, not a wine drinker?"

"I like it, but the first sip always tastes terrible."

"I'll remember that when I take you wine tasting."

Her eyes lit up. "We're going wine tasting?"

Whoa. Where had that come from? When had I even had the thought that I was going to take Morgan out? It was as if there was no processing from my brain to my mouth. I was just going to take her.

She might be overthinking things, but when I was with her, everything felt completely natural.

"Yeah. The Lubbock wineries are surprisingly good. Unless you want to go to Napa or something. I have to use up all my vacation before I start the new job."

Holy fuck! Honestly, did I just suggest going on a vacation with her?

"I wonder if I have access to the private jet now," she said with a mischievous smile.

"I'm pretty sure, if we don't want Jensen to know yet, taking his jet to Napa might tip him off."

She giggled that perfect laugh. "You're probably right. But it'd be hilarious to see his face."

"Can't argue with that."

She seemed to be brimming with excitement over the fact that I'd already confirmed a second date. I was starting to wonder who I was and what had happened with the normal Patrick Young. I'd never dated like this. Sex always happened on the first date, and then I'd get bored easily. I never cooked for other people. And the second date was never a guarantee and

I'd been worried that mentality would translate to Morgan as well. That I'd fuck everything up just by being me. But it seemed she brought out the best in me.

Twelve

Patrick

We finished up dinner, and then after cleaning up, we moved into the living room. I flipped a movie on in the background and wrapped an arm around Morgan's shoulders as we both pretended to watch the romcom on TV. All I could feel was the press of her hip into mine, her head tucked into my shoulder, our fingers threading together. The weight of her slight figure drove me crazy. I wanted to push her back into the couch and find all the ways to make her come. At the same time, I didn't want to rush her.

Fuck!

"Did I mention that Steph wants you to be a bridesmaid?" I asked.

"What?" Morgan sat up and looked at me. The movie completely forgotten.

"Yeah. She's thinking a New Year's Eve wedding. I think you might have to wear glitter or something."

"She would." Morgan rolled her eyes. "Are you in the wedding?"

I nodded.

"Oh, good."

"Why?"

"Weddings are so…" She made a face and stuck out her tongue.

I laughed. "Aren't you obsessed with that show *Say Yes to the Dress?*"

"I like TV," she said with a shrug.

"How do you have time for it?"

"It's good background noise. But I can't believe that Steph wants me in the wedding."

"Makes sense to me. Y'all are close. You've known each other since you were kids."

"True."

She leaned her head back against my shoulder and watched the movie again. I was distracted by the way her thumb dragged across my hand that I couldn't have told anyone what the movie was even about. Self-restraint was not my forte. I was dying to move forward.

"Patrick?"

"Hmm?"

Morgan sat up straighter. Then, she hitched her leg over my lap and straddled me. My eyes strayed to inch after inch of exposed thigh as her dress slid up dangerously high. My hands went to her hips. Half to keep her still and half to force her down. I wasn't exactly processing with her sitting on me like this. Well, my dick was.

It was saying, *Take this and run.*

She slipped her hands under my shirt, running her nails across my chest before tugging it up and over my head. Her eyes widened in appreciation. Even as her hands shook slightly, she moved them down to my belt buckle. Her eyes met mine for a second before she pulled it loose and snapped the button on my pants. My body jerked as she moved to the lining of my boxers.

"Fuck," I muttered, shoving her hips down hard against me.

Her eyes snapped back to mine. Then, she circled her hips in a hypnotizing figure eight. My fingers dug into her hips. Hard.

"Too much?" she asked slyly.

"Not enough," I told her. "Definitely not enough."

A part of me still couldn't believe that I was here with Morgan Wright. That she was the girl driving me crazy as she ground her hot body against mine. But I fucking wanted more.

She leaned forward until she had her lips against my ear. "Then, take more," she said, as if reading my mind.

My hands moved to her ass. I hoisted her up and then dropped her onto her back across the couch. She stretched out before me with her arms over her head. Her dark hair fanned out around her face. A coy smile played across her kiss-swollen lips. She looked like a fucking goddess.

I covered her body with mine, crushing my lips to hers. Our hips pressed together. I was sure she was all too aware of how much I wanted her in that moment. In response, she moaned and pulled her knees up to either side of my hips. I grasped her bare thigh before bunching her dress up to her waist. I traced the lace of her thong, and she moaned.

I pulled back to look at her, and she threw her arms around my neck.

"Don't stop," she said breathlessly.

Her cheeks were flushed and her breathing unsteady. And, God, she felt so good. I wanted to study every inch of her skin. Lick, kiss, and suck every sensitive part of her body until she trembled beneath me from release.

I pulled her back up, grabbed the hem of her dress, and tugged the whole thing up and over her head. She released backward and gave me the view of a lifetime. Her tits spilled out of a black lace bra that matched the thong I'd been fingering.

"Jesus Christ," I groaned.

"Probably not who you want to talk to right now."

I smirked and slid my hands back up her thighs. "Probably not."

She bit her lip and squirmed as I took my time moving up to the apex of her thighs. I dragged a finger across the damp fabric left covering her.

"Patrick," she moaned.

"Yes?"

"Tease."

"Mmhmm," I agreed.

I'd just hooked my finger under the material, ready to give her exactly what her body was demanding, when a banging came from the front door. Morgan and I both froze, eyes wide and fear palpable.

"Fuck."

Morgan jerked up and reached for her dress. "Fuck is right. Fuck. Are you going to answer that?"

Another knock sounded at her whisper. "Patrick?"

My head fell into my hands. *Austin.*

"Fuck," she hissed louder.

"Just…go into my bedroom. I'll convince him to leave."

"Are you kidding me right now? You want me to hide? How old are we?"

"Do *you* want to deal with him right now? Right after he got out of rehab?" I asked in frustration.

"Fine, fine," she spat, jerking away from me and walking into my bedroom.

She closed the door, and I cursed whichever god found this funny.

I threw my shirt back on, took a cursory glance of the room to make sure nothing was out of place, and then yanked the door open.

"What the fuck, dude?" Austin asked, stepping into my house. "Can't answer your phone?"

"I didn't have my phone on me."

I patted my pockets for dramatic effect. I hadn't looked at the damn thing since I got Morgan to my house.

I hadn't even considered that Austin would want to get ahold of me. It'd been different since he stopped drinking and started dating Julia. Our weekends had been all about getting wasted and going home with one of our normal hook-ups. We didn't hang out as much because of it, but I'd rather have him sober.

"Julia is out with Emery and Heidi tonight. I thought we could hang. What the hell were you doing in here?"

"Uh, nothing."

Austin gave me a solid side-eye. "You didn't answer your phone, and you weren't doing anything. Either you're jacking off or there's a girl here."

"Neither. Just here by myself."

"Is it Mindi?" Austin asked with a shake of his head. "I think she's crazy, but I'm not against you dating her …even if I can never say her roommate's name again if I want to keep my balls."

I laughed. "Not Mindi. It's no one. I'm alone."

"Whatever. Don't tell me. Just answer your phone next time. I'll leave you with your nobody," Austin said with an eye roll. He didn't believe me any more than I was telling the truth. "Are we still doing lunch tomorrow? We can catch the Tech game."

"I'll be there."

"Tell your friend I said hi," Austin said. He chuckled at himself, punched me in the arm, and then left.

I breathed a sigh of relief when he was out the door, and Morgan peeked her head out.

"He's gone?"

I nodded. "Yeah. I guess I should have been checking my phone."

"I guess so. Who knew my brother was so needy?"

"He says hello by the way."

"So I heard." She frowned.

There was a divide between us now where there hadn't been before. A few short minutes ago, we'd almost crossed a line that neither of us could come back from. Now, we were standing a half-dozen feet apart with nothing but space. Those few minutes had given her time to reconsider. I could see it on her face.

"Maybe we should take this slow," I suggested so that she didn't have to.

"No, we shouldn't."

I cleared the distance between us. "There's plenty of time."

"I don't get it, Patrick. Didn't you hear Austin? You normally have some new girl here. You don't think twice about moving forward or whatever with them. But it's different with me? You want to go slow with me? You're never the gentleman, but now, you insist on it?" She scoffed and looked away from me. "If you don't really want to do this, then just say so."

I grabbed her chin in my hand and forced her to look at me again. Anger at the accusation hit me. Maybe I'd been concerned before, but tonight had changed things.

"My past is completely wide open to you, Morgan. You know all about what I've done. I've never had to hide who I am from you because you've been there from the beginning. You've seen it all, just like Austin. It's not surprising that he thought you were another girl. Because, for me, there has never been anything else. Physical with no connection. You're damn right that I'm not a gentleman."

"So, that's it then?" she asked with that hardened strength I'd seen from her in the boardroom. The defense mechanism she deployed when dealing with the outside world.

She pushed me away, but I reached for her elbow and held her in place.

"No, that's not it." I tugged her close again. "I think we should go slow because I want to do this the right way for once."

She paused, and I saw the anger slip away. "You want to do this right?"

"Yeah," I said, suddenly nervous by my own outburst. "You're different, Morgan. You're *not* just some girl. You never have been, and you never will be."

Thirteen

Morgan

"Knock, knock," a voice said from the door of my office on Monday morning.

"Julia," I said with a smile. "Come in."

"Are we still doing lunch?"

"Yes, let me send out this email, and then I'll actually eat lunch today."

She laughed as she walked over and plopped down in a seat in front of my new desk. It had come in this weekend, and Jensen's office was finally starting to feel like my own.

"I'm excited that you invited me to lunch. I like having girl time with you," Julia said.

"Same. I didn't really have girlfriends before you all started dating my brothers."

"I've never been that great at girlfriends either," Julia said. She swept her rose-gold hair to one shoulder, revealing the myriad of piercings on her ear and the tattoos peeking from her shoulder. "Heidi kind of forced me to be friends with her."

"She and Emery are quite a pair." I sent out my last email and then stood. "Okay, I'm ready."

"Great! I was thinking Thai Pepper if that's all right?"

I glanced at my clock and sighed. "They're so slow though."

"Yeah...but the food is worth it."

"All right. I should probably let David know on the way out."

Julia sent me a sly look as we left the office. "David's cute, right?"

"Is he?" I asked, taken off guard.

"Come on. You've noticed. You work with him all the time."

"Haven't really noticed." I waved at David when we got to his office. "Taking a long lunch. Text me if you need me."

He was on the phone and held his thumb up. I really looked at him for the first time. Julia was right. He was good-looking. Tall and broad-shouldered with an energetic smile. No wonder Patrick had been worried about David when he saw us together.

Oh well. It was probably good I had no interest in my own CFO. Talk about trouble. That would make Patrick look like nothing in comparison.

"He is kind of cute," I admitted as we started to walk out of the building together.

"Right! Good. I'm glad you think so. I think you should go out with him."

"Are you crazy? He's my subordinate."

"As the head of HR for Wright Construction, I will agree that it is crazy and a horrible idea...but as your friend." Julia winked. "He's, like...barely your subordinate."

I shook my head. "That's an awful idea."

"The girls and I are determined to hook you up with someone by Christmas!"

"Uh," I said in response.

What the hell could I say to that?

It's not like I could say that I'd started talking to Patrick. That would get straight back to my brothers. Something I did not want to deal with yet. It was enough that Patrick liked me and wanted to see where this relationship was going. If it really went somewhere, well, then we'd cross that bridge when we got to it.

"It'll be fine," Julia said.

I didn't correct her. It was easier that way. It wouldn't come to that anyway.

We drove across campus in Julia's black Tahoe and parked in the back lot outside of Thai Pepper. It was a hole-in-the-wall sort of place that was always packed for lunch. It was noisy and hard to find a table, but the food was too good to pass up.

"Ah, there they are!" Julia said when we entered the restaurant.

"They?" I asked.

My eyes scanned the room and landed on Heidi and Emery holding a table in the corner. I laughed and shook my head. I should have known that she'd invited them. This was clearly an intervention. I was the only one who hadn't known what was happening.

We maneuvered our way across the crowded room. I pulled out a seat across from Emery, and Julia sat across from Heidi. They were a commanding trio. I was the CEO of a huge organization, but I was out of my depth with girl chat. The last time we'd had a girls' night was to celebrate my promotion. I'd gotten wasted and hung out with Patrick most of the time. I couldn't even remember what had happened at the end of that night, except that he'd gotten me home somehow. This was all to say that I failed at girlie things.

"Morgan, we're so glad you wanted to do lunch," Heidi said with a wide smile. Her blonde hair was in a slicked-back ponytail at the top of her head, and unlike her friends who preferred shades of black, she was in a fitted, long-sleeved pink top.

"What Heidi means is," Emery said, "thanks for letting us commandeer your lunch with Julia. Now, I hope you don't mind Heidi trying to butt her way into your love life."

"You should get used to it," Julia agreed.

"Hey, I'm not that bad!" Heidi cried.

"No, you're worse," Emery said.

"I don't hear any of you complaining now that you're engaged and shit."

"Whatever," Julia said. "We all know the real hook-up is you and Emery."

"I do love her," Heidi said, draping an arm across Emery's chair and batting her eyelashes at her.

Emery kissed Heidi's cheek. "You know it."

"Get a room," Julia groaned. She turned to look at me. "Can you believe these two?"

I laughed and shrugged. They all seemed pretty amazing to me. I hated that I always felt like an outsider, even when they were including me. That was how I felt about Steph inviting me to be in her wedding. We'd talked on the phone this weekend, and I still couldn't believe that she wanted me to be a part of it. I wished relationships came as easy to me as my loyalty to my family and my passion for work.

"Now, as we were saying," Heidi said, pulling out a notebook after we ordered our pad thai, "we're on a mission. We know there's the big Wright Christmas party coming up in, like, three weeks. We thought we'd help set you up on some dates."

"Heidi made a list," Emery said with a dramatic eye roll.

"Y'all, I really appreciate this," I said. I chewed on my lip. *How the hell was I going to get out of this?* I didn't want to go on any blind dates, and I didn't want to tell them about Patrick.

"Just give it a shot," Julia encouraged.

"Okay, option one is," Heidi said, "Todd Hammond. He's a pretty boy. He likes to wear Ralph Lauren polos and boat shoes. One of those frat guys, but he's not a douche. Emery will pull up his picture."

"Um, y'all…"

"Option two, Jeremy Masterson. He's one of those gym guys. Likes to wear sleeveless shirts sometimes. We'll forgive him because he's the hottest option."

"Heidi, stop!"

All three girls looked up at me with wide eyes.

"While I appreciate it, I'm not going on any blind dates. I've, um…actually started seeing someone."

Heidi put down her notebook and looked eager. "Oh my God, who?"

"Uh, you don't know him," I lied.

"Where did you meet him?" Emery asked.

I swallowed. *Shit.* "We were at a party together. We hit it off, and things have been going well so far."

"That's so exciting!" Julia cried. "What's his name?"

Fuck.

"Joe."

"Joe," Heidi said in delight. "That's amazing. We'll table the list for now. Tell us about Joe. Is he hot? Does he treat you like royalty? When do we get to meet him?"

"Um…it's still really new. I haven't told anyone about it yet. So, I'd appreciate it if you didn't all blab to my brothers."

Heidi zipped her mouth shut. Emery held up her hands.

Julia promised, "Don't worry about us."

Yeah, right. I'd probably have a call by the end of the business day, and that was if I was lucky.

I spent the rest of lunch feeling like a total idiot as I invented my fake boyfriend. I tried to keep everything as true as possible. Lies were better when they were mostly true anyway. Then, you wouldn't slip up. I'd learned that in business long before I ever had to apply it to a relationship.

By the time I got back from lunch, I was frazzled. I appreciated finally having friends, but, shit, it made everything much more complicated. I just needed to get back to work and piece together how that lunch had gone so wrong.

I was still reeling when I entered my office and found Patrick standing in front of my desk. I cleared my throat. He whirled around and smiled the most adorable lopsided smile. My stomach flipped.

"Hey," I said.

"Hey."

We'd spent most of the weekend together, but it was still surreal to see him here, in my office. Part of me kept wondering when the rug would be pulled out. That, all along, maybe I had just imagined this. But he was smiling at me with light in his eyes that said he was remembering everything we'd done all weekend.

"What are you doing here?" I stepped further into the room, toward him.

"I wanted to see you."

"Here?" I asked, glancing back to the door.

"Where else? Don't you live here?"

"Austin works on *this* floor."

"Yes, well, that will be a convenient excuse."

I rolled my eyes. "Excuses, excuses."

"Hey, I'm here to see you," he said, reaching for my hand and tugging me closer to him. "Why don't we hold the snark for a minute or two?"

"Not possible."

"Oh, believe me, I know."

"So, you just came to see me?" I asked suspiciously.

"No. I obviously have ulterior motives."

I couldn't even get the words out to ask what his ulterior motives were before he dropped his lips down onto mine.

Patrick Young was kissing me.

In my office.

At work.

Where anyone could see.

What was my life right now?

Amazing. Just like the taste of him and the way he fit against me and the desire that swept through my body.

I melted into him, delirious from the moment. His hands were on my face. Our breathing ragged and desperate. The kiss unimaginable, raw, and addictive. Just like the man before me.

I didn't want to pull away. If this was wrong, I didn't want to be right.

He gently released me and landed a light kiss on the tip of my nose. "That's why I'm here."

"I suppose you can visit me in my office anytime then."

"You suppose?"

I nodded, staring up into his baby blues and feeling my body floating off into the clouds. I could get lost here. It was tempting to forget everything else that I had going on, but I couldn't do that. Just because I finally had Patrick, it didn't mean I could slack off.

"Yeah. But…maybe not right now. I'm pretty swamped."

Patrick grinned. "All right. You free for dinner?"

"I probably should eat here," I said with a sigh.

"All right. We'll figure it out. I know how important your job is."

"Are you coming for Thanksgiving?"

"Can't. Austin asked me already, but I'm having dinner with the fam. Steph left, and I hate when they have to be alone for the holidays."

"Probably for the better anyway. The girls are snooping, and I'm not ready for my brothers to suspect something between us is happening anyway."

"It'll be fine. They won't figure it out." He dropped another kiss on my lips. "But maybe...come over whenever you're done?"

"Maybe," I said coyly.

"I like my chances."

He straightened and then exited my office. I sighed heavily, loving where my life was right now. Probably not the best idea to keep this from everyone or to be sneaking around and lying. It all made me frantic and unsure, but when I was in his arms again, everything else would just slip away.

A knock at the door made me jump. I turned back around, expecting Patrick to stroll back in for one more kiss, but I was disappointed to find Uncle Owen intruding instead. I suppressed a disappointed sigh.

"Owen," I said in greeting. "Our meeting isn't for another hour."

"Considering how you weren't prepared for our previous meeting, I figured we could use some more time."

There went the carefully plotted out afternoon I'd scheduled. Instead, I would have to deal with my douche uncle, who seemed to be making it his sole mission to piss me off. All I wanted was for him to go back to Vancouver. I'd much prefer our meetings be about raising Wright Construction into the new age. We were already above the bar for most construction companies, but we wanted to lead the pack in environmental awareness and new digital and technological advancements. Getting caught up on what the Canadian branch was doing and how to bring them closer into the fold was taxing. Owen had good ideas, but being in his presence was repulsive.

"By all means, let's get started," I said, gesturing for him to sit.

"I'm just curious. How did the board approve you?"

I wanted to snap back that it was none of his fucking business. Instead, I said, "Jensen recommended me, and I was approved unanimously. Just like Jensen was after our father died."

"Ethan," Owen practically hissed. "How charming that the board continues to think his children are as capable as he was."

There went all my good feelings from my kiss with Patrick. I needed to restrain myself. He was baiting me, and blowing up on him would just give him satisfaction.

"It is charming, isn't it?" I said with a broad smile.

His smile dropped at my flippancy.

Morgan: 1.

Owen: 0.

"Now, back to numbers…"

Fourteen

Morgan

Thanksgiving had never been a holiday the Wright family cared about.

None of us were particularly good cooks. We didn't feel the need to sit around a table full of catered food to say what we were thankful for. And, really, the only good thing about the day was football.

I was pretty sure most of that mentality was due to the fact that our father had worked every Thanksgiving that I could remember. Not just upstairs in his home office where he could come down and cheer on the Cowboys when he needed a break. Oh no, he'd actually go into the office from sun up until sundown. He'd leave all five of us to fend for ourselves. Without Jensen, I wasn't sure we would have even eaten on Thanksgiving, let alone had a real Thanksgiving dinner.

But that had all changed. Since my brothers were dating actual normal women from actual normal families who had actual normal Thanksgivings, that meant we got to have one, too. Emery, Heidi, and Julia came over to

Jensen's extra early and started cooking. I offered to help, but since I proved to be inept at even peeling potatoes, I was quickly cast back out to the living room.

By noon, when the Cowboys game started, the house smelled heavenly.

"Ugh, are you guys really watching the Cowgirls?" Julia asked when she wandered into the living room.

Austin shot her a lethal look. "Did you say that with a straight face?"

"Hardly."

"Don't mess with my Cowboys."

"They suck," she said with a shrug. "They're definitely going to lose to the Packers today."

"Don't you like the Browns?" I asked, butting into the conversation.

Julia gave me a wide-eyed look that said, *Whose side are you on?*

"That's right. My Ohio girl," Austin said. He pulled her into his lap on the chair. "Didn't they lose every game last year?"

"They won one!" Julia insisted.

"My high school team was better than that," Landon piped in from the corner.

"Watch it," Julia said.

"You're fighting a losing battle. Try college football next time," I said with a grin.

Julia hopped out of Austin's lap and pushed his shoulder. "Yeah! Morgan has a point. Ohio State is way better than Tech."

"Morgan," Austin groaned.

I shrugged. I was a shit stirrer; what could I say?

It was six o'clock before the girls finally told us it was time to eat. The Cowboys had ended up losing to the Packers, much to Julia's delight, and all the guys were bickering over what had gone wrong. Sutton was mostly ignoring everyone, except her son, Jason. Though I noticed David, who I'd invited over for the meal, was trying to engage her. A sight that made me internally giggle, considering the doe-eyed look he'd given me when he was talking about Sutton a week ago.

I was just glad to finally eat real food and not snacks and finger food. We had all gotten drinks and were about to sit down when the doorbell rang.

"I got it," Jensen said.

He hopped up from the table and went to the front door. Curious, I followed him. And, when he opened the door, my stomach dropped.

"Owen," Jensen said, holding out his hand.

"Jensen, my boy." Owen shook Jensen's hand and then pulled him in for a hug.

I just glared. *What the fuck was he doing here? Why was he here to ruin my first ever Thanksgiving?*

"Thanks for coming."

My eyes shot to Jensen. *Traitor.*

"Morgan," Owen said with the kindest smile I'd ever seen on his face.

When we were alone in my office, he was a mean-spirited dickface. He made me want to shoot fire from my mouth, stab him through the chest a couple of times with a poisoned knife, and stomp on his face with my high heels. And, now, he was smiling at me like he didn't know how I felt.

He tried to pull me into a hug, too, but I stepped back.

"What are you doing here?"

"Morgan," Jensen grumbled.

I questioningly arched a brow.

"I invited him."

"Why?" I couldn't hide my own distaste.

"Oh, I'm sorry," Owen said. He took a step backward and gave me a sympathetic look. "Am I not welcome anymore?"

I wanted him to stop whatever game he was playing. But one look at Jensen told me that he thought I was the bad guy.

"Of course you're welcome. Come on in. The dining room is straight through here. Make yourself at home," Jensen told him.

Owen smiled brightly. "Thank you. I'm so happy to be spending Thanksgiving with family. It's hard, being away from my boys during the holidays."

"I bet it is," Jensen said amicably.

"I bet it is," I muttered angrily under my breath.

Uncle Owen wandered into the dining room, but Jensen kept me from following.

"What is your problem, Morgan?"

"My problem? He's a dick. You said so yourself."

"He's a handful, and I know he can be a pain with business, but he's not that bad outside of the office. I invited him here for you anyway."

"Me?" I gasped.

"I know what he can be like at work. I thought you'd like some time outside of work to get to know him. Maybe to find common ground. I thought this was a good opportunity. You can charm anyone, Morgan."

I tried not to reach out and strangle my brother for the inconvenience. Apparently, I wasn't even allowed to have a day off. Always calculated. Always thinking one step ahead. I admired my brother's tenacity. I just wish that didn't make him right.

"Okay. I'll try to be friendly."

"Good. Now, come on."

Jensen wrapped an arm around my shoulders and ushered me back into the dining room. I took my seat across from Uncle Owen and watched the way he enchanted the room. If Jensen thought I was any good at this, then he hadn't really seen Owen work.

By the time we were through with the entrées and ready for dessert, everyone was eating out of his hand.

Everyone, except me.

As soon as dinner was over, I hurried to follow Heidi into the kitchen to help with dessert. I needed some fresh

110

air. I wasn't sure why *no one* else could see right through him. I had a radar for shitty, fake people. I'd employed it multiple times for my brothers' stupid exes. And I knew that Uncle Owen wasn't what he said he was.

"Do you want pumpkin pie or cherry pie or Kimber's famous chocolate cake?" Heidi asked.

"One of each?" I said with a laugh.

I was obsessed with Kimber's chocolate cake. She was Emery's older sister and had a bakery downtown. Her desserts were to die for.

"Why didn't you invite Joe?" Heidi asked.

"Joe?" I asked in confusion.

"Your boyfriend?" Heidi asked.

She shot me a weird look, and I immediately recovered.

Imaginary Joe. Right. Fuck.

"He, uh…had a family thing."

"Because I really want to meet him."

"Probably not best to bombard him with the entire Wright family for a first meeting."

Heidi sighed. "You're probably right. But he's welcome. I'm speaking for everyone here, of course."

"Of course you are."

"So, tell me," Heidi said, slicing off a piece of cake, "does he really go by Joe? Is his first name really Joseph? Because I might or might not have stalked you on social media, and you're not following or friends with anyone named Joe."

"Heidi!" I groaned.

Of course, there was no real Joe. So…she wasn't going to find anything.

"Who is Joe?" Landon asked, walking into the kitchen.

Heidi's eyes widened. "Nobody."

"Are you hiding a guy from me?" Landon joked.

Heidi held up her shiny engagement ring. "What do you think?"

"Austin! Jensen! Do you know anyone named Joe that I should be worried about?"

All three of my brothers stood in the kitchen and looked between me and Heidi. I wanted to crawl into a hole and die. I didn't want them to know about Patrick, but I didn't really want them to know about my fake boyfriend Joe either. I'd kind of been prepared for this at least since I thought the girls would spill about it earlier. But they hadn't...so I'd thought I was home free. No such luck.

"Joe?" Austin asked. "I don't know a Joe."

"Me either," Jensen added.

Heidi fidgeted. "Oh my God, I'm awful under pressure."

"Pressure about what?" Landon asked. "Wait...is this about Morgan?"

"Morgan has a boyfriend named Joe and I'm not supposed to tell you and I'm a horrible friend. Fuck."

"Thanks, Heidi," I said sarcastically.

"You're dating someone?" Austin asked with a sly grin.

"Weird," Landon added.

"I just have one question," Jensen said, holding up a finger. "Where do you find the time?"

"I don't want to talk about it."

"Well, we have to meet him," Austin said. "This should be fun."

Someone knocked at the door, and I sighed with relief as I bolted from the kitchen. I could hear my brothers discussing my new *boyfriend* between them.

God, I was not looking forward to that conversation. Nosy jerks.

I swung the door open and gasped. "Patrick?"

"Hey, Mor."

"I thought you were going to be at your parents'."

"I was. We already finished. I brought a pie. It's apple." He showed it to me.

I moved forward to inspect it and ran my hand up his. He stroked his thumb over my palm and winked.

"Did you make it?" I asked.

"Definitely no. I can't bake. My mom made it."

"Wow."

He chuckled at my reaction and I leaned closer, as if I were going to kiss me.

"Morgan," he said softly. "Everyone is here. This isn't the time."

I wrenched backward, startled at my own boldness. He squeezed my hand as if to apologize for turning me away and then flashed that smile I adored. "Are you going to let me in?"

"Oh, yeah. Uh, sure. Sorry."

I stepped back to let him pass and took the apple pie out of his hands even though I had no interest in going back into the kitchen to deal with my brothers. I also had no interest in going to the dining room and dealing with my uncle. And, now, Patrick was here.

Great.

Wonderful.

Fifteen

Patrick

F*uck*. Morgan had been about to kiss me right there in the middle of the entranceway. *What had she been thinking?* Anyone could have walked in, and then we would have single-handedly ruined Thanksgiving.

Oh, hey, guys. Yeah, I'm dating your sister.

That'd go over swimmingly.

I closed the door behind me and watched Morgan hustle into the kitchen. I was second-guessing coming over here now. I'd never second-guessed hanging out with the Wrights a day in my life. Everything had always been easy and comfortable with them. I fit in like I was one of the brothers. But, with this one secret looming between us, I automatically felt like the enemy.

When I entered the dining room, I found everyone but the Wright brothers I'd been dreading seeing. David had Jason on his lap, and Sutton was watching them play with a sorrow in her eyes that was impossible to miss. A strange man I'd never met before sat at the end of the table.

Emery and Julia were each eating a slice of chocolate cake and chatting.

"Patrick!" Emery said when she saw me standing there like a fool.

"Hey, Em, Julia."

"Hey, Patrick," Julia said with a wave. "The guys are in the kitchen. They're hounding Morgan about her new boyfriend."

My stomach dropped out of my body. *Oh, fuck!*

"Morgan, uh, has a new boyfriend?" I managed to squeak out.

"Yeah, I guess everyone knows now because of Heidi's big mouth," Emery said with an eye roll.

"We should probably intervene," Julia offered.

They both looked at the kitchen and then frowned.

"We'll give them another minute," Emery said.

I swallowed my pride and walked toward the kitchen. I didn't want to have this conversation today. I didn't want to fuck everything up. But I wasn't going to leave Morgan in there, alone, to deal with all three of her brothers. This wasn't one-sided. And I wasn't going to let her fend for herself.

When I entered the kitchen, I found Jensen, Austin, and Landon in a semicircle around Morgan, who was slicing a piece of apple pie and ignoring them. Heidi, however, was not.

"Just back off, boys," Heidi said, brandishing a serving knife. "Give her some room. No wonder she didn't come to any of *you* with this information. Why would she when you all act like Neanderthals?"

"Heidi, it's fine," Morgan said.

"We're not acting like Neanderthals," Landon said, throwing an arm around his fiancée. "We just want to meet the guy. Is that too much to ask?"

Heidi glared at him. "I'm just saying…she would have told you when she was ready."

"We just want details," Austin said. He walked over to Morgan and poked her in the shoulder.

Morgan rolled her eyes, but I could tell that she hated this. Hated them acting like she was a kid again. Some family dynamics never went away, no matter what age. Steph and I were a testament to that. Morgan being the CEO didn't change anything.

I took a deep breath and then pushed my way through. "You don't have to gang up on her about it. She should be able to date whoever she wants."

All three of the Wright brothers' eyes turned their full attention to me.

"Oh God," Morgan groaned, setting her serving knife down.

"Did Patrick know about the new boyfriend, too?" Jensen asked.

My head whipped to Morgan.

She arched an eyebrow, as if to say, *You're an idiot.*

"Oh, yes," Austin said, nudging me. "Spill the details. How do you know Joe?"

"Joe," I said tonelessly.

Who the fuck was Joe? Was Morgan seeing someone else? This was not the conversation I'd anticipated having. I'd thought I'd have to defend what was happening with me and Morgan. Instead, I was caught in the middle of something totally unexpected.

"Yes. Joe," Morgan said, "my new boyfriend."

Our eyes met in the short distance. Her face was blank. It showed none of the frustration she obviously felt at my interference. I'd thought I was being chivalrous, but instead, I'd just gotten in the way. Gotten in the way of her talking about Joe. God, I hoped he was just a cover-up and not a real dude. *Fuck.*

"I don't know Joe," I said, facing the guys again. I was careful to school my features, not to reveal anything else. "But Morgan is old enough date whoever she pleases."

"Thanks, Patrick," Morgan said, her tone sarcastic and argumentative. "I don't need your validation on dating any more than my brothers. Why don't we move on from this nightmare?"

Jensen laughed. "We've ignored our uncle long enough. We should probably be more hospitable."

"Smart," Austin said. "We can bug Morgan once he's gone."

"I've got a good idea, Austin," Morgan said. "Jump off a cliff."

"Don't make me come over there," Austin said.

"I can take you."

Austin laughed. "Yeah, right."

Heidi groaned. "You two are such children. Let's go. Come on. Go eat your dessert."

Everyone disappeared into the dining room, leaving me alone with Morgan and a plethora of desserts.

"So…Joe?" I asked, turning to look at Morgan.

"I should have told you," she whispered. "It was stupid. I'll tell you the whole story later."

She started back toward the dining room, but I grabbed her hand before she could move back into the line of sight by the rest of the guests.

"No other guy, right?"

"What?" she asked, wide-eyed.

"There's not really another guy?"

"No. Of course not. I made it up."

I breathed a sigh of relief. I hadn't realized how knotted up I was when I found out that they hadn't been talking about me. The idea that she was seeing someone else had hit me like a ton of bricks. Even worse than when I'd seen her with Travis or heard David ask her to dinner. No matter that neither of them had amounted to anything.

"Good. That's good."

She grinned up at me, and her eyes glittered. "Were you jealous?"

"Insanely."

"I don't know why…but I like that."

"Can we talk later? Alone?"

She nodded. "Sure. After all of this."

I let her walk past me and let my heart rate even out before following her. *Jealousy. Fuck, I'd been jealous.* Morgan Wright was bringing out a whole new side of me.

"Patrick, come over here," Jensen said when I entered the room.

He was standing next to the man I hadn't recognized, which I figured must be their uncle. I'd only heard horror stories about the man. So, I didn't know what to expect.

"Patrick, this is our uncle, Owen. He lives in Vancouver."

I held my hand out, and we shook.

"Nice to meet you, sir."

"Nice to meet you, too. Do you work for Wright Construction, Patrick?"

"I actually just quit."

Jensen sighed. "I still can't believe you left."

"Me?" I asked with a laugh. "What about you?"

"It was time."

"Yeah. Same here. I still love the company, but I want to do something on my own."

"I think that's admirable," Owen said. "What will you be doing?"

"I'll be working at Texas Tech in negotiations. I'll be handling all of the big clients that partner with Tech."

"That sounds like a great position. Congratulations!"

"Thank you." I couldn't keep the smile from my face.

I was proud of my new job. I'd always enjoyed my work at Wright, but it had always been hard, living under the shadow of the Wrights. And, now, with this thing with Morgan growing legs, I couldn't imagine how I'd feel if I were still working there.

"Dude," Austin said, coming up to my side and shoving me, "are you ever going to tell us about that girl you're seeing?"

"I'm not seeing anyone," I insisted again.

"It's Mindi, isn't it?"

"If I were seeing someone, don't you think I'd have told you?"

"Probably," Austin said with a shrug. "But you haven't."

"Because there's nothing to tell."

"Whatever, dude. Hey, what are you doing this weekend? We should throw you a going-away party."

"Can't. I'm going to San Francisco to see Steph."

"Wedding shit?"

"Yeah. Since I had this whole week off, I thought I'd visit."

"Damn, okay," Austin said. "Throw that idea out the window."

I laughed and then was glad when Landon came over and changed the subject. We moved into the living room for the evening football game.

It was strange, being in a room with Morgan now. I'd never noticed her presence so acutely before. Even though we were acting how we always had, it was different. I didn't want to come right out and say that Morgan and I were talking, but I didn't like going back to friends. Not after I'd had her body underneath me and her lips on mine.

I leaned back in the recliner and pulled out my phone. I jotted out a text to Morgan, who was seated across the room.

Hey, beautiful.

I waited for her to notice her phone display lighting up, but she was invested in the game, yelling equally at the screen and Austin. She glanced down at her phone for a second and then grinned from ear to ear.

Is this smart?

Probably not.

Morgan's eyes met mine across the short distance, and all the heat between us was in that one perfect glance.

What did you want to talk to me about earlier?

Follow me out of here, and I'll tell you now.

I pocketed my phone before waiting for her answer and exited the room, heading to the bathroom. I'd done a lot of dumb things in my life, but leading Morgan out of that living room had to be up there. My intentions were anything but pure, and her entire family was in the house.

Did I care? Nope. Not one bit.

I entered the guest bathroom on the first floor and left the door unlatched. A few minutes passed, and I about gave up when a knock sounded on the door.

"Patrick?" Morgan whispered. She pushed the door open. "This is a really bad idea," she said softly.

"I like really bad ideas."

I pressed the door closed behind her and backed her up against it. She tilted her head up to stare at me. She looked half-frightened of the situation we were in and half-desperate to keep going. The first half might be the sane part, but I had every intention of listening to the other part.

Our lips crashed together.

Our hands roaming each other.

Our bodies a tangled, frantic mess.

Her breath was my breath. Her heartbeat was my heartbeat. Her movement was my movement. We were perfectly in sync. Treading a line we'd come close to crossing over and over again. Not just a physical line either. An emotional line that seemed to stretch thinner each time we got closer. I could feel us both teetering over the edge, ready to move forward. Both of us knowing the consequences we'd have to deal with when we did.

Morgan threw her arms around my neck, jumped, and hooked her legs around my waist. I caught her ass in my hands and set her down on the countertop, knocking over a handful of toiletry items in the process. She laughed breathily against my lips at our own audacity. But neither of us pulled back. Neither of us stopped.

I couldn't stop kissing her. I couldn't seem to get enough of her lips. Or the way she writhed against me. Or her hands digging into my back. I definitely couldn't get enough of her legs tugging me closer.

I slipped a free hand to her thigh and then under her short black skirt. She moaned when I trailed across her inner thigh all the way up to her thong. I hooked a finger under the material and pushed it to the side. She stilled beneath me for a second. Then, I moved a finger against her clit, and she shuddered all over.

"Oh God," she moaned.

"Shh," I said against her skin.

She bit down on her lip to try to keep from saying more. I wanted to hear her scream, but right now, right where we were, she was going to have to hold it in while I made her come.

My thumb moved to her clit, circling in a tantalizing movement, and then I slid a finger into her pussy. She was wet and ready for me. Her whole body tightened at the movement. When she was beginning to relax around me, I added another finger. She whimpered in pleasure, and, God, my dick hardened at the sound. I moved my fingers in and out of her, desperately wishing that it were my cock instead. But I loved drawing this pleasure out of her.

"Fuck, I want you," I ground out.

She tilted her head back and gasped. That was answer enough.

Suddenly, her entire body clenched. I watched her face as she came just from my fingers. I couldn't wait to see what she looked like when it happened with my dick.

"Oh my God," she whispered. She repeated it another half-dozen times before opening her eyes and looking back at me with hazy sex eyes.

I withdrew my hand and gave her a cocky grin. "You're gorgeous when you come."

Her cheeks heated. "Maybe we could do that again sometime soon."

I laughed. "How about this weekend?"

"All right."

"I'm flying to San Francisco to see Steph. You should come with me. You could say it's for wedding stuff."

Morgan hopped down and straightened her skirt. "I want to, but I don't know if I can get away from work."

"It's only for a couple days. Live a little with me, Mor."

She smiled shyly. "All right. But I should probably get back out there before anyone notices we've both been gone for so long."

I grasped her chin and kissed her hard one more time before she slipped out of the bathroom. I washed my hands and tried to straighten my hair a little before following after her.

"Hey, Patrick," someone said behind me as I exited.

I whirled around with wide eyes as Emery materialized in front of me.

Shit. How much had she heard? Had she seen Morgan disappear from the bathroom before me? Would she tell Jensen?

"Yeah?" I asked nervously.

She stepped up to me and smudged a spot on my neck. "Lipstick," she said with a wink before going into the bathroom.

I blew out a heavy breath. *God, that had been close.*

I pulled my phone back out and texted Morgan.

Em knows.

Sixteen

Morgan

The entire company had Black Friday off of work. Even me.

I just wished that leaving with Patrick that afternoon to go to San Francisco to see Steph didn't make me feel so guilty. I knew work-life balance was essential, but I couldn't help it. I only took time off was for family activities. I didn't really take *me* time.

As a woman, I always felt like I had to work twice as hard and twice as long to get the respect I deserved. Stepping out of the office made me nervous, and I thought Patrick could tell. He kept cracking jokes to try to make me more comfortable.

I didn't really breathe until we landed in San Francisco. And then I let it all go. I'd committed. I was here. I just needed to enjoy myself.

"Better?" Patrick asked as he shouldered both of our bags.

"Much."

"Good."

"Sorry that I was in anxiety-attack mode."

"I'd kind of expected it actually. I know how you react when I take you away from work early. This is like that but on steroids. But you need a break. You work too much."

"So you keep telling me," I said with a smile.

He dropped a kiss on my lips and then exited the plane. We picked up our luggage and then grabbed a taxi. Steph insisted that we could stay with her and Thomas in their apartment for the night before we headed up to Napa on Saturday morning.

"I can't believe we're going to Napa," I confided. "I've always wanted to go. Though I feel guilty about leaving Steph."

He slipped an arm around my shoulders and pulled me into him. "I can only handle so much wedding talk. We can hang out with my sister, but it's still our vacation, right?"

"True. You're right."

The cab dropped us off at Steph's apartment. When we got there, Steph was stuck on her computer, shopping online sales for Christmas presents. Thomas was binge-watching the latest season of *Supernatural*.

It was nice, being with Steph and Thomas. Besides the fact that they were deliriously happy and recently engaged, it was a relief to have someone *know*. Just finally fucking know. I wasn't sure how much longer I could hold out at home like this. No matter how hot our incident was in the bathroom on Thanksgiving, I didn't want to hide forever.

And Emery wasn't enough. She hadn't seemed to care and promised not to say anything anyone when I brought it up at the end of the night. I hated that I'd had to do that to begin with. But I dreaded dealing with my brothers more. Their reaction to my imaginary Joe had been bad enough. They'd bugged me all night about it. I couldn't even begin to guess how they'd take it when they found out Joe was actually Patrick. But, at the same time, I wanted everyone to know that we were finally together.

I cornered Steph later that night in the kitchen while the guys were busy playing video games. "Can we talk?"

"Of course! What's up? How does it feel to have all your dreams come true?"

"Well...you know what they say about things that are too good to be true."

"Yeah. They usually are. But that doesn't have to be the case here."

"Can I ask you a kind of personal question?"

Steph laughed and leaned back against the kitchen counter. "I think we're beyond this. You can ask me anything. You know you're one of my closest friends!"

I heard the sincerity in her voice, and for the first time in a long time, I let the tension release.

"I do," I finally said. "I'm not so great at this sort of thing."

"Eh, that's fine. I like you as quirky, bossy, and ridiculous as you are. I find it endearing."

"Hey, I'm not bossy!"

Steph rolled her eyes. "Bossy girls are strong. Bossy girls take over the world. Bossy is a compliment. Don't let anyone tell you different."

"You have such a way with words, Steph," I said with a smile.

"Thanks! It's like I write lyrics or something."

I laughed. "Or something."

"Now, spit out your question, and stop stalling."

"Patrick told me that you'd slept with Austin."

Steph became suddenly interested in a fake piece of lint on her sweater. "That's not a question."

"Well, I never knew about it."

"Yeah," Steph said with big eyes. "Sorry. I was kind of ashamed at the time. I own my sexuality now and don't regret what happened. But, well...I was eighteen and stupid."

"Yeah. I can see why you didn't tell me. Especially because Patrick said he flipped out. When it happened, how bad was it between Patrick and Austin?"

Steph blew out a long breath. "Bad. It was right after their senior year of college, so Austin went on that internship in LA. I think that might have been why you didn't notice when the worst of it happened. And then Patrick didn't start with Wright right out of college because of it."

"Really?" I gasped. "I knew he took a year and worked for a competitor, but I didn't realize it was because of you and Austin. I feel like my world is upside down."

"Well, the whole thing was stupid." Steph rolled her eyes. "Are you asking because you haven't told Austin?"

"We haven't told anyone. Just you, Thomas, and accidentally Emery. I feel like we're past the point of hiding. I don't want to be his dirty little secret. I want to be his girlfriend."

Steph bit her lip. "You do know that Patrick doesn't really do labels on relationships."

"Trust me, I'm well aware."

"He seems different with you."

"You're just saying that because I'm your friend."

Steph shook her head. "No, really. It's like, when you're in the room, he's attuned to your presence. The world revolves around you, and he shifts to fit back into axis."

"Song lyrics, Steph," I said to deflect from what she'd just said.

Did Patrick really orient himself around me? Was he that different with me? Obviously, we weren't having sex yet. As much as it irritated me, I knew it was a good sign for him. For someone who rushed into everything, he cared about me and respected me enough to see where this was really going. But it was hard to believe that my life fit into the lyrics of one of Steph's songs. That Patrick really was that into me.

And yet, when I glanced off at him in the living room, it was like he could feel me looking at him. He turned around, caught my eye, and winked before going back to his game.

Steph's face said, *I told you so.*

I didn't contradict her.

———

We had a lazy Saturday morning in the city with Steph and Thomas, enjoying brunch at one of their favorite restaurants and a quick tour of the city. Then, Patrick borrowed Thomas's car and drove us out of town. The Napa countryside was stunning as we meandered through the hillside and out to a vineyard.

After we valeted the car, Patrick pulled me close and placed a soft kiss on my lips. It was nice to be here together like this. Neither of us was worried about my pesky brothers interfering. No work to take over my time. It was glorious. In fact, it was probably the best weekend I'd had in a long time.

"Why are you looking at me like that?" Patrick asked.

"I'm glad that we did this."

"So am I. Truthfully, I thought it would be harder to convince you to leave."

"Someone told me I needed to lighten up and live a little. I'm not even thirty," I said with a grin.

"Whoever said that must be really smart."

I snorted. "You enjoy complimenting yourself?"

"All the time."

"Of course you do."

"I'm a confident guy," he said with an easy shrug. "Come on. Let's go find the wine tasting."

"I'm going to get so drunk."

"No, you won't. I'll make sure you drink water and eat plenty of food. I bet there's pasta. There's always pasta."

"Or pizza."

"Mmm, pizza." He reached down and entwined our fingers together. "You're a woman after my own heart."

Staring up into his face and knowing that smile and that adoration was all for me made me fall all over again. I'd thought that what I'd felt for Patrick all those years was more than a crush. But it had been nothing compared to this. Not when I knew that this was real.

I followed Patrick down through the vineyard and to the indoor tasting bar. The room was crowded with people trying to escape the winter chill, but we found a spot at the bar and listened to the man as he poured sips. He was knowledgeable and charming. By the end of our session, we were going home with an entire box of red wine.

Both of us were giddy and a little tipsy from all the different pours. He had his arm around my shoulders as we walked back through the crisp weather and into the main arm of the vineyard. The place was massive with a hotel, spa, and fine dining attached. We found a pizza place and indulged.

I was in date heaven as evening approached. I hated that we'd have to go back to the city. I was a hundred percent not ready for that.

"Do you think we should head out soon?" I asked.

"Nope. I have something else planned."

I narrowed my eyes. "When did you have time to plan anything?"

"Last night while you were pretending not to work but were working."

"I..." I trailed off.

"Yes?" he asked coyly.

"I might have been working."

"That's what I thought."

"I was just checking emails."

"I don't care that you were working," he said, kissing my nose. "That's what you do. And I planned this while you were doing your thing. Come on."

Patrick walked us to the elevator and up to the top floor of the hotel. He slid the key card into the door. It opened up to a stunning suite overlooking the setting sun on the vineyard.

"Wow," I whispered, walking through the luxurious room and out to the balcony. "The view is breathtaking."

"Yes, you are," he said.

I turned back to face him with the hint of a blush on my cheeks. *How long had I dreamed he'd see me that way?* It was hard to imagine that my dreams were really becoming reality. That we were really standing here, in a swanky hotel room in Napa, as a couple.

"You seem surprised."

"Not surprised. Shocked. How long have we known each other, Patrick? I never thought you saw me that way."

"I didn't. Or I guess I chose not to," he corrected. He stepped up to where I was standing and drew me closer. "I think a part of me always recognized how amazing you were. It was just easier not to look too far into it. Easier not to rock the boat, you know?"

I chewed on my bottom lip. "I kind of have a confession."

"What's that?"

"You said you never saw me that way. I was always just your best friend's little sister. But, to me, you were so much more than my brother's best friend."

"Oh, yeah?"

"I've always liked you, Patrick," I whispered, releasing the secret I'd been holding in for so long. "Always."

"Like…how long is always?"

"You remember that time you and Austin came back to the house your freshman year of college?"

"We came back a bunch."

"The first time. It was homecoming at the high school. I had made the varsity cheerleading team my freshman year of high school. You and Austin showed up at the house, all big and bad college boys. And I stood there, in the hallway, in a skimpy cheerleading outfit. You turned around when I walked in the room. I think maybe you were going to say hi, but instead, you just stared at me."

Patrick nodded. "I, uh, yeah. I remember that now."

"Something changed about you. I've been a goner ever since."

"Just from that one look?"

"Well, that look started it, but it was everything about you. How easygoing you were and how well you fit into our family and the way you made me laugh."

"That was the day I decided I could never pursue you, you know?"

"What?" I gasped.

"Yeah. The thoughts I was having about a fifteen-year-old high school student when I was eighteen and in college were...obscene. I knew Austin would kill me. So, I just...stopped seeing you. I forced myself not to even consider it. Then, after what happened with Steph...well, you know."

All this time, Patrick and I had had our moment. Our one perfect moment. It had taken us a dozen years for it to happen again.

Seventeen

Patrick

"Well, you see me now," Morgan said. She looked up at me through sultry hooded eyes that said all the dirty thoughts I'd once had could come to fruition.

Here I'd been all this time, trying not to look at her. Trying to avoid seeing her as anything more than Austin's little sister. It turned out that I'd missed all the signs by burying my head in the sand.

"I see you. All of you," I said. I tugged her closer and drew her lips to mine. "I see you and feel you and want you."

"Mmm," she agreed.

"I want all of you."

"You already have all of me," she whispered.

And I could feel that truth in her statement in every kiss and every touch and every breath. Morgan Wright was mine.

"I have most of you," I said, working my way down the buttons on the front of her peacoat.

"Just most?" she whispered.

I slipped the jacket off her shoulders and let it puddle at her feet. Then, I pulled her shirt over her head.

"You'll know when I have all of you, Morgan. You'll be able to feel it."

I ran my hands up to the cusp of her bra. I flicked my finger against her nipple, and she shook at the feel of me.

"You'll be able to taste it."

Our lips collided once more as I deftly popped her bra off. My tongue was slow and luxurious against hers. She was practically shaking with my ministrations.

"You'll feel when not just our bodies connect, but our souls. Then, I'll have all of you and not before then."

She gasped. "Who knew you were such a romantic?"

"It's different with you," I told her as I walked her backward toward the bedroom.

She stumbled, and I caught her in my arms, whisked her off her feet, and gingerly deposited her on the bed.

"Different how?"

"I don't know. This is all new to me. I've never really been into someone like you before. Or really…interested in a relationship at all. But, when I'm with you, I feel like I'm my best possible self."

I popped the button on her jeans and peeled the skintight pair off her legs. She was staring at me, mesmerized and possibly…shocked.

"You seem surprised," I said.

She crawled back across the bed to me. Her beautiful tits and round ass were wonderfully on display. Her dark hair fanned in front of her face. Her lips and eyes screamed seduction. She moved onto her knees and slowly and methodically undid each of the buttons on my shirt. Then, she ran her nails across my shoulders as she pushed it off me.

"I thought you always thought of me as just a kid sister."

"I certainly don't see you like that now."

"That's a relief," she said with a smirk as her hands trailed my biceps. "This might have been awkward."

I laughed and shook my head. "You're ridiculous. Come here."

Then, I brandished a kiss like a weapon. I had every intention of finally tasting every inch of her skin. She wasn't completely mine yet. I'd waited. I'd been patient. I'd known that I couldn't treat her just like anyone else. She wasn't like anyone else. When we finally came together, I wanted it to be the right moment. I wanted it to mean something.

My hands moved to her waist as I dropped my mouth over her nipple. I bit and sucked and licked one and then the other until she was writhing beneath me. She was begging me for more and begging me to stop. And I just loved the sound of her begging.

I dropped to my knees on the floor at the edge of the bed and slowly dragged her thong off, baring her before me. I ran my fingers up the inside of her legs until she quivered. She moved her legs to my shoulders as I reached the apex of her thighs. I opened her pussy up to me and then slid a finger down into her. She was already soaking wet and moaned at the slightest movement.

"Patrick, please," she groaned.

"No rushing," I said. "I want you to feel everything."

I lowered my lips to her clit and indulgently circled my tongue across the sensitive nub. Her hips came off the bed. I used a free hand to hold her down as I worked her into a frenzy.

"Oh my God. Oh my God. Oh my God," she moaned over and over and over again.

My cock ached in my pants as I brought this gorgeous woman to the highest heights. Seeing how she reacted—every moan, gasp, twitch, and shake—made me just want to bury myself in her. I needed it like a man lost in the desert needed water. With the way she came undone on my face, it didn't even feel like an exaggeration.

She came up onto her elbows to look down at me. She had a happy, sated look on her face. My own little sex kitten.

Then, she crumpled backward onto the bed. I rose to my feet and watched her moments of perfect bliss. She raised her hands over her head, curled her toes, and laughed my favorite short, breathy thing that went straight to my balls.

I unbuckled my belt and shucked my jeans into a heap on the floor. Her eyes rounded at the sight of me through my boxers.

"My turn," she said. Her lips curled into a naughty smile.

"You don't have to reciprocate."

She arched an eyebrow as she sat up and moved to the end of the bed. "What happened to feeling all of you?"

I thought about arguing with her because I wanted to be fucking inside her right now. But she dropped to her knees on the carpeted floor without hesitation and knelt, eye-level with my cock. I pretty much lost all coherent thought at that point.

Her fingers ran along the edge of my boxers, and my dick twitched in response. She responded by yanking them off me and taking my cock in her hand. It looked enormous with her little hand, but, fuck, she knew what to do with it. She experimentally stroked me up and down before lapping her tongue across the tip.

"Fuck," I moaned like a prayer.

She smirked at me, as if she knew exactly how to torment me in the best way. Then, she opened her mouth and took me into her. I closed my eyes to keep from thrusting forward. I didn't want to deep-throat her on accident, and yet I wanted to feel all of that warm, wet sucking all the way down to my balls.

She began bobbing her head on my cock. Down, down, down and then all the way back to the tip. Her mouth made a little *pop* sound as my cock came out of her mouth. I had to hold back from coming all over her face.

She took me back in her mouth, and I moaned at the long strokes she was taking. She hummed in approval. The vibrations made me shudder.

I ran my fingers through her hair. "Mor, I'm going to come."

"Mmm?" she mumbled, glancing up at me with innocent, big eyes. Though we both knew there was nothing innocent about what she was doing.

"Oh, fuck," I said.

I jerked against her mouth, but she didn't stop. She seemed to have no intention of stopping. She was in control. A hundred fifty percent in control. This was Morgan Wright, who was the CEO of a Fortune 500 company and could take on the world. Right now, she was taking on my cock and winning.

I couldn't hold back any longer. My body convulsed, and then I shot cum right into her mouth until I was wholly spent. I leaned heavily against the bed as I watched her swallow.

Fuck, oh, fuck, it was a beautiful thing.

She wiped her mouth and shot me a confident smile as she pushed me on the bed and crawled on top of me.

"You're magnificent," I told her as I stroked her hair out of her face.

She blushed, but she didn't disagree. She was this glorious duality of a woman. Strong, fierce, independent, and loyal, but at the same time, there were cracks in her exterior that showed me her fears, doubts, and flaws. And it was seeing her in these moments of vulnerability that made me realize I adored the entire package.

Without her fears, she would have nothing to overcome. Without her doubts, she would have nothing to conquer. Without her flaws, she would be fake. Because no one was perfect. Her strengths and her weaknesses made her the person she was, and I didn't want her any other way. She was simply perfect for me.

I reached between our bodies and stroked her clit. Her body shook, but she didn't try to stop me. She just wrapped her hand around my dick and matched my pace. She stared down into my eyes, and I finally saw everything she had told me earlier. She really had liked me for a long time. And this here really was our moment.

My cock lengthened fully again at her touch. She released me and then angled her body over mine. I felt the warmth of her touch the tip of my cock. I wanted to pump up into her, but I paused.

"We should get a condom," I told her.

I flipped her over onto her back, and she gasped. I hopped off the bed and found a condom in my discarded jeans.

"I'm on the pill," she told me.

"Let's be doubly safe."

She nodded as I ripped the wrapper open and rolled the condom on. Then, I moved back onto the bed and positioned myself above her.

"You're sure?" I asked.

"I've always been sure about you."

Our lips locked as I thrust into her. She was so wet, and I slipped all the way into her without resistance. She tightened all around me. My head fell into the crook of her shoulder, and I grunted something inaudible.

"Oh God," she moaned. "You…"

"Yeah. Fuck."

Her pussy clasped around my cock and held on for dear life. It was like nothing I'd ever experienced. Our bodies were intertwined, her heart beating a crescendo against my chest, and something seemed to shift ever so slightly. Like everything was suddenly right with the world.

I started moving inside her, picking up tempo. She matched my pace with her own movements. Our bodies slapped together. My hips pressed against her own. I filled her over and over again.

Then, out of nowhere, she cried out, and her entire body tensed like a snake ready to strike. I couldn't seem to hold on. I wanted her to have another orgasm, but there was no way. The strength of her coming set me off like dominoes falling.

When we both finally stilled, we were panting and sweaty. I looked down at her in amazement, wondering what the hell she had just done to me.

"Now, you have all of me," Morgan whispered.

What I hadn't entirely realized until that moment was that she had all of me, too.

Eighteen

Morgan

Returning to work and reality seemed impossible. I didn't want to live in a world where I had to hide Patrick. I'd understood at first when it was just a fling. A totally uncertain possibility. But, after Napa, there was no going back.

As I entered work on Monday morning, I felt like I was walking on clouds. *Had I ever been this happy? This blissful? This relaxed?*

I felt like a different person. A new person. And, God, I loved it.

My dopey grin carried all the way to my office before it disappeared entirely at the sight of Jensen standing there with none of my dreamy giddiness.

"What's wrong?" I asked.

"I know what's going on here, Morgan."

Oh no.

"You do?" I whispered.

Fuck. Who told him? Who said something? Emery? God, I really didn't think she would divulge this!

"Yes. You're finally taking your moment to rebel."

"Jensen, that's not what this is about," I said quickly. I needed to figure out a way to salvage this conversation. Dating Patrick was not my rebelling moment.

"There are a million things I want to say to you right now, but I mostly just want to hear your side of the story. I think all of this got completely out of hand. I don't want you to make the same mistakes I made. You haven't been CEO that long."

"Wait," I said as I processed his words. "What are we talking about here?"

"You missed work on Friday and disconnected all weekend," he said and then arched an eyebrow. "What did you think we were talking about?"

"Nothing. I'm confused. What does it matter if I missed Friday? We had the day off."

Jensen sighed. "The CEO never takes a day off."

"I know, but…"

"The board is concerned about your commitment to the job."

My jaw dropped. "The board? You're on the board now!"

"Yes, I'm aware. But I didn't find out about this until after they all convened without me."

"What the hell?"

"They don't think I can be objective about my sister and handpicked successor. How can I blame them about that?"

"This is bullshit. All because I missed one day when the company was closed?" I asked, fuming.

"I'm not saying that any of it is fair, Morgan."

"You missed a shit-ton of work every time you went to New York."

"Yes, but I didn't go to New York as much when I first started as CEO. So, I missed too much of my son's young life. And, when I was actually there, I would *always* check in with the New York branch. We're a huge company. We have offices all over the country. We have them in San Francisco for instance."

"It's not like I was completely absent. I answered emails while I was gone."

"It's not the same. Fuck," Jensen said, turning and walking away.

"How do I fix this?" I asked.

Panic was starting to set in. I needed to make the board feel more secure about me. I'd done everything above and beyond for years, and still, it didn't seem to make any difference.

"We'll let it blow over. I think everyone has too much to worry about right now with going into the holidays anyway. Just stay on top of things and try not to leave again unless you have to leave for the business. I thought I'd addressed everything I needed to in our transitional period." He shook his head and then sighed. "I'm really surprised the board is this upset with you about it."

"Me, too. It doesn't even make sense."

"No, it doesn't. I think our uncle might have something to do with it."

I groaned. "Uncle Owen? He hates me."

"He doesn't hate you. I just think he's very serious about the business, especially since he is here and can see what's going on."

"So, you think he went to the board behind your back?"

"I'm not sure. But be careful around him."

"You think I should be careful?" I asked in frustration. "He's speaking to the board about my behavior and way overstepping his bounds, and *I* should be more careful? I think that I should go find Uncle Owen right now and have it out with him."

Jensen sighed. "I had a feeling you'd say that."

"He's trying to ruin my job!"

"He's baiting you. Just ignore him. Stay cool. Remember, you want this to all blow over. The reason you're CEO is because you're already dedicated and invested in this company. Let your actions prove your worth."

I ground my teeth but nodded. Jensen was probably right. He usually was. He'd run this company successfully for a long time. If I wanted to follow in his footsteps, then I had to be above and beyond. I couldn't risk having any complaints against me. Not a single one.

And then I got this...all because I'd left for the weekend. A holiday weekend at that. Some part of me thought the whole thing was unfair...and probably a bit sexist. But the other part of me wondered if maybe...it was true.

Ever since I'd started talking to Patrick, I'd definitely been at work less. He'd been convincing me to leave early and avoid work on the weekends. I'd actually been loosening up and enjoying myself. Then, I had gotten hit with a two-by-four.

Maybe this thing with Patrick was changing me. Work had to come first. That was a lesson I'd learned long ago.

"Morgan," Jensen said.

"Sorry. I just...nothing," I said when I saw his eyes crinkle in concern. I straightened up and washed all the worry from my face. I was strong. I had the weight of the world on my shoulders. I could do this. "I'll double down, and everything will be fine. If I need to console the board, then I'll handle it. Thanks for coming to let me know."

"I know you can do it." Jensen frowned. "Just find some work-life balance. It's a hard line to walk; I know."

"I'll figure it out."

"I know you will. I should probably get back to my office now. Ribbon-cutting is getting closer and closer. We have to be ready."

"Good luck," I said as I walked him out.

"Hey, I like what you've done with the place, too." He gestured to the office. "More modern, sleek, very you."

"Thanks. I thought it could use a woman's touch."

"How was your trip by the way? You and Patrick in San Francisco." He wiggled his eyebrows up and down.

All of my brothers knew of my crush on Patrick. They'd always known, and they thought it was hilarious. Especially because of Patrick being so oblivious to it. In fact, it had become a huge joke among them. I was pretty sure they wouldn't find it funny if they found out we were banging.

"We were there for Steph's wedding stuff."

At least, that was the cover story. And we had done some wedding stuff. Just…not that much.

"Yeah, I know. I'm just messing with you."

"Go back to work," I said with a grin, playfully shoving him out of the office.

"Yes, ma'am."

I watched my brother's retreating back as he went down the hall. Fear crept into me from all sides as soon as he was out of sight.

He'd made it seem like none of this was a big deal. As if it would all just blow over. But, if that were the case, he wouldn't have come down here to talk to me about it. He wouldn't have left his cushy new office to be the bearer of bad news. A phone call would have sufficed.

This was more serious than he had been letting on. I knew it in my bones.

My uncle had the ear of the board. That was the nugget I was taking away from this. He had it out for me. He'd had it out for me from the first day I met him. It seemed he would do anything to make me suffer.

I didn't know why. I had no idea what his reasoning was. But he was here on behalf of the Canadian branch of Wright Construction through the holidays, and I would have to deal with him. When all I wanted to do was fire him. He was already a pain in my ass, but I knew I couldn't. He hadn't actually done anything wrong, and I didn't want to get in any more trouble with the board than I already was.

Jensen had talked about work-life balance, but what he'd really meant was, *Find a way to put your life on hold.* At least for now.

I chewed on my thumbnail as I considered what that meant. I'd just gotten him. I'd put it all on the line. And, already, it was overloading me.

I needed to be serious about my job. I was already serious about my job. I was the hard worker. I had all the pressure on me. Just once, I'd love to walk in one of my brother's footsteps where everything came easy to them, and they had no problems they couldn't overcome. I might be the brains of the operation and seem like the smart, determined, and sarcastic one of the bunch, but it didn't stop anyone from second-guessing my every move.

It had taken me years to earn the respect of my employees at the company. Something that had naturally happened to Jensen when he walked into the room. And, now, it was crumbling all because of my new relationship. A relationship no one even *knew* about!

Fuck, I'm going to have to talk to Patrick.

It was his first day on the job at Texas Tech. I couldn't just leave here to go talk to him. Not when I was under scrutiny. But maybe I could make time for a quick lunch. It was just across the street anyway. No one would notice me if I left for a quick break. I hoped...

"Hey, Morgan!" David said, popping out of his office.

I jumped slightly at the interruption to my deep thoughts. "Hey, David. How was your break?"

"Good. How was yours? How was San Francisco?"

"It was great, but...I think we really need to buckle down. We still have the Disney contract that we have to dig in on."

"I'm all for it."

"I'm thinking late nights all week."

"That's fine. You know I enjoy it." He leaned against the door and casually crossed his arms. "Oh, wait, you know, I can't do late Thursday though."

"Why not?"

"I promised Sutton that I'd babysit Jason. She wants to get out of the house."

My heart constricted. Of course Sutton wanted someone to babysit. *God, I'm a shitty sister. How did Jensen actually manage his work and home life?* Because, right now, I didn't think I was handling either of them. My sister was suffering, and I couldn't even find time to babysit.

"Of course. Maybe I should come with you?"

"If you want to. But…it might be nice, if you don't mind me saying…"

"What?"

"If maybe you went out with Sutton instead. I can take care of the boy. He's no problem. I have a few nieces and nephews his age. I…well, I'm not sure anyone can take care of Sutton. She might appreciate it if you tried though."

"You're right." I felt like I had a golf ball in my throat as I tried to swallow around the tears threatening me. "I'll…I'll call her. Thanks, you know, for being there for her."

"Oh, Sutton is great. She's the strongest person I've ever met."

"She really is," I agreed.

David grinned and then ducked back into his office, leaving me reeling. Another thing to add to my list of things to do. Something I should have already thought of.

Fuck, I'd been so blind lately.

Just trapped in my own vortex and unable to see everything else disintegrating around me. I needed to break free of its grip, or I'd end up losing it all.

Nineteen

Morgan

I hadn't made it to see Patrick at lunch. In fact, I hadn't even eaten lunch. I'd been slaving away at my computer until my eyes became blurry and a headache began to morph into a migraine. And, still, I pushed through the pain.

I had to. I had four meetings, three conference calls, and at least a week's worth of backed up emails and messages that needed to be sorted. There was never a shortage in work.

When David came by to say he was going to get dinner and would be back in a half hour, I was half-delirious and stuck on *another* conference call. I waved him off when he offered to get me something. I couldn't even tell if I was hungry anymore. There was just too much to do and a headache to ignore.

My call finally ended, and I hung up with a sigh. I was rubbing my temples therapeutically when I heard a knock at my door.

Great. Another meeting.

"Come in," I said.

"Good to see you, too," Patrick said with a crooked smile.

"What are you doing here?" I asked, jumping to my feet. Then, immediately, I regretted it as a wave of dizziness hit me. I had to clutch the desk to steady myself.

"Are you all right?"

He stepped up to the desk, as if he wanted to help me stand. I straightened and backed away from the help. I didn't need help. I didn't need anyone's help. I never needed anyone's help.

"I'm fine."

He frowned and furrowed his brows at me. As if he couldn't possibly understand why I was acting like this.

"You seem upset. Did something happen? Have you eaten anything today?"

"I said, I'm fine," I repeated with more venom than I'd intended.

He stepped backward at my force. Then, he seemed to shake it off and smiled again. "Maybe I should get you out of here. You seem like you need a break. I could cook you dinner and tell you about my first day."

"I said, I'm fine!" I yelled this time. "God, don't you get it? I don't want to leave. I have too much to do. I'm the CEO of this company. I can't just flit after you whenever you want to be together. Work has to come first. Okay?"

Patrick's eyes rounded in shock. "Morgan, I'm not trying to interfere with work. I was simply offering to make you dinner."

"You don't understand."

"Help me understand. I feel like I'm missing something here. This weekend, we were together, and now, you're yelling at me."

I let out a frustrated sigh and released the tension I'd had in my shoulders all day. "I know. It's not you. Not really."

"Can I be clued in on what's really going on around here?"

Patrick walked around my desk and pulled me into his arms. I went with little resistance, closing my eyes and listening to the beat of his heart. It soothed my aching head and brought back some clarity.

"I'm sorry. Jensen was here this morning. The board is worried about having me here as the CEO because I was gone this weekend."

Patrick reeled back. "That's outrageous."

"I know."

"You were still working this weekend. You answered emails and everything. I saw you."

"I know."

"Plus, Jensen used to leave all the time, and no one said he wasn't fit to be CEO."

"I know."

"And you're the most dedicated person I know. You *are* Wright Construction."

"I know all of that. But that doesn't seem to matter. It only matters what lies are being spread about me and how my new position is perceived. I feel like, when I'm with you…I forget about work. I let it slip away, and I just…am."

"Morgan, I hate to break this to you, but that's how life is supposed to be. Your entire life isn't work. You should relax at home and remember to eat and live a little."

I chewed on my lip. "I want all of those things, and I want them all with you. It just seems like whatever balance there is in my life needs to be tipped toward my job right now."

"Okay. I understand that. But I don't think that means at the expense of your health and sanity."

"I could maybe compromise on that. But it's harder with my uncle snooping around here right now."

"What's going on with your uncle? I saw him on campus today."

"You did?" I asked in surprise. "What was he doing there?"

He shrugged. "I don't know. I went to get a snack at the Union, and he was talking to some administrators. He said hi to me when he recognized me and asked about my new job, and that was it."

"Hmm," I said. "Weird."

"It's not that weird. He's an alumnus. I'm sure he's a big donor."

"I'm sure he is. But, right now, everything about him gets on my nerves. He was talking to the board and telling them that I wasn't working, trying to sabotage me. I don't even know why."

"Have you asked him about it? I mean…maybe he actually thinks he's being helpful."

I rolled my eyes. "Yeah, right. He might have everyone else fooled, but he has never said a kind word to me in private. He acts like I should be the hot little secretary."

"Wait," Patrick said, raising his hand, "can you be my hot little secretary?"

"You can't afford me," I deadpanned.

"I was thinking something a little more sexual."

"Chauvinist."

He grinned. "I'll let you into the good ole boys' club."

I gagged. "Hard pass."

"It was a euphemism," he said with a wink.

"Now, who is ridiculous?" I asked with a grin.

"Aha! There it is!"

"What?"

"Your smile." His hands cupped my jaw and pulled me in for a slow kiss. "I was waiting for that."

"I can't believe you won this."

"I can't believe I won you."

The next kiss was like nothing before. He didn't just taste me. He devoured me. I forgot where I was and explored his body, channeling all my frustrations from the day into that kiss. It was hot and heavy and made me think about throwing him down on my new desk and taking advantage of him.

A throat cleared behind us, and we launched apart. Our chests were pounding as the realization of what we had been doing and where hit us.

"Sorry to have, uh...interrupted," David said from the doorway. There was a small blush on his cheeks.

"Patrick was just leaving," I said quickly.

David held up a bag. "I got you dinner. I knew you hadn't eaten today."

"Thank you. I really appreciate it."

"I'm going to, uh, you know, leave this here." He dropped it onto a chair by the door and then disappeared.

I sank back into my own chair and put my head into my hands. "Well, that went well."

"David is fine," Patrick said. "He'll be fine."

"I know. He's not going to say anything, but I just...I don't know. I'm so stressed. I should take this week to get caught up."

"Do what you have to do," he said. "Just come over to my place, or I can meet you at yours whenever you finish. I don't care what time it is."

"Are you sure?" I asked with hopeful eyes.

He dropped to his knees in front of and forced me to look at him. "Of course I'm sure. We're together, right?"

I nodded.

"I might be new to being in a relationship, but I'm pretty sure I already knew what I signed up for with you."

"Oh, yeah?"

"A slightly neurotic workaholic with a heart of gold."

"That sounds like me," I said with a short laugh.

"I like you just the way you are. So, come see me when you're finished here."

"All right. I'll do that."

He kissed me again and then left. As soon as he was out of the office, my headache returned. I sighed and got back to work.

———

It was Thursday before I finally left the office on time. I'd made plans to hang out with Sutton and her best friend, Annie, while David watched Jason. I knew it was important to spend time with my sister right now. She was only five months without her husband and still fragile.

I changed quickly at my apartment and made it over to Sutton's house right on time. She trotted out of the house in an all black ensemble that would make Emery and Julia proud. Annie followed close behind in forest green pants and a black sweater. Her red hair swayed behind her. They both hopped in the car.

"Thanks for coming out with me," Sutton said by way of greeting.

"Sut, of course! I'm glad we get to spend some time together." I grinned at Annie in the rearview mirror. "Hey Annie."

"Sup, Morgan.

"So what's the plan?"

She sighed, and I suddenly noticed that she looked like she'd aged beyond her twenty-three years. I felt bad for noticing.

"Can we just go to a movie? I'd really like to be somewhere quiet without any responsibilities."

"Sure."

I pulled away from her house and started to drive to the local Alamo Drafthouse. I didn't know what was playing, but it really didn't matter.

We bought tickets for some obscure indie film that none of us had ever heard of. The theater was empty, and we picked seats in the very back.

As soon as we sat down, Annie's phone started ringing. She groaned. "It's Todd. I'll be right back."

She disappeared back down the stairs. I arched an eyebrow at Sutton.

She waved her hand. "New guy. I don't like him."

"I see."

"So, what's been going on with you?" Sutton asked.

"Just work stuff."

She raised an eyebrow. "I don't think so. You seem off."

"I'm here for you, and you're the one interrogating me?" I asked a little defensively.

"What's there for you to ask me? My husband is dead. I have an eighteen-month-old son who will grow up without his father. I'm pretty much the same."

I winced at her harsh words and wished that I hadn't. This anger, I knew, was part of her grieving. I couldn't be upset that she was taking some of it out on me. For a while there, she'd hated the entire world. The fact that she was leaving the house, even for something as mundane as seeing a movie, was major progress.

"You're right. I'm sorry."

"Don't apologize to me," she said. "Just talk to me. I'm tired of being treated like I'm made of porcelain. Everyone tiptoes around me. I won't break."

"We don't think that."

She shot me a classic Wright look of indignation. It was so perfect, I actually laughed.

"What?" she gasped.

"You just…remind me of Jensen."

She sighed and sat back heavily. "I don't mean to act like this. I can't control how angry I get at everything."

"It's okay. You can be mad at me. I'm used to that from you." I laughed, and Sutton rolled her eyes. "I guess there is one thing I could ask."

"Oh, great, here it goes," Sutton said.

"What's up with David?"

"What do you mean?"

"He's great with Jason. He seems really interested in helping."

"He is," Sutton agreed. "I don't know what's up with him, but I appreciate his help. It sucks, being a single mom."

"You're a great mom though."

"Thank you. But there's nothing between David and me, if that's what you're asking. I don't know if I'll ever be ready to start dating again. Let alone right now when, most days, the only reason I get out of bed is because of my son."

"I wasn't suggesting—"

Sutton held up her hand. "It's fine, Mor. Now, tell me why you're acting so weird."

I took a deep breath and decided it was time. I couldn't hold everything in, and I figured a test run on Sutton would be smart.

"I've...kind of started seeing someone."

"Really?" she asked, brightening. "Who?"

I paused uncomfortably before saying, "Patrick."

Sutton squealed. She actually squealed. I stared at her in utter shock. My little sister was back for that one moment of pure joy. And it was all for me.

"Finally! I'm so happy for you! Oh my God! When did this happen? How did this happen? Why aren't we celebrating with everyone?"

"Because...other than you, only four other people know, and they all found out on accident."

"Why?"

"I'm not sure if you're aware, but we have three scary older brothers, and one of them is Patrick's best friend, who just got out of rehab."

"So?"

"Austin slept with Steph when she was in high school. Patrick blew a gasket, and he doesn't want to lose his friendship with Austin."

"Okay. So, he thinks it'll either be you or Austin, and he can't have both?"

I shrugged. "I think he's just nervous, and he doesn't know what to expect. When we first started, I was all for it. You know our brothers are nosy and get in our business and are all judgmental. This is so new and fresh. I just want to experience it without anyone else's thoughts about it."

"But now?"

"But, now…I don't like hiding."

"Then, don't hide."

"It's not that simple."

"It is that simple. If you love someone, then there are no obstacles too great."

"I mean…love," I whispered, choking on the word. "I've liked Patrick for years, but love? Love is something that takes time and dedication. It takes reciprocation. It takes, you know, actually saying the words and meaning it and having the other person say it and mean it back."

"You two have been circling each other for years. *Love* is not too strong a word to use when you've crashed into each other's orbit."

I blushed and looked down. "When did you get so wise?"

"Trust me, you don't want the life experience it takes," Sutton said. "Just appreciate what you have when you have it. And tell Patrick how you feel. You don't want to wake up one day and remember all the things you never said."

Twenty

Patrick

I stood between Austin and Julia outside of the Wright Construction building.

It was two weeks since Morgan and I had returned from San Francisco and the day of their annual Christmas party that they threw for the entire corporate headquarters. The top floor restaurant would be cleared out for dancing while hors d'oeuvres circled, and an open bar would pour drinks all night. I'd gone every year since college when Austin and I would crash his dad's party for the drinks. It was strange, not to be here as an employee, and I found it was equally strange not to be here on Morgan's arm.

Ever since she'd gone out with Sutton, our relationship had been even better. She was still working herself into the ground, but it was pretty much impossible to deny that this was the best and most stable relationship I'd ever been in. The only one I'd ever really thought of as a relationship.

That should have been an indication that it was time to come clean to Austin. To her whole family. But, every time I thought about it, it was with dread. She hadn't brought it up again, but I knew that she wouldn't stand for it much longer. A girl like Morgan deserved more than hiding anyway. I hated that I just wanted to enjoy the bliss with her rather than deal with the inevitable drama...but I did.

Fuck.

I couldn't do it. I didn't want to. Not yet.

"Your tie is crooked," Julia said.

I snapped out of my melancholy and adjusted my tie. "Better?"

"Eh," she said noncommittally and then fiddled with it herself.

"What would I do without you?"

"You'd be lost," she confirmed.

"Definitely."

"Hey, hey, hey," Austin said, bumping in between us. "That's my girl."

I laughed. "I'm well aware of that. I remember all the groveling and single-man tears."

"There were no tears."

I held my hands up in defense and displayed my classic smile. "Sure, bro."

"Fuck you."

"I know. I love you, too."

"Okay. If you two are finished with your little bromance, can we go inside?" Julia asked. "It's fucking freezing."

Austin pulled the door open. "After you."

When Julia walked in, he butted in front of me and tried to shut the door in my face. I flipped him off. He laughed and then let me inside.

"You're a real dick, you know that?" I said.

"I think that's why we're friends."

We both laughed as we moved into the elevator and upstairs. I wished that I had come here with Morgan, but

I'd been stupid and said I'd come with Austin. Too late to fix it now.

"How does it feel to be back?" Austin asked. "Can't believe you've been gone from the company this long already."

Of course, Austin didn't know that I'd been at the company a lot after-hours. Now that David knew about my relationship with Morgan, it was easy to be there with dinner and ruin their evening work sessions. Both of them worked too fucking much anyway. But saying that to Morgan was a whole lot of in one ear and out the other. She was a workaholic. That was just who she was.

"It's good. Feels like home."

When we exited onto Morgan's floor, we all piled out and found Sutton and David chasing after a particularly rambunctious Jason. I laughed as he ran around my legs and clung to the back of Austin. He scooped him up and onto his shoulder.

"Who's the biggest now?" Austin asked, bouncing him up and down.

"Me!" he called. "Da, go!"

Sutton gasped softly and covered her mouth. I could see her threatening to break down.

"Excuse me," she muttered and then disappeared down the hall to the restrooms.

We all stood there in awkward silence at what had just happened. No one was willing to acknowledge that Jason had just called Austin the D-word. And not the one I'd used earlier.

"Hey, slackers, are you going to get in here?" Landon asked, stepping out of Morgan's office.

"Yeah," I answered for everyone.

Austin pulled Jason off his shoulder, and we all entered the office as a group.

"What's going on?" Landon asked. "I feel like I walked in on a ticking time bomb."

"And where's Sutton?" Heidi asked next to him.

Julia shook her head as she strode eagerly toward Heidi and Emery. "She'll be back."

At Julia's comment, Jensen glanced at Jason in Austin's arms. Then, he pushed his way out of the room without a word. I was sure he was on his way to talk to Sutton.

My eyes drifted away from the rest of the Wright family and significant others to the stunning woman standing behind the desk. Morgan was radiant in a slim black cocktail dress. Her hair was down, and she looked fierce and beautiful. All I wanted to do was force every single other person out of this room and take her right then and there on that desk.

She caught my gaze, and the room heated. Fuck, she was wearing red lipstick. Gorgeous fucking red lipstick. It suited her. Maybe I could convince her to wear it all the time. I didn't care if it got on all my clothes…and anywhere else, too.

Her smile dropped when she realized I hadn't made a move to walk forward. Our distance was suddenly that barrier again. The one that kept me from announcing to our friends and her family that we were dating. There was so much history keeping me from speaking the words.

She glanced away from me without a word. "Once Jensen gets back, we can all go upstairs. The party has already started. I'll give my speech soon, and then we can all enjoy ourselves. Thanks for another successful year. And thanks for believing in me to be CEO of Wright Construction."

"Were you practicing your speech on us?" Austin joked.

"Ha-ha," Morgan deadpanned.

"It was pretty well done if that's part of it," Landon agreed. "I'd keep out the part about believing in you as CEO. That's sentimental."

Morgan rolled her eyes. "You know I can fire both of you, right?"

Austin clutched his chest. "Threats! I'm going to take this to the head of HR." He turned to his girlfriend, who was the current head of HR. "The CEO threatened to fire me for making fun of her."

"Eh, you deserved it," Julia said, crossing her arms.

"Whose side are you on anyway?"

"Probably Morgan's."

Austin scrunched up his face at her and then smacked her ass. Her eyes rounded, and she smacked him back.

"Watch it! That hurt!" she shrieked.

He grinned like a fool. "I meant for it to."

"Please keep the sexual harassment claims to a minimum," Morgan said dryly.

"Or just in the bedroom," Landon muttered under his breath.

"Children," Jensen said, entering the room, "are we fighting again?"

"No, Dad," Morgan said with an exaggerated eye roll. "We're well behaved, competent, and productive members of society."

"I wouldn't go that far," Jensen said.

Everyone laughed.

It was a good day when Jensen got in on the jokes. He was usually too busy with fixing everyone's problems and acting like the only parent of the bunch to join in on the antics. When he cut loose, he was a really fun guy though.

I usually stayed out of all of it. I was treated like family, but I wasn't family. They all had their own dynamic that no one else, even people like me who had been there from the beginning, could entirely breach.

"Sutton is going to meet us upstairs in a minute," Jensen announced. "And our other guest should be here"—he glanced out of the office—"now."

The Wright family's uncle walked into the office.

Owen had been perfectly nice to me both times I met him—at Thanksgiving and on campus. He seemed like an upstanding guy. Maybe even one who had been misunderstood all these years he was away in Vancouver. It might have helped all the Wright siblings if they'd actually had a parent or relative around to help raise them. Their mom had died too young, and their dad had been a chronic, abusive alcoholic. Jensen acted more like a parent for a reason.

But I could feel Morgan's death glare from where I was standing. She had every reason to believe that Owen hated her. It had made her do a one-eighty, too. Working a hundred hours a week and pushing herself to the brink of collapse. Even if he wasn't really trying to harm her, he was doing it anyway.

"Hey, everyone," Owen said with a bright smile and wave.

They all seemed happy to see him. Relieved even. Like he just seamlessly fit in with their family. But I knew Morgan was silently seething and trying not to erupt.

"Glad that I could be here for the annual Christmas party. Of course, I'm sad to be missing the one back home. It's a lively affair. I usually make a big speech." His eyes landed on Morgan. "If you need help with yours, let me know. I've been doing this a long time."

Morgan clutched the desk until her knuckles turned white. "I think I've got it covered."

"That's a nice offer though," Jensen said.

"Yeah. Super nice," Morgan said flatly.

"Also, I brought this," he said, holding up a bottle of Moët & Chandon champagne. "I thought we could all toast to another great year at Wright."

I froze in place. And then, suddenly, all eyes shifted to Austin. He'd only gotten out of rehab six weeks ago. The fact that he was coming to the Christmas party at all was a big deal. It was his first event where he'd be around alcohol again. But to just toss it in front of him like Owen was doing was tantamount to treason.

"We don't drink," Morgan bit out. Her voice was clipped.

"Oh," Owen said. "I'm sorry. I thought it was an open bar upstairs. I wanted to bring my favorite champagne to toast with."

"I said, we don't drink. Not here. Not between us," Morgan snapped.

"Mor," Austin muttered, "it's fine. It's a nice gesture. I'll just go outside."

"You are more part of the family than he is. You're not leaving."

"Morgan," Jensen hissed.

Owen's eyes were round with concern. I didn't know if it was fake. If it was, he was a good actor.

"I'm sorry. I didn't realize. It seems the family has inherited Ethan's problems," he said about his brother. "I should have known better."

"It's fine. You didn't know," Jensen said. "Come on, everyone. Why don't we all go upstairs?" He said it to the room, but his eyes were on Morgan.

I couldn't read whatever conversation passed between them, but it wasn't good. Morgan was already all over the place between working too much, not eating enough, not sleeping enough, and now this speech. She did not need this shit about her uncle, too.

I acted like I was following the rest of the family out of the office but stopped. "Hey, man, I'll be up in a minute."

"Cool." Austin nodded his head and hurried after Julia.

He was swatting her ass, and she was busy with trying to land a decent punch.

I waited until everyone was on the elevator before pulling the door closed behind me and turning to face Morgan. She'd dropped down into her office chair with her head in her hands.

"Hey," I finally said.

"Oh, am I worthy of your speech now?" she grumbled.

"Morgan."

"Just don't. All right?"

"Should we talk about your uncle?"

"No," she growled low.

"He shouldn't have asked you about your speech."

She slammed her hands down on the desk and looked up at me. "I said, no. I don't want to talk about Mr. Doucheface. I don't want to talk about his passive-aggressive attacks on me or the fact that I look like the bad person when I call him out on his bullshit. I have to deal with his smug face enough during the hours I'm here at work, so I really don't want to fucking talk about him now. Not when I'm supposed to stand on that stage and give a speech. Not when I'm supposed to be holding things together, and it all seems to be falling apart."

I stood there, frozen from her anger. Her blistering anger. But I knew it wasn't directed at me. Not really. This was about work and her uncle. I just happened to be the only person in her life who would let her vent it all out of her system and not care.

"Come here," I told her as I stepped around the desk.

"I don't want to do this tonight, Patrick."

"What don't you want to do? The speech? Cool. I'll do it."

I reached for the piece of paper on the desk, and she snatched it away from me.

"You can't do it."

"Why not? I'm funny and charming, a little goofy, but I've been told I'm a pretty good public speaker."

"You're not funny. Stop trying to be funny."

"You know what you need?" I asked, holding my hand out.

She scrunched up her eyebrows. "What?"

"A dance."

"What?"

"Just give me your hand."

"Patrick."

"Trust me, okay?"

She sighed and then placed her hand in mine. I pulled her away from the desk and out in the middle of the room. Her high heels brought her up to my shoulder as we swayed in time to the music in our heads.

"What are we dancing to?" I asked, moving her in closer until our bodies touched.

"Nothing," she whispered.

She tilted her head up to glance into my eyes. All I saw was *her* in that moment. This unbelievably strong woman who took on the world. There was weariness but also hope and determination and joy in those eyes.

No matter what that uncle of hers was putting in her head, Morgan Wright was the future of this company.

She was my future. I could feel it then. And, without thinking another thing, I crushed her closer to me and pressed my mouth against hers.

It barely registered when the office door opened or when someone stepped into the room.

I only heard the words out of Austin's mouth. "What the fuck is going on here?"

Twenty-One

Morgan

No.

> *No, God, this couldn't be happening to me right now.*

After putting this off for so long, we'd been caught red-handed. And by the last person I'd wanted to see. Jensen might have laughed it off and given me grief about it later. Landon would have maybe even pretended like he never saw it. But Austin…

"Seriously…are either of you going to tell me what the fuck is going on?" Austin asked.

Patrick and I backed away from each other at the same time. Not that it made us look any less guilty. We were so guilty.

"Austin, I…we," I said, suddenly tongue-tied.

His eyes locked on mine before switching to his best friend. "Are you with my little sister?"

"She's not so little anymore, Austin," Patrick said coolly.

How is he so confident? I was actually shaking. I'd wanted to tell everyone what was happening. Yet I was the one who was terrified with how this would fall out between Patrick and Austin. It wasn't like my brothers could disown *me*.

"Yeah, I noticed you'd figured that out when you had your tongue down her throat."

"Austin," I groaned.

"Don't you have a speech to give upstairs, Morgan?" he bit out.

"We should talk about this."

"Yes, we should. Patrick and I are going to talk about this."

"I think we should all talk. It's not like we meant to hide this from you."

"Yes, we did," Patrick said.

I glared at him. Of course, he was right. We had held this back from everyone on purpose. Especially Austin. He'd been there that first night. We could have told him then, and we hadn't.

"It's been Morgan this whole time. When you asked me who was at my house, it was Morgan. It's still Morgan. And, yeah, we purposely didn't tell you or anyone else because we knew this would be your reaction."

"No one else knows?" Austin asked.

I cringed. "Uh…not exactly."

"Go give your speech, Mor."

Patrick turned to look at me and smiled his cute lopsided grin. "Go on. I'll handle this."

"Patrick," I whispered, "I don't want you to do this alone."

"I know. But we'll deal with it together after the party."

I frowned between Patrick and my brother before nodding. I couldn't believe I was actually walking away from this right now. I could stay and ignore my speech. But, with all the drama going on at work, I didn't want to give anyone a reason to second-guess me. Even for something as little as a speech.

I walked toward Austin, who was still standing in the doorway. He moved aside, so I could pass.

"This isn't his fault, you know."

"I think I can handle this."

"Go easy on him," I whispered before leaving.

My heels carried me down the hall like a scared little mouse. I'd just *left* Patrick there with Austin. It didn't matter that Austin had told me to leave and that Patrick had agreed that it was okay. I felt like a traitor.

I jammed my finger on the button in frustration and then circled back to face my office. I had to go back. Yes, I needed to worry about work, but it was just a speech, right? This was *Patrick*.

The only man who seemed to understand my crazy and still liked my work ethic. He took care of me and cooked for me and made sure I was still sane at the end of each day. He didn't try to change me. He didn't try to put me in a box. He didn't try to make me conform to a standard. I was just me, and he was fine with that.

I took a deep breath and was about to walk down the hall when the elevator dinged open. I glanced back at the giant metal box and was surprised to find Emery standing there.

"Shit, am I too late?" she asked.

"Just a bit."

"Austin was coming down here, and I just realized why you and Patrick were missing together."

"Yeah. He found us in a compromising position."

"Fuck," Emery spat. "Should I go in there?"

"They kind of both forced me to leave."

"Do we need to get Julia?" Emery asked with concerned, wide eyes.

"I don't know. I feel half like I should go back in there and try to fix everything and half like...maybe they should duke it out."

"Yeah. Men!"

"I mean...right!"

"Why is it even a big deal anyway?"

"For so many reasons. But I told Patrick up-front that, if it came to this, I'd handle my brothers, and now, I'm running away at the first sign of trouble."

Emery put her arm around my shoulders and guided me onto the elevator. "You're not running from trouble. You're running the company. This will blow over. Austin is going to be shocked, and then it'll be fine. I'll talk to Jensen for you if you want?"

"I appreciate it but no. I should probably do that myself."

"I respect that."

The elevator dinged open on the top floor, revealing the hundreds of employees who worked at Wright Construction. All of my employees. Every single one of them. Despite the issues in my personal life, my heart swelled with pride at all the happy faces. I loved this company. Frankly, I adored this company. Like Jensen, I made sure that I knew everyone's names and faces. I didn't want to just completely lock myself away in my glass tower and never know the people who were doing the hard work.

I smiled, hugged, and shook hands with people as Emery and I meandered through the crowd to the front of the room. I could tell that people were taking full advantage of the open bar. A sea of happy faces without a care in the world. And here I was, their leader, terrified to face her brothers and about to go onstage to address them as shaky as fuck.

"Where have you been?" Jensen asked as soon as I reached the rest of my family.

"I—"

"It doesn't matter. I wanted to introduce you to some people before you had to be up there, but it's time to get up onstage."

I looked between Jensen and Landon and then on to Sutton. She gave me a half-smile and nodded her head, as if she could read my mind.

"I'm dating Patrick," I told my brothers. "You might want to save him from Austin downstairs."

Jensen's and Landon's jaws dropped open at my declaration. Then, before I could second-guess myself, I walked away and onto the stage. My stomach was churning, and my hands were trembling. Out of my periphery, I could see both Jensen and Landon disappear and head for the elevator. I tried to block it out and concentrate on my speech. But, yeah, there was no chance of that.

Still, I stepped up onto the stage. I cleared my throat into the microphone and got everyone's attention. I smiled like I was cool and confident. Even though I was kind of dying on the inside.

"Thank you all so much for coming tonight," I began. "It's been another unbelievable year for Wright Construction. I'm so grateful to have stepped into the CEO position and to see the growth and trajectory of this company. I have high hopes and, let's be honest, intense, strategic plans to continue to move onward and upward."

I couldn't believe that I was talking about this right now. My mind was a hundred percent on the conversation that was going on downstairs. I hated that this speech was tainted by all of this. We should have just told the guys after we got home from San Francisco. I knew that Patrick didn't want to tell because of his relationship with Austin. But I was clearly at fault too. I'd made up an imaginary boyfriend instead of telling them!

I continued through my planned speech. I told them about the work we'd been doing with the environmental upgrades. How our company was moving toward better digital equipment in the field. Plus the success we'd had with our prized Disney World project.

"Not to mention, the amazing contract we're negotiating with Texas Tech right across the street," I added. "We've always been top of the line, helping to build the university so many of us graduated from. And, once we close that out at the end of the year, it will be thirty straight years of Wright Construction on the Tech campus!"

The crowd cheered. And, over the tops of the heads, I saw Jensen and Landon schlep back into the room without Austin or Patrick behind them. Nerves bit at me as the applause died down.

I needed to end this thing. I just needed to get off this stage and figure out what was going on. *Fuck.*

"Here's to you! Wright Construction would never be as successful without all of you. I hope the annual bonuses going out next week help to show just how much we appreciate you."

The screams were even louder than before. I laughed and raised my hands to quiet everyone down. Even though, on the inside, I was squirming.

"Enjoy the party and the open bar! Happy holidays!"

I stepped off the stage in relief. The weight of the world fell off my shoulders. One huge struggle down. Another even bigger one to deal with.

Jensen was waiting for me. He looked like a walking thundercloud.

"We need to talk."

"I know."

"But I need you to keep that smile on your face for a little bit longer."

"Okay," I muttered.

"Be on your best behavior."

"Why?"

Jensen didn't answer. He just tugged me across the room over to where our uncle stood with two men I'd never seen and definitely never met before. But my uncle was one of the last people I wanted to see right now.

Douchecanoe.

"Owen, we're so pleased that you've been able to stay through the holidays," Jensen said easily.

The look I gave him said that I completely disagreed. He narrowed his eyes at me, and I plastered that smile back on my face.

Why the fuck am I talking to these people when I have other shit to deal with? I was already at my wit's end with work. Add everyone finding out about Patrick, my dick uncle, and these two random men, and I was about to break.

I didn't have another fake pageant girl smile. I only had resting bitch face and zero fucks to give.

"I'm happy to be here, too, Jensen," Owen said when I didn't respond. "I'm also happy that my two boys were able to make the trip to stay with me for the rest of the holiday season."

I did a double take.

"Morgan, these are our cousins from Vancouver," Jensen supplied. "The rest of the family met them while you were…otherwise occupied."

I didn't miss the edge to his voice.

"Wow," was all I could muster.

The taller of the two just laughed and held his hand out. We shook.

"I've heard a lot about you. I'm Jordan, and this is my younger brother, Julian."

Now that I knew who they were, it was impossible to miss. They could be my brothers, and no one would disagree with me. It was eerie. Tall, dark hair, dark eyes, and handsome. I wondered if they had the Wright charm, too. Or if they were as big of dicks as their father.

"Nice to meet you." I shook Julian's hand, too.

"We'd love to get to know you better while we're in town," Julian said.

Great. Just what I needed. Eager cousins I'd never met before wanting to get in on my life.

"I'm sure we can set something up," Jensen said before I could snark back.

"But, right now, we have some important business to handle."

"Business?" Owen asked. "It's the Christmas party. Can't it wait?"

"No, it can't."

"Take the night off, Morgan. You've earned it."

I narrowed my eyes. "It's bad when I take time off. It's bad when I don't take time off. Make up your mind."

Jensen sighed heavily and looked to the ceiling.

"I don't think I know what you mean," Owen said.

"I think you do."

"No, I really don't," he said, holding his ground.

"It's called a double standard. Look it up in the dictionary if you're confused," I snapped back at him. I turned my attention back to my cousins. "Great meeting you."

Then, I more or less fled that conversation.

What the hell is with this night? Is it a full moon? Is Mercury in retrograde? Something had to be happening in the cosmos to bring me this much negative energy. Because…damn.

"You're going to have to make that up to Owen," Jensen said when he jogged up behind me.

"Whatever." I angled for the exit. "Let's get this over with."

"Morgan," Jensen said, stopping me, "you can't storm out of here, looking pissed off. Stay and mingle for a while. We'll deal with this after the party."

I arched an eyebrow. "I can't. I'm not built that way. It stresses me out to wait to deal with anything. I'll get worse than I was with Owen and his uninvited children who we'd never freaking met."

"They're his kids. They don't have to be invited."

"Whatever. I don't like to be in the same room with him. I'm pretty sure I wouldn't have cared to ever meet his kids."

"I'm not going to touch that," Jensen said, trying to conceal his laugh. "Just stay for an hour. Calm down. Breathe. We'll talk it out."

My eyes slid to his, and my anger began to dissolve. The fear that had threatened to strangle me slowly eased. "How are Austin and Patrick?"

"Austin was in shock. You know how he is. Plus, there's alcohol nearby. We're trying to manage him. Julia is trying to talk some sense into him."

"I don't want to ruin their relationship," I whispered. Tears got stuck in my throat, and I tried to swallow them back. I absolutely could not start crying. I hated crying to begin with. I doubly hated crying over stupid shit. Nothing was worth my expensive mascara.

"They've been friends a long, long time. It'll work out," Jensen said soothingly. "Make your rounds. Let everyone cool off for a minute."

"Ugh," I groaned. "Fine."

Cooling off was the last thing I wanted to do. I wanted to take my fiery anger and wreak havoc on the world. Burn everything that stood in my way. I wanted this nightmare to be over.

Twenty-Two

Patrick

There were a million things I wanted to say. A thousand defenses. A hundred arguments. More than a dozen cuss words. But not a single apology.

I wasn't here to apologize for Morgan.

And I never would.

That didn't mean that the last hour had been any better though. After having it out with Austin, he'd stormed out of the building. Jensen and Landon had come in at the tail end of that, and Jensen had immediately gone off to find Julia. Landon had given me a short laugh and crossed his arms over his chest, as if to say, *You're in it now.*

Currently, I was in the conference room with Landon, Jensen, and Sutton seated around the table. I couldn't sit. I was too nervous. I was too pissed that Austin hadn't come back yet. Too worried that Morgan wasn't here either.

The last thing I wanted was for this to be a repeat of what had happened when Austin and Steph hooked up. I deserved a chance to explain that this wasn't the same situation. At the time, Steph had only recently turned eighteen. She had still been in high school. Austin had been drunk and an idiot with no intention of ever seeing her again.

Morgan and I had been together for weeks. We might have hidden our relationship, but it wasn't for the reason that Austin thought.

I could still hear his accusation before he'd stormed out of the office.

"You lied to me. To me. And, worse, you've been lying to my sister. Hiding whatever the fuck this is and trying to act like you're not just going to toss her aside the second you get bored, like you did with all the others."

I closed my eyes against the pain of those words. Of course that was what he thought. I'd never given any indication that I was interested in a relationship. Not with anyone. Certainly not with Morgan. Not Morgan, who he'd always been protective of. They all had.

It was his unsaid implication that kicked me where it hurt. I wasn't good enough for her.

That part might have been true. Morgan Wright was out of my league. Still, I wasn't going to back down. Not when she'd chosen me. I might not be good enough for her, but I'd damn well keep trying to deserve her.

A noise broke me from my thoughts, and I whirled around to see Morgan standing in the doorway. Our eyes locked. Everything clicked into place. I smiled at the sight of her, and she returned it. We might not have intended to be here tonight, but we were. And we'd work it out.

"Where's Austin?" Morgan asked.

Jensen sighed. "He's with Julia."

"Is he coming up here?"

"Yeah. She said he'd be up in a minute."

Morgan frowned and then bypassed her family to come stand next to me. "How are you?" she asked, concern etched into every feature.

"Oh, you know, walk in the park," I said with a strained smile.

"Yeah. Pretty much, right?"

I reached out and threaded our fingers together. "How about you?"

"Ready to just get this over with. My head is killing me, and this day has been a disaster."

A knock sounded on the door, and we both tensed as Austin entered the room. He crashed into the seat next to Sutton. She arched her eyebrow at him.

"Took you long enough, jerk," Sutton said.

He shrugged. "I needed to meditate and shit."

"Did it help?"

"Are you being snotty?" he asked.

She poked him. "I actually wasn't."

"Can we convene this family meeting?" Landon asked. "We totally missed the party for this."

"Yes, I believe we should. It's been a long night for everyone already. I'd like to go home," Jensen said.

"Can I just ask a question?" Landon said.

"You just did," Austin grumbled.

"What happened to Joe?"

Morgan rolled her eyes. "Joe is Patrick."

"Patrick is Joe?"

"Yes. Joe doesn't exist. I made him up."

"Huh," Landon said and sat back.

"I liked Joe better," Austin muttered under his breath.

Morgan looked like she was about to tear into him, so I cut in. "Before we say anything else, I'd like to say a few words."

All eyes turned to stare at me. This was definitely Morgan's domain. I wasn't the leader, but I wanted to say the things that I hadn't been able to say to Austin. I'd been on the defensive, and I should have just tried to explain.

"Morgan and I started seeing each other a couple weeks ago. It was unexpected. Neither of us were ready to tell you what happened. I worried about your reactions to our relationship, especially Austin's," I said in a rush. "Obviously, that fear was warranted. However, I don't intend to break up with her just because you don't approve of us being together. We've all known each other a long time. I know this must be strange, but Morgan and I *are* together. And that's not going to change."

Everyone stared at me, speechless. Even Morgan.

"Uh, yeah. What he said. Though, to be completely honest, I wasn't too keen on having all of you in my business," she spat. "Considering how you're reacting right now."

Sutton held up her hand. "I was perfectly happy for you two when I found out."

"When did you find out?" Austin demanded.

"Morgan told me on our girls' night."

"You told Sutton and not us?" Landon asked with his hand over his chest. "I'm wounded."

Jensen rolled his eyes to the ceiling. "Dear God, we're not upset with you two. Can you sit down, so it doesn't feel like you're addressing the class?"

"You're not upset?" Morgan asked, surprise laced in every word.

"I'm not upset because I guessed," Landon volunteered.

"You didn't guess!" Morgan cried. "You were just asking about imaginary Joe!"

"I'm observant."

"You're not that observant," I said.

"Hey, you're on the chopping block," Landon said. "Sit your ass down."

I grinned at him, relief flooding my system. Morgan and I took our seats across from the rest of her family. The only one who still looked pissy was Austin. He was my best friend and entirely unpredictable. I didn't know if he was about to relapse and go on a bender or laugh it off like the whole thing was a joke.

"The most important question that I have to lead with is," Jensen said, ignoring Austin's sullen behavior, "did this happen when you were still an employee? Especially since she's become CEO."

We glanced at each other. Technically, yes. It had started while I worked here. But it hadn't been serious…and I'd already put in my notice.

"Trust me when I say that you do not want another situation like what I went through," Landon said. "Heidi still kicks me for that sometimes."

"Yes," Morgan finally said with a sigh. "But it didn't get serious until afterward."

"Wait," Jensen said, holding up his hand, "is this the real reason you two went to San Francisco?"

"Uh," I muttered.

Morgan looked guilty. "Yeah."

"I was already going. It was to see Steph about wedding stuff. But…it was also because we were together."

Jensen pinched the bridge of his nose. "No wonder you didn't do any work."

"Hey! I did work," Morgan muttered.

"Okay, okay," Landon said. "So, they went away together before they told anyone. Heidi and I did that. You and Emery did that! And it wasn't all rainbows and unicorns."

"Oh, Waffle," Austin muttered under his breath, naming the stuffed unicorn that he and Julia had gotten on their first date.

"I don't want this to come back and bite you in the ass," Jensen said. "I don't actually care that you went or that you're together. It's not my business."

"Yeah. As long as Patrick treats you right, I won't have to beat his ass," Landon said.

Austin pushed back his chair. "So, we're just going to ignore the fact that they lied?"

"And you've never lied?" Morgan shot back.

"Sure, I've fucking lied. But, fuck," Austin said. His eyes shifted back to me. "After what happened to Steph, you expect me to be cool with this?"

"This is a different situation, and you know it," I said.

Austin pushed out of his chair and leaned forward with his hands on the conference table. "You didn't speak to me for a *year* after that. I've only had an hour to deal!"

"You're right," I said. "But Morgan and I are together. That doesn't change because you're upset. You hooked up with Steph and ditched her. I have no intention of doing that. In fact, I have no intention of going back to the way things were. You of all people should know what it's like to have a woman change you. So, hear me when I say, Morgan is it."

"Really?" Austin asked in disbelief. "Just like that?"

"Just like that."

He plopped back down in his seat and then glanced between me and Morgan. "Huh."

"What?" Morgan asked.

"I always joked about you dating Patrick for so long. I mean, we all knew how you felt about him. It was obvious to everyone but him."

"Thanks for the heads-up," I muttered under my breath.

"I never thought it'd actually happen. Like, it was a joke for so long that, now that it's a reality, it's not really funny. Maybe I'm just an asshole."

Sutton snorted. "Maybe?"

"Hey!"

"Why did you even go bother them?" Sutton asked.

"I…" Austin paused. "Owen told me to go get them."

"What?" Morgan shrieked, jumping out of her chair. "Owen sent you?"

"Yeah. Dude said that I should get you for the speech."

"He knew," she growled.

"He knew what?" I asked.

"He already knew about us. He must have. That's why he sent Austin downstairs. He's out to get me."

"Morgan," Jensen said with a sigh, "are we really doing this again?"

"I don't understand why no one believes me. Owen is trying to sabotage me. He might charm everyone else, but he hasn't charmed me. He doesn't want to charm me. He wants me to suffer."

"Uh, are you talking about Uncle Owen?" Landon asked. "He doesn't really seem like the type to want people to suffer."

"Oh, yeah? Well then, why was he sent to Vancouver? You don't exile someone out of the country for no reason. How come we've never met him before? How come Dad never talked about him, and he never had pictures of him? Doesn't anyone else think this is fishy?"

"I do," I said.

"You don't count," Austin said. "You're not part of the family."

"Never mattered before."

"Y'all!" Morgan snapped. "He's manipulating you. He did this on purpose to derail me. Just like he's been doing with everything since he arrived."

"I really think you're over—" Jensen began.

"I swear to God," Morgan growled like a feral animal, "if you say I'm overreacting…"

Jensen held his hands up. "Okay."

No one could go toe-to-toe with Jensen, except Morgan. Seeing his miniature give him hell was actually pretty satisfying.

"I don't know about all of you, but I'm just happy I could be here to watch that showdown. Morgan has the biggest balls of us all," Landon said.

I grinned like a fool and tried not to say aloud the dirty comment flitting through my head.

Austin groaned. "I was on my way to forgiving this shit, and then you made that face. About my sister. I know what that face means."

I laughed. "Guilty."

"Guy! Back on topic," Morgan muttered. "Something is going on here. I can feel it in my gut. And it has to do with Owen."

"Say it does," Sutton cut in. "What does he want? Why is he doing it?"

"I don't know. But I intend to find out."

And I was certain that she wouldn't rest until she figured it out. That was just who Morgan was. But, by the looks on the rest of her family's faces, she wasn't the only one contemplating what Owen was up to.

"Okay. Let's look into it," Jensen said finally, breaking the tension.

"Can we talk?" Austin asked, nodding his head toward the door.

"Yeah."

I kissed the top of Morgan's head before leaving her alone with the rest of her family. Austin and I needed to have this out anyway. We stepped outside and closed the conference room door behind us.

"Why didn't you tell me?" Austin asked.

"Why the hell do you think?"

"She was the girl at your place that night I came over, right?"

"Yeah."

"You were still working at Wright then."

"Yeah."

"She could get in trouble for it. Especially if what she's saying about Owen is true."

"I'd already put in my notice, and it was my last real day at work. Nothing happened before that."

"God," Austin said, running a hand back through his hair, "do you know how many times I made fun of her for liking you? And you didn't even notice. Like, that night we got her wasted at First Friday Art Trail. You brushed my comment off like she was *your* little sister."

"I know," I said, remembering that night. "I don't want to cause a rift in our relationship, but I didn't intend to fall for Morgan. Once it happened, there was no going back. I know I've been a dick with women in the past. I know that I'm not relationship material, and she is. I know all of that. But I can't walk away."

"Do you love her?" Austin asked point-blank.

I balked at the question. Love. *Shit. Did I love Morgan?* It was so soon. I'd never said those words to a woman before. I'd never even considered it. But it was becoming clearer and clearer to me that there was no other woman in this world, let alone the universe, that was like Morgan Wright. She was the deal-breaker.

"Yeah," I finally said. "Yeah, I do."

Austin held his hand out. "All right."

I took his hand in mine, and we shook. "You're cool with this?"

"It's not that I don't want you to be with her. My shock came out as anger when, really, my anger was just shock. And then I was pissed that you'd lied to me. Plus, I know the kind of women you gravitate to."

"Crazy women."

"I mean, Mor is crazy but not your flavor of crazy."

"I've come to realize that she's the only flavor I ever want to taste again."

"Dude, stop. That's my sister," Austin said.

"I just mean—"

"No, I know. It's fine. If you love her and treat her right, then we're good. I was a shit and overreacted."

"Did Julia tell you to say that?" I asked with a laugh.

"Maybe."

"She's good for you."

"Yeah. What is it with these women?" Austin asked.

"They drive us crazy and pull us along on one hell of a ride, but it's all worth it in the end."

Twenty-Three

Morgan

"What a night."

Patrick took my hand in his as we stepped through the doorway into his house. "You can say that again."

"I cannot believe that all happened."

"It was certainly unexpected."

"I know that we hadn't talked about telling them again."

"I know. I would have liked to have waited a little longer, but I knew we couldn't wait forever. You're not the kind of woman who deserves to be hidden. You're not my dirty little secret."

"No, I'm your Wright secret."

He laughed. "Well, now, you're just my Wright."

"I'll take it."

"You know what I regret the most?"

I shook my head and looked up at him with curious, round eyes.

"That Austin interrupted our dance."

"Seriously?" I asked with a laugh. "We didn't even have music."

"I don't need music to dance with you."

"I'm not a great dancer."

"You're perfect," he assured me as he took my hand and started to sway me around his living room.

We got swept away into our little dance. My hands around his neck. His hands sliding down my hips. I leaned forward into his chest and listened to his heartbeat.

We'd survived. I couldn't believe that we were here right now. And I wanted to make sure it stayed that way.

"I feel like I'm still riding the adrenaline of the evening," I told him. I untucked his shirt from his pants and slid my hands up his chest.

"Right?"

"I was terrified that you'd bail after Austin's reaction."

"The thought never even crossed my mind."

I started at the top of his shirt and undid the buttons all the way to the bottom. He stripped off his shirt as I moved to his belt buckle.

"I know you've never done relationships before."

"Morgan," he said, snatching at my hands, "you are not like anyone else."

"Obviously, I know that," I said with a smirk.

"Of course you do. That's what I like about you. I didn't know that I wanted a relationship before you. I didn't want a relationship before you. You've changed everything."

"But...why?"

"The girls I dated before you weren't relationship material. I never thought I'd even be interested in a woman who was. But, when you opened my eyes, it was like a lightbulb."

I laughed breathily. "So, any woman who is relationship material would have done?"

"You know that's not true. It's just you. You're it for me."

A light switched in that moment. One second, we were dancing around the living room to music only the two of us could hear, and the next, Patrick was grabbing the backs of my legs and wrapping them around his waist. His hands crawled across my body. His lips crushed against mine. We couldn't seem to get close enough. It was as if something had snapped.

All that pent-up energy of not knowing when we'd tell people and then the stress when everyone found out. Suddenly, there was nothing left between us. No one keeping us apart. No more barriers.

The tension broke like a tidal wave.

We barreled toward his bedroom. My shoulder bounced into the wall, and I only broke apart long enough to laugh. It'd probably hurt later, but right now, who the fuck cared?

He backed into the room, kicking the door all the way open with his heel. We stumbled over something in the middle of the room. I laughed and dropped out of his arms. Then, I pushed him backward into the door, slamming it shut with a force.

"Fuck," he said at my aggression.

"Claim me," I breathed.

I was aching for him in all the best possible ways. There were no inhibitions left between us. We stood before each other, stripped bare to our souls. He could see the desire and lust and…more in my eyes. The things I couldn't say yet. But they were written clear as day through the windows into my heart.

He grabbed my shoulders and whirled me around, so my back hit the wall. His hand found my underwear, yanking it to the ground. I kicked off my heels, dipping me the several extra inches they had given me. But he didn't seem to care.

He dropped his pants and pulled out his dick, which was already hard me. Hoisting my leg around his waist, he pressed himself up against me. The tip was poised and ready against the opening to my pussy. I could feel him there, and I nearly screamed with want as he paused.

I teased his dick by making little circles. He slammed his fist into the wall and groaned my name. It was hot as fuck.

But I didn't have to tell him twice. He grabbed my ass in his hands and thrust up into me. My head whipped back into the wall. My hands dug into his shoulders.

"Oh God," I moaned.

"Morgan," he said against my shoulder, "you feel so fucking good."

He picked up his tempo and moved into me harder and harder and faster and faster. It was exhilarating. Nothing gentle about it. Just him wanting me. Me wanting him. The knowledge that we never had to hide this again. That we could just be ourselves. It took me to a new high.

I hadn't even realized quite how much it was all weighing on me until that weight was lifted. I was no longer a secret. Patrick had stood up for me. For us. He wanted this. He definitely, a hundred percent, wanted to be with me. He had to if he'd stood up to my brothers like that. Especially standing up to Austin and his temper. It was exhilarating and made me feel overwhelmingly happy.

As if all the puzzle pieces had finally been fit together. And not as a metaphor for what was happening right now.

Though…that was a great benefit.

For a long time, I'd thought Patrick and I would never really happen. And then, when we had gotten together, I'd thought we would crash and burn. That the hiding had been his way of keeping me distant. Even when things had been going so well, I still hadn't known.

But, now, I knew.

Patrick wanted me and only me.

He picked me up off the wall and then dropped me backward on his bed. He yanked me toward him until my ass was practically hanging off the bed. Then, he stood over me and entered me again, holding my legs open wide for him.

I clutched the bedspread and bit back a scream of pleasure. I was seeing stars as our bodies collided. It was too much. Everything felt too strong, too bright, too good. I'd never even known it was possible for me to feel this much. To just completely delve into this right here. Nothing compared.

Patrick moved forward onto his elbows, and I wrapped my legs around him, drawing him in closer. He pecked a kiss on my lips.

"Fuck," he groaned.

"I'm…so…close," I got out.

"Oh God, I can't wait to feel your pussy come all around me."

My entire body clenched at his words. Erotic and filthy and totally fucking turning me on.

He pulled back a little and grinned. "I like that reaction." Then, as he continued to fuck me, he moved his lips to the shell of my ear and whispered every utterly filthy thought he'd ever had about me.

My brain stopped functioning, and my body went with it. I came with an unrivaled force. My body convulsed around him, tightening and shaking from head to toe. My release was so hard that he came directly after me, finishing in a heap on top of me.

The mewling sound that came out of my mouth was incomprehensible. I didn't even know what I was saying. I was sure Patrick thought I was speaking in tongues.

Eventually, Patrick slid out and rolled onto the bed beside me. His chest was still rising and falling heavily. But he wrapped an arm around my shoulders and drew me closer.

"That was…the best sex I'd ever had in my life," he said.

I propped myself up on an elbow and looked at him with shocked, big, round eyes. "Ever?"

"Ever."

I opened my mouth and then closed it. I couldn't believe it. I mean...I could. It was just crazy. I knew Patrick had slept around a lot before we dated. He wasn't the dating type, which meant there had been a revolving door of women in his life. I'd always just...assumed that at least.

"Really?" I asked again.

He laughed and kissed my shoulder. "If I'd known we could have been doing this for all those years, I would have started a long time ago."

I swatted at him. "You're joking."

"I'm not. Why is it so hard to believe?"

I shrugged. I didn't say it was because he had more experience than me. I just lay back in his arms and enjoyed the fact that I was the best.

"I'm the best you've ever had," I whispered.

"Damn straight."

He got up to go clean up, and I went when he was finished. As I crawled naked into his bed, I noticed he looked more contemplative than when he'd told me I was the best sex of his life. Like he couldn't quite believe what his life was right now.

"What?" I asked.

"Can I ask you something?"

"Sure. Shoot."

"Why me?"

I cocked my head to the side. "What do you mean?"

"You said you always liked me since high school. But...why me?"

"You weren't like other guys."

He laughed. "I was exactly like other guys."

"Not to me. You always took me seriously, even before I was formidable enough to be taken seriously. You always treated me with value. You never made fun of my aspirations, and you were never intimidated by them. I

194

guess I always felt like you got me. Like maybe you were the other side to my coin." I blushed at that.

He stared at me in wonder. "You thought all of that, even in high school?"

"Well, first, I thought you were, like, so cute," I said with a high school cheerleader accent, batting my eyelashes.

He laughed.

"Then, the rest solidified over time."

"I might have missed some time with you all those years," he said, sliding back over my body and pressing my legs apart, "but I'm going to try to make up for it."

Twenty-Four

Patrick

"Are you serious right now?" I asked my boss, Bailey, on Monday afternoon.

Up until this point, work had been great. I loved my new job and the clients I had already started building relationships with. I enjoyed working with Bailey and my other coworkers. But I didn't like this. If I had been courted for this job because I knew the Wrights, then they were going to have another thing coming. I was not going to use my connections with them for business.

"Patrick, it's not like I'm asking you to do something illegal."

"The fact that you have to clarify should give you a clue."

"I'm just saying that you have an in with Wright Construction. You're *dating* the CEO. You could talk to them for us."

"No."

"Why are you being so obstinate about this?"

"If you want a lower price, then go with Jim Hogan Construction, Escoe Industrial, FX Contractors. There are a million options out there, but you and I both know that Wright is the best. They're local, the highest quality, and the hardest workers by far. So, don't ask me to do something I'm not comfortable with. Just figure it out without me."

I grabbed my suit jacket off my chair and left the office. My mind was reeling. I probably should have stayed for the last half hour of the day, but I needed to clear my head. I couldn't stand there and talk to her about all this shit another minute. She hadn't wanted to bring it up, which meant she knew that I wasn't going to be happy that she was fucking bringing it up.

I didn't even know how she had found out about me and Morgan so fast. We'd only been out to the world for a total of three days, and suddenly, even my boss knew that I was dating Morgan Wright.

I'd been stupid happy all weekend with Morgan, and now, I was dealing with this. All I wanted to do was go talk to her, but she really didn't need more shit on her plate.

Ready to take out my frustration on the first person who looked at me wrong, I headed to the gym. I always kept my bag in the back of my truck for occasions like this when I didn't get in my typical morning workout. I usually went with Austin. That, at least, hadn't changed. But, today, I didn't want to see anyone I knew. I wanted to vent into the weight room.

I stripped out of the workday suit and into running shorts and a Dri-FIT T-shirt. I grabbed gloves out of my bag before heading into the room. The gym was already filling up with the afternoon crowd. People who came in to get their workout in after work were usually the ones who weren't morning people. I went through a quick warm-up and then started with free weights.

I'd thought that this would make me feel better. Less angry at my boss for trying to use my relationship with

Morgan to get ahead. But I wasn't feeling less angry. If anything, I was feeling more so. With each bicep curl, I got more pissed at the situation I'd found myself in.

Had I only been recruited to the position because of my friendship with the Wrights? Because I'd worked for the company for that long? Did everything in my life revolve around the Wright family?

I loved them. They were great people. Austin was my best friend. Landon was a close second. Jensen had gotten me out of more than one bind. Morgan was my new girlfriend. Sutton was like a baby sister. But, Jesus Christ, my entire life sometimes felt overshadowed by their greatness.

Sure, they were Texas royalty here in Lubbock. Sure, they had a Fortune 500 company. Sure, they were a landmark family in the community. But I wasn't chump change. I was something outside of the Wrights.

Fuck, I knew this wasn't the main issue. I was taking out my own irritation on the fact that it was associated with the Wrights. The real issue was being taken advantage of. As if it was an appropriate thing to do to try to convince me to use my friendship to help my boss get ahead.

I moved to the bench press, and one of the gym employees moved in to spot me. I'd seen him around, and I probably knew his name if I thought about it. But I wasn't really in the mood to be the friendly guy I normally was.

The thing I hated the most was that I should be able to take this to Morgan. That was what a relationship was for, right? But it was dumb. She was the CEO. She didn't need to be dealing with my petty squabbles with my boss. She had enough to deal with as it was. Plus, I was pretty sure I'd made my position about this clear to Bailey. There was no way I was going to use my relationship to further her agenda.

I'd never even had a real relationship before, and I knew that was against the rules.

I felt really alone with this. If I told Austin, he'd take it to Morgan. She'd wonder why I hadn't told her first. An unexpected downside of dating your best friend's little sister. If you could even consider there being a downside where Morgan was concerned.

I eased the bar back into place and sat up, dripping sweat.

"Good work today, Patrick!" the employee said behind me.

"Thanks," I said with a half-grin.

"Hey, can I ask you a question?"

I toweled off. "What's that?"

"Is it true that you're dating Morgan Wright?"

"Wow. Good news really does travel fast."

"So, yes?"

"Yeah, we're dating."

"Man, what's that like? She's so uptight and brainy."

I arched an eyebrow. "You're saying that about my girlfriend."

The guy raised his hands. "I didn't mean anything by it. I just didn't think she was your type of girl. What does Austin think?"

"First, there's nothing wrong with Morgan being a strong, successful woman. If you think that makes her uptight and brainy, as if brainy is a bad thing, then you don't know her. And, second, I don't think I really had a type of girl before Morgan. And Austin's cool with it. Thanks for asking."

I started to walk away, and I could hear the guy trying to apologize. But, really, even though he'd been nosy and kind of a dick, my reaction had been heightened by my current anger. I was a ticking time bomb.

I finished my workout in the weight room and then ran a couple of miles on the treadmill. I was worn out by the end of it. The last mile really did me in. Finally, I was able to stop thinking so much. This newfound aggression was something I was not used to. I was usually a laid-back kind of guy. The one who didn't have a care in the world.

But, when it came to Morgan, everything was different. She had turned my world upside down. Brought meaning in my life that I hadn't even known I was lacking. I had been waiting my whole life for Morgan, and I hadn't even known it.

Twenty-Five

Patrick

When I left the gym, the sky was already dark. I texted Morgan to let her know I was leaving. It wasn't strange that I hadn't heard from her since lunch. I doubted she'd actually eaten lunch when she texted me. She didn't normally get out of work for another hour or two, if I was that lucky. So, I had some time to kill.

I was glad that I'd taken a shower at the gym, but, fuck, I was already feeling drained. I wanted a beer and some comfort food before passing out. Wake up and deal with the aftermath of that conversation with my boss tomorrow.

As I pulled up, I noticed a black Mercedes parked in front of my house. "What the hell?"

I parked my truck in the garage and then hurried outside. And there she was. Morgan was sitting in her car in the dark with her head on the steering wheel. I knocked on the window, and she jumped nearly out of her skin. She rolled down the window.

"You scared the shit out of me!" she cried over the sound of rap music blasting through the speakers.

"What are you listening to?"

"'Hypnotize.'"

"Yeah, I know. I mean…since when do you listen to The Notorious B.I.G.?"

"Don't dis one of the masters."

I held my hands up. "You are an enigma wrapped in a mystery."

She turned down the music as it changed to "Big Poppa." "You'll have to accept that there will always be something more for you to learn about me."

"I look forward to that."

She smiled brilliantly before hopping out of her car.

"To what do I owe the pleasure of you leaving work this early?"

Her smile disappeared. "Ugh, Jensen. I don't really want to talk about it."

"Come inside. I'll cook us dinner."

I didn't really want to talk to her about my day either. And it was clear by the look on her face that she really didn't need to know.

"That would be great," she said with a relieved sigh.

I changed out of my suit for the third time today and into sweats. Morgan had stashed clothes here since she came over so often late at night and didn't want to go home. I got distracted as she stripped out of her suit.

"Why don't we stop right there?" I suggested when she was down to her bra and thong.

"Because you're all the way across the room." She teased her bra strap down and bit her lip.

Fuck, I could just devour her.

"Is that an invitation?"

"Most you're going to get."

I strode across the room and tugged her against me. Our mouths collided, and all the frustration bottled up in us came loose at the seams. Whatever I hadn't been able to unravel at the gym was pushed into that kiss. That maybe this moment here with her would help. I shoved her back into the footboard, and she toppled backward onto the bed with an irresistible giggle.

"Come here," she said, hooking her finger at me.

My eyes roamed her body. Everything about her was seductive as fuck. And it would be so easy to forget myself in her. But it also wasn't exactly healthy. It was the kind of behavior I'd indulged in before Morgan. I wanted to have sex with her. Shit, I wanted to fuck her into next Tuesday, but I didn't want to do it to forget. I didn't want her to do it to forget either.

I crawled on the bed toward her. She smiled coyly up at me, but I just pulled her against my chest.

"You don't want to?" she asked, surprised.

"Oh, I do."

"Then, why…"

"For one, you haven't eaten today."

"What's your obsession with food?"

"And, two, when I fuck you, I want to be the only thing on your mind."

She huffed. "I can multitask."

I brushed my lips against her ear. "When you multitask, I want it to be because you're fucking me and screaming my name at the same time."

"Patrick," she gasped, sitting up and glaring at me. "You say those things and then don't fuck me?"

"I'm going to fuck you, Mor," I promised. "But after I take care of you first."

She flopped back on the bed. "So unfair."

I laughed gruffly and then slid down between her legs. I grabbed a knee and moved it to my shoulder as I kissed my way up her leg. I trailed my fingers down her sensitive inner thigh, and my lips followed, stopping just before the apex and then moving up the other leg. She writhed her hips, aching for me to move back to where she wanted.

I took my time in getting back between her legs. Then, I put my mouth against the lace of her thong and blew hot air on her pussy through the material. She moaned out loud. It was a satisfying sound, to say the least.

I hooked one finger underneath her thong and slowly slid it down her legs. I tossed it to the ground with a sly smile.

When I moved back to that spot where she so desperately wanted me, I pushed her hips down to the mattress and then brought my tongue to her clit. I licked slowly and languidly up and down until she was making these adorable mewling noises. Then, I gently nibbled on her as her pussy pulsed in anticipation. Just as she was trying to escape my insistent movement, I sucked on her clit, causing her to scream. And, still, I didn't stop. I slicked two fingers through her wetness before inserting them into her pussy.

"Oh, fuck," she groaned, panting around her words.

I wanted her to feel this. I wanted to drag her pleasure out. I wanted every orgasm I could milk from her body.

She needed the release like no one else I knew. And this was definitely one way that I could take care of her. She needed someone who was present for her. She was so complex and not used to people who could keep up with her. We might be opposites, but it didn't matter. I was determined to give her all the things that she didn't even know she needed.

As I curled my finger inside her, touching the G-spot, she cried out with release. Her walls contracted around my fingers. Her hips bucked off the bed, even as I tried to hold her down, as she rode out the wave. Her face was pure ecstasy.

And, even though I was rock solid from her orgasm, I was feeling pretty satisfied myself.

Finally, she lay flat again on the bed. Her chest was heaving and eyes closed.

"That was…"

"I thought you should come at least once before dinner."

"My turn?" she asked, eyeing my bulging cock.

"I'll let you reciprocate later. I wanted this to be all about you."

"How did I get so lucky?" she whispered.

"I'm the lucky one."

Her eyes drooped as the tension finally left her body, and she relaxed back into the bed. She looked like she could fall asleep right then and there. And, as someone who was notorious for sleeping less than six hours a night—sometimes only as much as three or four hours—it wouldn't even be a bad idea for her to get a solid twelve hours in.

"Jensen is worried about our relationship," she muttered.

I froze. "What? I thought he was fine?"

"I thought so, too."

"What happened between the party and Monday morning?"

She shrugged. "He remembered I was CEO?"

"He was both married and dating at one point or another when he was CEO."

"I know. He said, and I quote, 'Would it kill you to wait a year?'"

"What the hell does he think a year will do?"

She shook her head and sighed heavily. She found her discarded underwear and changed into leggings and a T-shirt before she answered me, "He thinks I'll be more secure in my career. Right now, I'm an untested CEO. He said the first year is the most important and that it sets the precedent. He doesn't want the board to doubt me."

"Isn't he on the board? Can't he tell them to trust him and you?"

"No. I'm being tested in my new position. He claims that they want me to succeed, but I have to prove myself. And my fucking uncle is not helping anything."

"Did he do something else?"

"Besides try to sabotage me and our relationship?" she snapped.

"Right. He's done enough."

"And Jensen won't listen to me about this. I'm supposed to suck it up. I can throw down with the best of them, but this is different. And, now, Jensen has invited Owen and my cousins to his ribbon-cutting ceremony next weekend. He told me I had to play nice." She rolled her eyes dramatically and made a vulgar gesture.

"Is it even possible for you to tone down your sarcasm?"

"I do fine in professional settings, thank you very much!"

"I know. Maybe you should take Jensen's lead on this one. Kill your uncle with kindness."

"Yeah, yeah. I'd rather kill him with my well-pointed sarcastic wit."

I laughed. "Come on. Let's not stress about it yet. I think I have some chicken curry and rice."

Her stomach grumbled just then, and she laughed. "I guess I am hungry."

I arched an eyebrow and ushered her out of the bedroom.

"Sorry I unloaded on you," she said as we wandered into the kitchen.

"It's all right."

"Your text earlier was obscure. Why did *you* leave work early?"

I stared down into her big brown eyes. She finally looked relaxed and happy again. She was too young to be like stressed all the time. She didn't need me to add more stress to her life. Let alone something as stupid as issues with my boss.

"I went to the gym."

"Twice in one day?" she asked. "Who are you trying to impress?"

"You, hopefully," I said, tugging her in for a kiss.

"You don't have to impress me, Patrick. Life is better when I'm with you."

I kissed the tip of her nose. "I couldn't agree more."

Twenty-Six

Morgan

Standing outside of Jensen Wright Architecture for the grand opening ribbon-cutting was utterly surreal. The building was a combination of brick and stone and had a homey feel. It was in complete contrast to the sleek, modern exterior of Wright Construction. I'd already toured the interior with Jensen earlier in the week. It had clean lines while with an easily accessible atmosphere.

The building had been his first pet project for the company. So, it was perfect. It had all the care and character that he put into his work. It made me consider building a house finally instead of living in the top-floor apartment I'd been in forever. Not that I was living in it much right now. Between long hours and Patrick's house, I hadn't had much incentive to spend time there.

But maybe eventually.

Jensen would make sure it was what I wanted when it came to it.

I was nervous about how the event was going to go down. In theory, it should be no big deal. Jensen would cut a ribbon. The building would open officially.

In practice, the least that I would have to deal with was my uncle and cousins. This was my first official event out with Patrick. We'd been out in the open since the Christmas party, but this was our first real time out in the world as a couple. And, of course, it was at a huge ribbon-cutting ceremony.

Hopefully, it would be no big deal, and everything would go as planned. But nothing was going that well for me right now. Especially not with my uncle around. I knew I needed to put on my happy face about the whole thing, but I couldn't deny that I was worried about how it would all go.

"It's going to be okay," Patrick whispered in my ear. He squeezed my hand.

"I know," I said with confidence.

This was Jensen's big day. That was all that mattered.

A crowd had formed outside of the building, including reporters from the local newspapers. A group of us were all huddled inside for warmth. The temperature had dropped out from under us out of nowhere. This happened every year, but it was no less shocking when it was seventy-five degrees at noon and eleven degrees by five.

It was just about time to head into the frigid temperature when Owen and his two sons, Jordan and Julian, entered in through the side door. I sighed quietly. A small part of me had still hoped that they wouldn't show.

"Sorry that we showed up so late," Owen said with a big smile for everyone. "Julian couldn't seem to find a tie."

Julian rolled his eyes, and Jordan elbowed him in the ribs. I laughed at the display. But, of course, the room had gone quiet, and my laughter rang out loud and clear. I couldn't catch a break.

"I thought it was entertaining as well. He had to borrow mine," Owen said.

I took a deep breath. *Kill him with kindness.* "Actually, I thought it was funny how Jordan and Julian were acting. Reminded me of me and my brothers." I shot him a bright, winning smile.

Fuck, I hope this works because it was killing me.

"I think you'd find that, if you get to know them, you have more in common with Jordan and Julian than you know."

"I'm looking forward to it," I lied. "Glad that you'll all be here through the holidays, so we can play catch-up."

Patrick coughed next to me, as if to say, *Don't milk it.*

I tried to hide my smile.

"That's great," Julian said. He seemed to be the most genuine of the three. "Maybe we could meet up for drinks somewhere around here. Does Lubbock have bars?"

"You realize this is a college town, right?"

"It's pretty small. I didn't know."

"It just feels small," I assured him. "I'll take you downtown and make you fall in love with my city."

"As long as there are hot girls, I'm in."

I laughed, actually amused by him. Though it seemed both his older brother and his father were less so. Apparently, he was supposed to be on his best behavior, too.

"Morgan, do you mind if I have a word with you before we all go outside?" Owen asked.

"Sure," I said, standing my ground.

"In private."

I ground my teeth. Of course, he was going to want to talk to me in private. He was going to dig into me, like he always did as soon as we disappeared from public sight. Honestly, being alone with him was a recipe for disaster. Jensen wanted me to make nice, but that was going to be next to impossible if Owen opened his big fucking mouth.

Patrick pushed me forward a step.

"Sure," I said. "Let's take Jensen's office."

Owen hadn't been here yet, so I showed him through the building and into Jensen's open office door at the end of the hall. It was immaculate. Jensen was one to bury himself under a stack of paper, like the rest of us, but this office clearly hadn't been broken in yet.

"Nice place," Owen said.

"Yep."

"Morgan, we only have a minute, so I'll come right out and say it."

I braced myself for what was about to come out of his mouth. I'd been blunt and angry with Owen at the Christmas party. I hadn't apologized for what I said. Nor did I have any intention of doing so. But I'd pushed him off to David more times than I could count, and I had known I'd have to deal with this eventually.

"I think we got off on the wrong foot," Owen said.

I tilted my head in surprise.

"You're not what I expected. And, to be honest, that's a good thing."

"Um…thank you?"

He laughed. "I know I can be a hard-ass. I know I take a lot of this really seriously. But I think we have the same concerns for this company. We both want it to be the best that it can be."

"That is what I want. That's what I've always wanted. I've dedicated my life to Wright Construction."

"See? We have that in common."

"I guess so."

"Can I confide something in you?" he asked.

I raised my eyebrows. "Sure."

"The reason my brother, Ethan, sent me away to Vancouver was because the board wanted me to replace Ethan as CEO."

"What?" I gasped.

He nodded. "Hard to imagine now. He's revered around here, but at the time, he was a raving alcoholic. He was obstinate and opinionated. He was sarcastic to a fault, narrow-minded, and egotistical. He made few friends and a whole host of enemies. This was before you were born, of course."

Well, that *did* sound like my father. But I'd never heard that they wanted to replace him.

"When we first met, I thought you were just like my brother."

I winced. "Well, thanks."

"See? That dry sarcasm is classic Ethan."

"Is there a point to all this?" I couldn't help asking.

"I've been here for several weeks now, and I think I was wrong. I let old wounds impact our relationship. I'd like to start over." He held his hand out. "What do you say?"

With hesitancy, I stared down at that hand outstretched toward me. I was still reeling from what Owen had said about my father. I couldn't believe that anyone had ever wanted someone else to take over the company. That Owen had been a favorable alternative and that my father had sent him out of the country to get him out of the picture. But, at the same time, the way he'd described my father...was so on point. He hadn't been an easy man to have as a father. That was certain. And...I was like him. In more ways than one. I was sure I had as many of his baser qualities as I had his ambition and strong work ethic.

But, if Owen was extending an olive branch, would I be an idiot for refusing?

Swallowing my pride, I held my hand out. We shook. And, just like that...things were different.

Not wholly different. I still had my guard up. But at least this was a start. An unexpected one for sure.

"How'd it go?" Patrick asked when I stepped to his side.

I shook my hand from side to side to say, *So-so*. "I think I made a deal with the devil."

He laughed and then tried to cover it with a cough. "I'm sure it's not that bad."

"We'll see. He said we got off on the wrong foot. Still skeptical as to whether he thinks that foot is him calling me a secretary or me not treating him like he's royalty."

"The apology at least was something."

"Better than the way he'd been treating me up to this point."

I braced myself for the chilly weather as we all stepped outside. This ribbon-cutting reminded me of how much I loved being close to my friends and family. Jensen was surrounded by his new staff, but Emery stood by his side through it all. Heidi and Landon were laughing at each other. Austin kept swooping down to kiss Julia. She'd swat at him, but I knew she didn't mind. Sutton had Jason on her hip while she listened to David speak animatedly. She would need more time to recover, but I was glad that she was here with everyone else. That she had David, even just as a friend, to help her through this hard time. Even having Owen, Jordan, and Julian here wasn't completely awful.

The whole thing was over in a record fifteen minutes. Jensen made a speech and used some giant scissors to cut a red ribbon. Everyone applauded. There were a series of photographs, and then we all rushed back inside where snack food and drinks were waiting.

"I'm so proud of you!" I told Jensen when he was finally free.

He pulled me into a hug. "Thanks, Morgan."

"Big brother, all grown-up."

"Just now?" he asked with a laugh.

"Just now."

"I was CEO for all those years and not grown-up?"

"Nah," I said. "Not until at least Emery."

"I appreciate that," Emery said with a grin. "See? You weren't complete without me."

"That's a fact," he agreed.

"You certainly wouldn't have listened to anyone if they'd told you to wait a year for Emery," I said, nudging him.

"Oh God. I'll say it again. That's not what I meant," he groaned.

Emery eyed him. "What's this all about? Are you bothering her about Patrick still?"

"No," he said.

Emery turned to me. "Well?"

"He suggested that it might make more sense for me to wait a year before getting a boyfriend."

"That's not what I said! You took it the worst way possible."

"How else was she supposed to take it?" Emery asked.

"It was a joke. I was only saying that it's easier to be CEO and single."

Emery's eyebrows rose. "Well then, what are we doing together?"

He sighed and shot me a death glare. "Thanks. Now, I'm in trouble."

"Anytime," I said with a broad smile.

"Morgan is a great CEO. She and Patrick are great together. You boys all just need to get over it. Don't make me get Heidi over here. She'd have a thing or two to say."

"She's my handpicked successor. I think I know that she's perfect for the job. And it was a purely theoretical suggestion. I didn't think they'd actually break up."

"Good," Emery said with a head nod.

I laughed. "You two are adorable."

"Just trying to keep him in his place."

Jensen rolled his eyes. "And where is your place?"

"Probably right here."

"Probably?"

She shrugged. "You're kind of stuck with me."

"That's good," he said.

Then, Jensen pulled a powder-blue box out of his pocket and sank to one knee. Right then and there, in front of everyone.

Emery's mouth dropped open in shock. "What are you doing?"

"Proposing," he told her.

Her head swiveled from side to side in disbelief before landing back on Jensen when she realized this was real life.

"Emery, will you do me the honor of marrying me?"

"Can I wear a black wedding dress?"

Jensen chuckled. "Whatever you want."

"Oh, we're already off to a good start."

"Is that a yes?"

"Of course it is. Stand up already."

Jensen obliged with a pointed head shake. Then, he slid the Tiffany ring onto her finger and dragged her in for a kiss. The entire room erupted with cheers and calls and whistles. I was clapping and smiling so hard, my cheeks hurt.

I couldn't believe this. Jensen had been so adamant earlier this year about not getting married. He'd already done it once. Once was enough. He and Emery were happy the way they were. I'd completely written off the possibility.

My eyes found Patrick across the room where he was standing with Austin. His smile was magnetic, and when he met my eyes, he did a little dance that made me laugh.

Goof, I mouthed to him.

He did the dance again. I had to cover my mouth to keep from laughing harder.

Everyone started to crowd in around Jensen and Emery, so I moved out of the way. I watched Austin and Patrick step up for congratulations and took that opportunity to pull out my phone. I'd left the office early for this, and I knew I'd have to play catch-up tomorrow. I absentmindedly scrolled through my emails, categorizing them by subject and priority. My system was pretty intense.

"Are you freaking out?" Julia asked.

"Oh my God, it's amazing!" I told her, glancing up from my phone. "Sorry, work."

"No big. I can't believe he proposed. Emery said they didn't want to get married."

"I know. Jensen said that, too."

"I wonder what changed his mind."

Both our eyes drifted across the room to where Sutton stood with Jason. She wore a sad smile but was putting on a strong face for all the excitement. Both of us had a pretty good guess as to what had changed Jensen's mind.

"Are you excited to be a bridesmaid?" I asked.

"Do you think I will be?"

I laughed. "Um…yes. You and Heidi are her best friends!"

"Weird. I hadn't thought about that."

I shook my head and glanced back down at my phone. Another email had just come in. I checked the recipient and frowned.

"Huh," I muttered.

"What?" she asked.

I opened the email and started to read it. My stomach dropped.

I read it again. My heart raced.

I read it again. I thought I was going to be sick. I reached out to steady myself against the wall as all the color drained completely from my face.

"Morgan, are you okay? You've gone pale."

"Do I need to get someone?" Julia asked.

I could hear her. I could tell she was worried. But fear and horror were the only things that crossed my mind.

"Morgan!"

I finally glanced up at her with glassy, wide eyes. "We lost the Texas Tech construction contract."

"What does that mean?"

"I'm totally fucked."

Twenty-Seven

Morgan

"Don't tell anyone where I went," I told Julia before disappearing down the hallway and into Jensen's empty office.

I dialed the phone number I needed and waited for the inevitable voice mail. It was the end of the day on a Friday afternoon. This email had been sent at this time on purpose. They hadn't wanted to hear shit from me. And, worse, it had been sent only five business days before Texas Tech would be closed for the holiday break. If I didn't get this resolved by then, my job would be on the line.

Fuck, it might be on the line anyway. Just at the thought of losing one of our biggest contracts.

How had this fucking happened? We'd been negotiating for weeks. Jesus, they had been in talks with Jensen before I even took over.

The last contract had been for ten years where Wright Construction was the sole contractor on campus. We basically had a monopoly on the system, and we'd had it for years. It was one of the things that had jump-started the company from the ground up.

It didn't make sense. Why would they deny us the contract in the middle of negotiations? Sure, it had been taking a while, but we hadn't come to a compromise. Part of the reason Owen was here in the first place was to work on moving all of our existing contracts into environmental efficiency. Since this one was already up, we'd been trying to work out the details to pair with what was already in place. It was hard to believe that it could go from all these negotiations to absolutely nothing in such a short period of time.

The number went to voice mail, as expected.

"Fuck!" I cried and then searched my previous emails. I'd spoken with our contact on campus numerous times. I was sure I had another number. "Aha!"

I dialed what I assumed was a cell phone. It rang twice before someone answered.

"This is Bailey."

"Bailey, this is Morgan Wright."

Bailey sighed. "Yes, Morgan. I thought I might hear from you."

"You thought right. You sent me a form email, rejecting the contract. What happened?"

"I thought it was clear in the email that we'd decided to go in a different direction. We're hiring Escoe Industrial for the construction contract going forward."

I saw red and nearly punched my fist through Jensen's brand-new wall. "There's nothing clear about that. We've been in talks for weeks. What could have changed that fast?"

"Well, for one, I don't have a couple of more weeks to continue negotiating with you. I wanted to get this done before the end of the semester when the current contract runs out."

"That's another week."

"Did you honestly think that we'd compromise between now and then?"

"That's why we have lawyers," I bit out.

"I figured that you'd already seen this coming, Morgan."

"Why?" I asked her, as if she were a crazy person.

"Well, it was Patrick's suggestion."

I froze in place. "Patrick who?"

She laughed a little tinkling laugh that made me want to rip her throat out. "Patrick Young, your boyfriend."

"I don't understand. What do you mean?"

She paused for a second. "You do know, he works for me, right?"

"He…he works for you?"

"Well, yeah. And he suggested that the other company would be cheaper. So, we pursued it, and he was right. He's a real asset to the team. You can tell him *thank you* for us."

I regrouped, putting away all the ugly things I wanted to say to this woman. I wasn't fragile or vulnerable. Those things were not how to handle this woman. They would get me nowhere. They would only leave her with satisfaction. I could reserve all my anger for the person it needed to be directed at.

"I see. I'll be sure to do that. Is there any way we can reconsider this decision?" I said in my most professional voice.

"The decision has been made. Contracts have been signed. I'm sorry."

She wasn't.

Sorry was an empty word. A word that meant nothing and said nothing and did nothing. A word that was utterly pointless when it had no actions to back it up. When it was a total lie.

"I understand. I'll be in touch on Monday morning."

Bailey sighed heavily into the phone. "Fine. I'm already out of the office. I'm going to go. Talk to you on Monday."

I hung up the phone, knowing it was likely that there was absolutely nothing that could be done on Monday that could have been done today. The contract had been sold out from under us.

That meant two very real things: I was very likely out of a job, and Patrick was at fault.

I leaned forward against Jensen's desk and took a few deep breaths. It didn't seem to matter how many I took because I still felt like I was hyperventilating.

Rationally, I could probably fix this. I might be able to spin what had happened to the board. I could probably talk it over with Jensen. We could come up with a game plan. We could stay on top of this before it spiraled out of control.

In reality, I was freaking the fuck out. And I was pretty sure my life was over. What the fuck did it say about me that I would lose such a huge contract after just starting this job? It had to mean that I was a train wreck. That I wasn't cut out for this. That I couldn't hack it.

Everything I'd ever second-guessed about myself was a reality. I was living my own worst-case scenario.

Worse even then I'd thought because I never pictured that Patrick would be the one to fuck this up. Of course, I hadn't thought that Patrick would be in the picture until he was. But him ruining my life? Fuck.

I couldn't breathe. I couldn't think. A migraine was coming on strong.

I needed to get out of there. I needed to walk out the back door and not look back. Because, if I had to deal with anyone right now, it was not going to be pretty.

Without a backward glance, I shouldered my purse and headed out of the office. I reached the back door when I heard my name. I closed my eyes for a second before pushing the door open and walking out into the cold.

My breath fogged in front of me. I hadn't had time to put on gloves, and already, my fingers were cold. I stuffed them in the pockets of my peacoat as I hurried away.

"Morgan!" Patrick called behind me.

I didn't turn around. I didn't look back. I didn't do anything, except continue to rush toward my car.

I'd never been a runner. It was inherent in my personality to take things on headfirst. But this was different. This was Patrick. This was my dream. And I knew that, if I faced my dream, it would shatter and reveal the nightmare.

"Morgan, where are you going?"

He was closer this time. He was following.

Fuck. I'm going to have to do this.

Right here. Right now.

I whirled around. "I'm leaving."

"Julia sent me to check on you. She said that you'd gone pale. That you looked sick. Are you okay?"

"No. No, I'm not."

"What happened? Are you sick? She wouldn't say what was going on."

"Sick," I said with a tight laugh.

"Uh…fuck, you're pissed."

"You think?" I nearly growled.

"Yeah. Tell me what happened. How can I help?"

"Help? No, I think you've helped enough."

He stepped forward toward me, and I took a step back.

"Stop."

He froze in place. I could see anguish on his face at my resistance. "Morgan, please. Why are you upset?"

"God, as if you don't know!" I cried, losing my temper.

"Know what?"

He gave me the perfect dumbfounded face. I wondered if he'd practiced that in the mirror. *Had he considered carefully how he'd stand here and lie to my face?*

"Do you think I'm stupid?"

"What? No, of course I don't think you're stupid. If you'd just tell me, I could…"

"I lost the Tech contract."

"Shit."

I ground my teeth together. "Yeah. Why didn't you ever tell me that your boss was Bailey?"

"You didn't know?" he asked.

"Oddly enough, you never mentioned it."

"It wasn't on purpose."

I held my hand up. "Just don't. I don't want to hear it. I really don't want the excuses."

"I'm not making excuses, Morgan."

"Ugh!" I screamed and turned away from him.

Of course, he was going to make this difficult. He'd hide it. Try to cover it up. Fuck, I hated this. I just wanted to lay into him. I wanted to pound my fists into his chest for the betrayal. I ached, and it was his fault.

He placed a hand on my arm, and I yanked it back.

"Don't touch me!"

"Morgan, I'm sorry that you lost the contract. It fucking sucks, but I don't understand why you're so upset with me."

"Oh, so you weren't the one to suggest to Bailey that they should go with Escoe Industrial?"

He opened his mouth. The *no* was on the tip of his tongue. His lips shaped into the word I so desperately wanted to hear. I wanted it to be a lie that Bailey had told. But then he scrunched his face up, and I knew. I knew what I'd already known. It wasn't a lie. It had never been a lie.

"I did," he said slowly, "but…"

"No! No, *but*! Don't even bother," I said, cutting him off. "That's all I needed to hear. You betrayed me to your boss. I don't even fucking know why you did it. Were you using me all along? Was none of this real? You must be a spectacular actor. Was fucking me a bonus for using me, or did you actually hate it all along?"

"That is not what happened at all," Patrick said.

"Whatever. I'm sure you have some formulated answer for all of this, but I wouldn't believe it anyway. Fuck, I'm such an idiot," I groaned. "I should have known better. You know what they say when something is too good to be true."

"It usually is," he supplied.

"Exactly."

I took one last look at the man I'd wanted to be with for so long, and then I let that hope fly off. I sighed and then started back toward my car.

"Please, Morgan, let me explain," Patrick said, following after me.

"Save your breath."

"This isn't what you think it is." He reached for me again.

I wheeled around and snatched my arm back. "It's exactly what I think this is! Fuck, I loved you! Do you know that? I loved you and you betrayed me and you ruined everything!"

Patrick's jaw dropped open. "You…love me?"

"Past tense," I spat.

"I love you, too," he said.

"No!" I yelled at him. "You don't get to say that to me! You have no right! If you loved me, then you wouldn't have done this shit. You wouldn't have sold me out to your boss. You certainly wouldn't have stood back and put my job on the line. You don't love me, Patrick. You love yourself. So, basically, nothing has changed."

Twenty-Eight

Patrick

S now fell all around me.
It blanketed the world in a clear, crisp white.

It covered the remnants of that fatal argument.

It erased any trace of Morgan's tire tracks as she'd peeled out of the parking lot.

I couldn't even comprehend what the hell had just happened. Everything had been going so perfect. Too perfect, but who was I to question it? This was everything I'd never known I always wanted, and I wasn't going to get off the train. I certainly wasn't going to jump off the train while it was still moving at full speed. And the aftermath of that conversation felt like hurtling off the train and the searing pain after the fall.

The first snowfall of the year couldn't have had better timing. Now, I was cold, wet, and freezing inside and out.

I stood there for who knew how long. Until I couldn't feel my fingers or toes or ears. Until Julia came rushing out the back door and to my side.

"Patrick, you don't even have a jacket on! You're fucking freezing. Get back inside," Julia said, actually pushing me back toward the building. "Tell me what happened."

I didn't say anything until she dragged me back into the warmth. I shook the snow off myself and then blankly stared at the wall.

"Patrick!" she said, snapping her fingers at me.

"I think Morgan just broke up with me."

"Oh, shit! What happened? The contract?"

"She told you?"

Julia nodded. "She told me not to say anything, but she looked like she needed you."

"Morgan doesn't need anyone."

"That's not true. Morgan's strong but not invincible."

"Fuck."

"Yeah," she muttered. "Do you want me to try to talk to her?"

"I don't think anyone is going to get through to her right now." I shook my head in frustration. "Fuck, I am such an idiot."

"I don't know all the details, but I think maybe you guys need to talk about it once she's calmed down. Speaking from experience, nothing good comes from discussions when you're angry."

I closed my eyes and shook my head. *Fucking fuck fuck.* I couldn't believe this had happened. I should have told her about my boss. I should have told her about what Bailey had wanted me to do. I should have just fucking confided in her. Instead, I had been so worried about piling more bullshit on top of her that I ended up making it worse. Now, she didn't trust me. She didn't even want to be around me.

"I need to leave," I told Julia.

"Okay. Will you be all right getting home?"

"Yeah. Just...don't tell anyone what happened. I'd rather deal with this before I have three Wright brothers breathing down my neck."

Julia zipped her mouth shut. "I won't say a word."

"Thanks," I said in a hollow voice.

She frowned in dismay and looked as if she wanted to say something more to me, but I didn't give her the chance. I grabbed my coat and got the hell out of there. I couldn't be around her happy family in the midst of Jensen finally proposing to Emery and the ribbon-cutting and all that. So much happiness. And then there was me.

I didn't think I'd been broken up with since high school. Since that dick Travis Jones had taken my girl out from under me. I'd played it cool since then. Never gotten too close. Never really been interested in a relationship. Definitely not interested in girls who wanted to be in a serious relationship. I'd had a good life.

And then Morgan had happened.

Everything had changed.

Everything.

Suddenly, the life I'd been living before her felt meaningless. The world I'd found myself accustomed to didn't matter. The casual sex, the late nights of drinking, the fake relationships—it all meant nothing.

Until Morgan, I hadn't realized what I was even doing with my life. Austin's drinking problem and rehab had been the wake-up call. But I'd turned it all around for Morgan.

Now, that was gone.

I crashed back into my house in a daze. My body felt leaden. My heart, an empty hole in my chest.

She'd said she loved me.

I couldn't get over the words. The three words I'd wanted to say to her. That I'd traced against her skin and said in my mind every night before she went to sleep and kissed against her lips. But I hadn't said them. Even after I realized that was what I was feeling. I'd been afraid to say them to her. Afraid it was too soon. Afraid she didn't feel the same. Afraid I'd fuck it up.

Like I just had.

I turned the shower onto boiling and stripped out of my clothes. My fingers were still stiff from the cold. When I got under the spray, they stung from the heat. I curled my hand into a fist and threw it into the tiled wall.

"Fuck!" I cried.

I shook my fist out in anger and then slammed it into the tiles again and again. I could feel the knuckles split open. Red seeped between my fingers and ran down to the drain.

The pain didn't help anything. It didn't fix what had happened with Morgan. It didn't bring her back.

I stuck my head under the water and stayed there until the water began to run cold. Then, I stayed a little longer, lost in my own thoughts. My own idiocy.

After I got out, I changed into sweats and moved into the kitchen. I found the bottle of top-shelf whiskey Austin had left me and poured myself a knuckle's worth. I drained it and then gave myself another, ignoring the pain in my hand along the way. I knew I was probably going to regret what I'd done when my hand was swollen and painful tomorrow, but what else was new? I already regretted a whole hell of a lot more than that.

Morgan had said that, if something was too good to be true, then it probably was. She had said that about our relationship...and she was right. But not about me. About her. Morgan Wright was too good to be true.

I'd known that she was entirely out of my league. That I couldn't possibly deserve her. But, once she had been mine, I'd done everything I could to make sure she never realized that.

Yet here I was with a busted hand, an empty whiskey glass, and a broken heart.

I looked like shit. I felt like shit. I was a piece of shit.

Because I *had* suggested that Bailey give the contract to someone else. I'd named three other companies she could use instead of Wright Construction. Even if I explained to Morgan that it had been because Bailey wanted to use our relationship to get to her or that I'd said it in conjunction with the fact that Wright was the best and that these other companies weren't even a real option, it wouldn't matter.

I hadn't pulled the trigger, but I'd loaded the gun and aimed.

No, there was nothing I could do to change her mind right now. Not when that contract meant everything to her. I knew what she hadn't said in her anger. That she could lose her job over this.

She was already on thin ice. A crack big enough to split the ground would surely send her floundering... drowning.

And, if I were the reason that she was no longer CEO of Wright Construction, our relationship would be doomed. The company was the most important thing in Morgan's life. It always had been.

I didn't hold a candle to her love for her job. I'd been okay with that. I loved her passion. Her fire. The way she handled everything with poise and dedication. The stress that only fueled her forward. The insanity and obsession that just screamed Morgan. She did everything with an unrivaled intensity.

Being with her and in her undivided attention was like being trapped in her orbit. You moved with her force and found steps with a new gravity. And she flung you out of orbit just as quickly as you had been dragged in.

I stared at the empty glass in my hand with a sigh. It was a sorry state of events of my life that I was hungry and actually didn't want to cook. Cooking was my happy place. The one thing I always reserved for myself. Fuck, I hadn't even really cooked for Austin much, and we'd known each other forever.

But, now, when I thought about cooking a meal for one, it felt pretty depressing. Cooking had been for Morgan. It had been the break in her day where I could take care of her. Slow her down and give her something she couldn't do herself. I'd been cooking for us for weeks. And I didn't want to go back to meals for one.

I shoved my glass away from me and exited my kitchen. I couldn't do it. I was too frustrated. Too pissed.

I ordered pizza and sank into my couch, wanting nothing more than to forget all of this.

The best thing that had ever happened to me had just walked out of my life. I'd ruined everything. And I wasn't sure that I deserved a chance to fix it.

The doorbell rang.

"Finally," I muttered under my breath.

I was still starving, and pizza had taken forever. Sometimes, I hated where I lived. You would think it would be faster to get pizza to a centrally located area of town, but I suspected the pizza places near here were all busier.

I pulled the door open and sighed. "Austin."

"Man, you really fucked up, didn't you?"

"Julia tell you?"

"Are you fucking kidding? Of course she did," he said, shoving past me. "As if you and Morgan running away from the ribbon-cutting wasn't suspicious enough."

"Yeah. Didn't really think about that." I was about to shut the door when I saw the pizza car pull up. I waited until the guy reached my door. "Busy night?"

"It's snowing," the guy said as way of explanation.

"Right. No one wants to be out in the weather."

"Yeah. Lucky me."

I handed the guy an extra twenty for a tip. My life was shit enough. Might as well make someone's night.

"Hey, man, thanks!" the guy said, brightening.

I nodded at him and then brought the large supreme pizza into the living room.

"Perfect," Austin said. "I'm hungry."

"I was going to eat this whole thing by myself."

"And, now, you're sharing, dipshit."

"Fair enough."

We each grabbed a slice of pizza, and I flipped on *SportsCenter*. It was all Bowl Game talk and National Championship hopefuls. I didn't really care about any of the teams in the finals, but it was mind-numbing. And that was what I needed.

"So, are you going to tell me what happened? I only got the hysterical version from Julia."

"Her version was probably right."

"Probably."

"Morgan lost the Tech contract. She didn't know that the contact at Tech was actually with my boss."

"How did she not know?"

"Because I never told her."

He gave me the look that said I was an idiot. "That was smart."

"Look, I knew she was negotiating the contract with Morgan, but I wasn't involved. I didn't think it was a big deal."

"Until…" Austin guessed.

"Until she asked me to use my relationship with Morgan or you or any of your family to help her get ahead."

"And you said?"

"I said, of course fucking not," I said, sitting up angrily. "I would never sell y'all out. I've known you my whole life. I don't want to be involved in business deals. It would be a conflict of interest."

"Did you tell Morgan that?"

I sighed and tilted my head back. "No."

"Yeah. That's where you went wrong."

"I didn't want to burden her with more bullshit. She's been so tense lately."

"I don't know if you've met my sister before, but she's always high-strung."

"Not always."

Austin gagged. "Please do not ever put that mental image in my head again."

I choked out a laugh. "I didn't mean…that. Whatever. Let's not talk about that."

"Fine by me."

"The shitty thing is that, when my boss was trying to convince me to help her out with this, I made the mistake of suggesting other companies that she could use for cheaper."

Austin smacked me upside the back of my head. "What the fuck, bro?"

"Ugh!" I groaned. "Thanks for that."

"What were you thinking? Suggesting other companies?"

"It isn't how it seems or how it was portrayed to Morgan. I said the companies would be cheaper but that Wright would always be better. I said the company was local, loyal, and quality business. That choosing someone else would be idiotic. Apparently, that didn't get conveyed to Morgan when my boss threw me under the motherfucking bus."

"Okay. So, say that's all fucking true."

I narrowed my eyes at him. "It is."

"I'm just saying…say it's true. I don't want to believe that you fucked my sister over, Patrick. You're like my brother. We've known each other forever. You're family. But, fuck, you have some incriminating evidence against you. So, I'm going to believe you fucked this all up until you prove me otherwise. How are you going to fix this?"

"What do you mean?"

Austin smacked me again. "I said, how the fuck are you going to fix this? You can't fucking make this right by sitting around your house, watching football, and eating pizza."

"Fuck."

"Oh, I see the lightbulb."

"Fuck you, dude."

Austin laughed in my face. "It's not like you to wallow and give up."

"I've never had a girlfriend before. How the hell would you know how I'd react to one dumping me?"

"If it were anyone but Morgan, I'd assume you wouldn't even care."

"Yeah. I think that's true."

I straightened in my seat. Austin was right. I couldn't sit here and do nothing. Sure, I'd fucked up. I should have told Morgan what had happened with Bailey. I should have been more up-front about the fact that the contract was even being handled in my office. But I hadn't maliciously suggested the other companies. There was no way that I could let her think that I didn't care about her or that I wanted to purposely hurt her.

"I need to make things right."

"Yeah, you do," Austin said. "Like I had to with Julia. Because, let's face it, there's no way that we weren't going to fuck something up with women as amazing as ours. We just have to man up when the time comes."

"I'm going to call her."

"Knock yourself out. I'll be here, eating all your pizza."

I rolled my eyes. "Leave me a slice."

Austin gave me a middle-finger salute as I disappeared into the bedroom and called Morgan's number. After three rings, it went to voice mail. I tried again. Same thing. The third call, it immediately went to voice mail, which meant she was seeing my calls and deliberately avoiding them.

This time, I let the voice mail go through to the end. I listened for the beep, and then I began to speak, "Morgan, I understand that you're angry with me right now. I get that you feel hurt and used and betrayed. I don't blame you for feeling that way when I didn't confide in you. But I never meant to betray you. I know you need time to deal with the ramifications of this contract and that you'll be busy with work. But I'm not going to just disappear. I'll be here for you through everything. I'll be at your side, trying to make things right, no matter what is thrown your way. No matter what, full stop. If you want to talk, I'm here for you. I'm never going to stop fighting. Never. You are the best thing that has ever happened to me. Love doesn't halt in hard times. That's when you need it the most."

Twenty-Nine

Morgan

I didn't listen to Patrick's voice mail.

I didn't delete it either.

Instead, it taunted me all weekend while I worked on trying to fix everything that had snowballed into a disaster for me. I had a plan. A game plan. I was ready—or at least, as ready as I would ever be to walk into the office on Monday morning and put my job on the line.

The email had only been sent to me. I had to think that someone else had heard that Escoe Industrial had received the contract, a company that was now pretty high on my list of companies I wanted to acquire. Either way, it meant that I would be on the hot seat on Monday. I would have to figure out a way to keep my job, or the board would replace me.

I couldn't imagine Wright Construction in the hands of someone who wasn't a Wright. So, getting fired was out of the question. I could do this.

When I made it up to the top floor on Monday morning, David was already sitting at his desk. He was always earlier than me, but I'd come in early to begin with. I'd filled him in on the situation on Saturday afternoon. I hadn't wanted to tell anyone, but David and I were partners in this. He didn't want someone to replace me either.

His head snapped up when he saw me standing in the doorway. "Morgan, I'm so glad you're here." He hurried up from his desk and over to where I was standing. "Thank God you're here early."

"Why?" I asked. My stomach dropped with worry at his tone. "What happened?"

"Owen showed up as soon as I walked in the door, and he's holed up in the conference room."

"What? What is he doing here? Why didn't you text me?"

"I did. You didn't respond. A couple of other people showed up. It feels like an ambush."

"Fuck. You think they know?"

He shrugged. "What else could it be?"

"True." I took a deep breath. "Okay. Wish me luck."

"You don't need it."

I grinned halfheartedly at him. Then, I straightened my shoulders and walked into the conference room. My uncle was sitting at the end of the long table, looking like a king holding court. Four members of the board of directors were present. Of course, Jensen wasn't there.

"I didn't realize that a meeting had been called for the board," I said, setting down my messenger bag on the table and staring down half of the board. As CEO, I was technically a member of the board, but I wasn't included in matters regarding me unless disciplinary measures were to be taken. That meant, we were only missing three people, including Jensen, from the eight-person board that would decide my future.

"I'm glad that you're here, Morgan," Owen said.

"I'm inferring that there's a reason that the majority of you are assembled today. Though I don't know why you're here, Uncle." I stared him down. "Last I checked, you were not a member of the board of directors."

"He's here as a courtesy to us," one of the other members, Curt, said from the end of the table. "We've recently discovered that you lost the Texas Tech contract, and we are worried about the financial future of the company with you as CEO."

"The contract isn't lost. Not officially. I am still talking to the administration on campus to right this error."

"I thought you said that it was confirmed," Luke said to Owen.

"I was told that Escoe Industrial had acquired the contract," Owen said.

"They had, but we were still in negotiations. I went a step up from the woman I had been dealing with on campus, and I think an inquiry is going to be opened to find out what happened. We should know by the end of the week."

"Is it true that it was your boyfriend who made you lose the contract?" Curt asked.

I ground my teeth together. "He works in the same division at the university."

"We're worried about the state of the company. That Tech contract has been part of Wright Construction for thirty years," Luke added.

"I am also worried about it, but I am doing everything I can at the moment to rectify the situation."

"We think, at this time, it would be prudent to select an oversight committee for you," Janice said across the table from Luke. "Truly, this kind of catastrophe would warrant firing."

I paled.

"Especially after all the trouble we've been having with your transition to CEO. But we don't have another successor in line, like when Jensen handed the company to you. It would be a nightmare to find someone again."

"I wouldn't mind helping to transition into CEO," Owen said. "In a temporary capacity, of course."

"Of course," I ground out. "Unfortunately, we don't need you."

Suddenly, his motives were crystal clear. Why hadn't I seen it before? Owen wanted my job. No wonder he had treated me like shit. Of course, that conversation at the ribbon-cutting made no sense. Why defend me, only to throw me under the bus here?

"Actually, it's not a bad suggestion," Janice said.

"Owen is a valuable asset to the company, and he is a Wright," Curt added.

"I think we should see if she fixes this first," Luke said, cutting off that scenario before it got wheels under it. "I think we give her until the end of the week to collect more information about the financial impact this might have. And, if she doesn't come up with a solution, then we explore other alternatives."

"Agreed," Janice, Curt, and the otherwise quiet Jake said.

Owen looked like steam was about to come pouring out of his ears at the suggestion. He'd clearly thought that I was going to be fired. And how could I blame him? I'd thought I was going to be fired. Especially with an ambush like this.

"I'll be happy to notify the remainder of the board about this," I told them. "Next time, we should include Jensen as well, considering he lives in town."

No one made a comment about that. Excluding Jensen on something like this had clearly been on purpose. It was a message. And I read it loud and clear.

I had one more chance. I was out of the frying pan but not out of the fire. If I didn't figure this out by the end of the week, they wouldn't be as lenient.

I spent the remainder of my day putting out fires and dealing with everyday management stuff. All while I still had to deal with how I was going to make things right. It was the last full week of work before the holidays, and I was mired down in utter bullshit.

My call with Jensen had been fucking wonderful after that meeting. I hadn't told him about what had happened this weekend. He'd just gotten engaged, and I hadn't wanted to ruin everything. I'd known that, if I'd told him what had happened, he would disappear and help me. That wasn't fair to him or Emery. He wasn't the CEO anymore. He didn't have to always be putting out my fires.

I wanted to be able to handle this myself. But I hadn't wanted him to find out from someone else about what had happened or the board meeting that he hadn't been invited to. He'd been pissed. Raving about how deceitful they'd been to exclude him.

At least one good thing had come from the meeting; he believed me about Owen now.

Owen was out for my job.

He'd probably been out for my job since day one.

His douche-bag attitude toward me had been to undermine me. He'd been playing mind games. And he'd been playing them well.

He had slowly dismantled years of my service to the company in a matter of weeks. He'd made me look sloppy and like he was a better alternative to me. It was heartbreaking and also pissed me the hell off. Even if I were fired from this job, it would be over my dead body that they gave it to Owen.

My head was so far up in the clouds, I didn't even notice that it was past five, and there was a knock at my door.

"Come in," I called, shuffling papers around and then typing fiercely into the memo I'd been working on.

"Hey, Mor."

My head snapped up. "Patrick."

"I didn't hear from you all weekend."

"I know."

"I called."

"I know."

"I left you a voice mail."

"I got it."

"Did you listen to it?"

"No," I admitted.

He laughed softly. "Of course you didn't. Were you doing this all weekend?"

"Yes."

"You still have a job."

"For now."

"Can we talk?"

"What have we been doing this whole time?" I asked with emphasis on the snark.

"I couldn't leave it the way we left things on Friday. I know you have a lot on your plate. I know you're dealing with this contract issue. But I won't let our relationship dissolve because of this."

"Patrick, I have one week to make this all right," I said, holding up one finger. "I have to prioritize that above all else."

"I realize that. I don't want to take away from your work. But I also want you to know that, when I suggested another company for this contract, it was a throwaway comment. I said it as if it were absurd to even consider someone like Escoe. I said they weren't local or loyal or quality and that Wright Construction would always be the best. And I believe that. I might have made an error in wording, and I take responsibility for that, but I don't want you to think that I would use or betray you. You mean too much to me for something like that."

I sighed and let the stress of the weekend bury me for a second. There hadn't been a moment in all this where it wasn't attached to Patrick. The man I had wanted more than anything, except the CEO position. Now, it seemed both of the things I wanted were on the line.

I'd been harsh on Friday. I'd said some things I probably shouldn't have. And, fuck it, I couldn't catch a break here.

"I know this wasn't all your fault, Patrick," I told him, standing and looking up at him. "I'm sorry that I unloaded on you on Friday. That wasn't fair to you."

He startled, as if he had been expecting me to scream at him again. But I didn't have the fire for it. I wasn't angry with him. I didn't have the energy for anger. I should have waited to talk to him after I figured this all out. But here we were.

"It's okay."

"It's really not. Maybe Jensen is right. Maybe I do need to take a year off from dating while I'm CEO."

"Morgan, that's ridiculous."

"Is it? I was a hundred percent dedicated to my work before we started dating, and now, I'm being investigated for a negative financial impact on the company. I clearly cannot accurately manage both. I can't do this right now. I need to be married to my work. If I even have a job after Friday."

"No, I don't accept that," Patrick said. "I don't accept that you can't juggle two things at once or that you need to take a year off from dating. I don't accept that we can't be together. We are better when we're together. You are less stressed and more relaxed. You laugh more. You smile more. You have more fun."

"Yeah, and I lose ten-year multimillion-dollar contracts, too."

"You're better when you're with me."

"Maybe," I ventured.

"Life isn't just your job."

"That might be the case," I said with a resigned sigh. "But, right now…it is. I wish there were another way. But, I really can't do this. It would be easier for me if you left."

"Morgan—"

"Please, Patrick. I have to reserve my strength for this problem. Don't make this any harder than it has to be," I said as my heart broke.

"I'm going to prove you wrong."

"I hope you're right."

Patrick stepped around my desk and stood close to me. He placed a kiss on my forehead. "I'm not going to stop fighting for you. I'm going to figure this out."

Then, he was gone. I collapsed forward into my chair at his absence and did the thing I hadn't done all weekend. I cried.

Thirty

Patrick

Working was a lesson in self-control. Trying to stay in my own lane and get my shit done while I worked only steps from Bailey's office seemed impossible. I kept telling myself that I only had to make it through the end of the week, and then I wouldn't have to deal with this again until the New Year.

In the meantime, I'd watch the clock tick and wait for the end of the day. Even though I wasn't really doing shit at home. It felt empty without Morgan in it. So much had changed in my life, and going back to who I had been before her wasn't an option.

I pushed away from my desk and stared at the ceiling. I was so fucking frustrated. I'd put everything on the line, and she'd walked. I hadn't been lying when I said I'd keep fighting for her. I would. I was just terrified that she wasn't going to change her mind. That, if she got fired, it would be the end of us for good. I couldn't imagine her coming back from that.

"Am I interrupting something important?" Bailey said from the door.

I immediately straightened. "No. Deep in thought. Can I help you?"

"I was seeing how you were doing."

"I'm fine. Why wouldn't I be?" I kept a straight face. Of course, there were a million reasons I was not fine right now, but I wasn't going to show that to her. I certainly wasn't going to talk about Morgan.

"Just curious. I wasn't sure if you knew what was going on at Wright right now."

"Why are you talking to me about this, Bailey?"

She leaned her hip against the doorframe. "I want to know what they're up to."

"And why would I know that?"

"Because you're dating the CEO."

"If I didn't make it explicitly clear last time, I have no interest in discussing my personal life at work. So, even if I knew what Morgan was up to, I wouldn't tell you."

"So, she's up to something," Bailey said, fishing.

"If she is, then you should be worried."

Bailey scoffed. "Why's that?"

"Because, when Morgan sets her mind to something, she always wins. Always."

"Yeah. I'm sure. Just tell her to stop trying to go over my head."

"I'm not going to tell her anything."

"Well then, I'm going to go over *her* head again," she said under her breath.

"What does that even mean?"

"Nothing. This whole thing is a nightmare."

"You know that there's no one over Morgan's head at Wright Construction?"

"Yeah," she said, waving it off. "Just frustrated."

Did she want me to sympathize with her? Because I didn't. She had purposely gone behind Morgan's back and given the contract to someone else. And, now, she was saying that she was going to go over Morgan's head. Seriously, what did that even mean? Jensen? Or the board of directors? I didn't even know.

What I did know was that Bailey was clearly outmatched. Even if I wasn't head over heels for Morgan, I was confident that she could take down someone like Bailey blindfolded with her hands behind her back. I hoped she could do it by Friday.

"Why did you do it, Bailey?" I asked before she left.

"Do what?"

"Why did you give the contract to Escoe Industrial? You and I both know it's not because of my offhand comment."

She shrugged. "It was a smart move."

"Really? You're this frustrated, and it was the smart move?"

"The Wrights have a monopoly on the university. There's no reason that someone else shouldn't get a share of the pie, and if that means we get the work done a little cheaper, then that seems fair to me."

"You get what you pay for."

"Well, you would say that."

"You're the one who asked for my opinion."

"It was enlightening."

I watched her retreating back with disdain. It wasn't that her argument was illogical. It just wasn't the right decision to make. Not just because of the Wrights, but because their company was better. She should want to be working with cutting-edge technology and innovative design. She should want everything that Wright had to offer.

And, still…my head was stuck on her one statement.

Go over Morgan's head…again.

Did that mean she'd done that once before?

My gut told me that I shouldn't ignore this. I texted Jensen to see if he was free, left work, and then drove out to his new architecture firm. His assistant let me go back to his office.

"Hey, Patrick," Jensen said, standing from his desk and shaking my hand.

"Hey, man."

"What's up? Your text sounded urgent."

"I'm not exactly sure. I'm worried about Morgan."

Jensen frowned. "Yeah. We all are. I heard what happened at the ribbon-cutting."

"Uh, yeah. That sucked. It wasn't much better when I tried to talk to her this week. Didn't help that you told her to take a year off from dating, and now, she thinks she should listen to you."

"That's not what I said—or at least—it's not what I meant."

"Well, this is Morgan. She took it literally."

Jensen sighed. "Yeah. I was playing the big-brother bit a little seriously, I guess. I want her to be happy. If she's happy with you, then great."

"Right now, she's not happy with anyone."

"Not even herself it seems."

"Especially not herself," I clarified.

"Sounds right. I'm doing what I can to help her with this contract. I wish that I could do more."

"That's kind of why I'm here. You know that my boss is Bailey."

"Right. I heard that."

"Well, she said something kind of strange to me today at the office. She was pissed, I guess, that Morgan was going over her head to try to get this worked out."

"I think it's perfectly reasonable that she's doing that," Jensen said. "If she needs to get it done right, then she needs to talk to someone else."

"I'm not arguing that point. I know Morgan will do what she has to do. She always does. The weird thing is that Bailey said that she'd go over Morgan's head again."

Jensen paused. "There's no one over Morgan's head."

"That's what I said. So, do we think that means that she met with someone else at Wright? I thought maybe that was you?"

"No. I haven't met with her. I'm only on the board anyway. I'm not over the CEO."

"Right. So, unless she's spoken to the board, I don't know who else she would be referring to, but it seemed suspicious."

"I'll look into it. Another thing to add to the list."

"I bet you thought, when you left the company, you wouldn't be dealing with this kind of stuff."

Jensen laughed and shook his head. "This was why I waited so long to leave. I didn't want to dump everything at Morgan's feet. But, at some point, the training wheels had to come off. I knew she was ready, but even I couldn't have anticipated something like this happening."

"I don't think anyone did. She's had so many problems with the company that she never had when she was CFO."

"Yeah. It's a different ball game. I think that, if this had happened to me, it would have been swept under the rug. I'd been successful for so long there. Maybe if I'd waited through the end of the year, we wouldn't be in this position."

"Well, this isn't your fault. And Morgan will work it out."

Jensen nodded. "I know she will. But I'm the fixer of the family. I'm the one who is supposed to hold everything together. From where I am right now, there's little I can do for her, and I don't like the feeling."

"That makes two of us," I told him.

"I know she's giving you shit right now, but I'm glad that she has you. And I respect you for coming to me about this thing with your boss. I know you're caught between a rock and a hard place."

"Something like that. I want to fix this shit, so I can get back to my life. So, how are we going to fix it, Jensen?"

He nodded at me in approval. "Okay…this is what we're going to do."

Thirty-One

Morgan

"How did you coax me into doing this again?" I asked Steph as we walked into a bridal shop downtown.

"I told you that, if you didn't come shopping with me, I would pick out the most hideous dress imaginable and make you wear it."

"Oh, right. What makes you think I'd wear it?"

Steph chuckled. "Because you don't back out of anything."

"Unfortunately, true," I grumbled. "How are you here right now anyway? Don't you have to be at work?"

"Actually," she said with a sly grin, "I haven't announced it yet, but I'm going on tour after the wedding."

"Oh my God! Steph! That's incredible. How did that happen?"

"Thanks. It kind of came out of nowhere. One of those insane stories that you don't believe actually happened. I was singing something in the freaking grocery store, and a guy approached me. I thought he was a skeez, but he turned out to be the real deal. I'm going to play as the opener for his band."

"Wow! I cannot even believe that happened. I'm so happy for you. Your life is so awesome."

"I know! It so is. I'm ready to quit waitressing and playing local gigs. I'm not getting my hopes up, but I'd rather be living my dream than sitting at home, wondering what could have been."

"What does Thomas think?" I asked as I shifted through a million shades and styles of bridesmaid dresses.

"He's so happy. Also…worried. And I don't blame him. He's a planner and headstrong and all that. And he'll miss me."

"Of course he will."

"But he's supportive. He believes in me. You know, when you find someone like that, it's important to hold on to them." Steph gave me a knowing look.

"Why do I feel like the conversation has switched to me?" I muttered.

"Probably because you broke up with my brother."

"Right." I became suddenly very interested in the burgundy taffeta dress in my hand. "What about this one?"

Steph rolled her eyes. "As if you're getting away from this conversation that easily."

"It was worth a try."

"I don't understand how this happened. You've liked Patrick forever, Mor. Like, literally forever. And ever."

"I get it. I know."

"I thought your obsession was kind of ridiculous and pretty gross, but I let you have your little thing."

I laughed. "You would think that. Though I don't know how you can talk after sleeping with Austin."

Steph shot me a sheepish look. "Uh, yeah…about that."

"Whatever," I said, waving my hand. "Ancient history."

"You're changing the subject again!"

"I'm adept at that."

Steph poked me in the side. "Well, cut it out. I don't want to deal with CEO Morgan right now. I'd like to talk to my friend about my brother for a minute."

I shelved the dress I'd been looking at and turned back to face Steph. "There's only one of me, you know. I can't switch it on and off like a lightbulb."

"Sure, you can."

"And, anyway, separating Patrick from work right now is pretty difficult."

"I heard."

"I had one ambush this week. I really wasn't looking forward to a second."

Steph dramatically rolled her eyes. "As if this is an ambush. You knew I was going to ask you about Patrick when we hung out. Calm your tits, woman."

I laughed a real full-bellied laugh. It had been a while since that happened. "God, I missed you. Can you move back into town? I feel like less of a loner when you're here."

"Going on tour, remember?"

"Right. Coming through Lubbock?"

She snorted. "Yeah, right. We'll be in Dallas. You can fly the private jet out to see me."

"Done."

"Now, talk to me," Steph said. She turned back to the dresses and started throwing ones she'd picked out into my arms. "You have one hiccup with work, and suddenly, you're giving up on your relationship? That doesn't sound like you."

"It's more than a hiccup. I might be fired."

"Okay, well, worst-case scenario, you get fired. What do you do then?"

I shuddered. "I am not even considering that."

She passed me a pink monstrosity. "Consider it. Say, by Friday, you're no longer CEO of Wright Construction.

You're still sitting on a trust fund most people would kill for, and you have marketable skills that you could get a job anywhere you wanted. Would it suck? Sure. You'd earned this position, and it was short-lived. Now, imagine that life alone. You have your family, but wouldn't you rather have someone there who loved you?"

I saw the picture Steph was painting, and it wasn't a pretty one. I didn't want to end up alone. But I wasn't even thirty yet. I could find someone else. But this was Patrick. I'd liked him longer than I could remember and wanted this so bad for so long.

Logically, I knew that I shouldn't let my work interfere with that. But the situation I was in was *not* logical. It was fucking stupid. An error I should be able to fix. An error that never should have even occurred.

"I see the wheels are working in there," Steph said. She nodded her head to the side, and we moved into the giant dressing rooms. "What are you thinking?"

"Maybe I should get a cat."

Steph laughed. "You are not becoming a crazy cat lady!"

I stuffed all the dresses into the first available dressing room and tried on the ugly pink dress first. When I stepped out, Steph covered her mouth, and her eyes widened.

"Wow," she said.

"If you make me wear this, I'll be heading straight to crazy cat lady. Definite spinster."

"You're twenty-seven!" she cried as I went to change. "You can't be a spinster yet."

"Actually, I think, historically, that would have made me a spinster for sure. I never would have found a man to impregnate me and force me to make him sandwiches and shit."

"You're so ridiculous!"

"Me?" I gasped, stepping out in another dress. "Look who's talking!"

"You want to be with Patrick. Why do you have to suffer for this?"

"Of course I want to be with Patrick. I also want twenty-five-hour days and a million dollars, but you don't get everything you want," I said, going back into the dressing room.

"Wait, but don't you already have a million dollars?"

I groaned as I tried to pull on some slinky gold sequined dress. "It's an expression!"

"It's a bad one."

"You're a bad one," I grumbled under my breath.

"Good one."

I stepped out of the dressing room, and Steph gasped.

"What? What now?"

She pointed at me and smiled from ear to ear. "That's the one."

"The what?"

"The dress, silly!"

I twirled in place and looked at the dress in the trifold mirror. Steph was right, of course. This was definitely the dress.

"Will the other bridesmaids look okay in it, too?" I asked.

"I, uh…didn't ask anyone else," she admitted.

"What do you mean? I thought there was going to be a dozen people in your wedding! Patrick said it was going to be a huge affair."

"It was. It totally was. But then we moved the date up to New Year's Eve, which didn't give us a ton of time to plan. I thought it would be easier for us both to have one person. More manageable."

My mouth fell open, and then I moved forward and pulled Steph into a hug. "Thank you so much. I'm honored, Steph."

"You know I love you. Even when you're being stupid."

"Well, thanks."

"And you are being stupid."

"What do you want me to do, Steph? I'm so fucking stressed about work. I have two days to fix this issue with the contract. I might lose my job. I probably shouldn't even be out with you right now. I can't handle a relationship. I can barely handle friendships. I feel like I know myself well enough to know that this isn't a good idea for me. I want to be with Patrick, but Patrick deserves someone who is...I don't know...sane?"

"Psh. Excuses. Patrick has never wanted a relationship before with anyone. This isn't an option of whether or not he should be with someone less crazy than you. Because crazy is totally Patrick's type. You're just a new brand of crazy. More sensible workaholic and less butcher-knife-wielding psychopath."

"Doesn't change how I feel."

"Oh, yeah? How would you feel if Patrick actually dated someone else? If he got serious and found a great girl and got married?" she shot back at me. "Could you stand at his wedding while he married someone else and tell yourself it was all better because you still had your job and worked a hundred hours a week? Could you wish him well and mean it?"

"No," I whispered, horrified at that thought.

"No," Steph agreed. "You couldn't. Right now, you live to work instead of the other way around. Who cares how much you work if you can't enjoy yourself when you're *not* working? How can you even be creative and productive without the downtime? You're happier and healthier with him."

The wheels in my head started turning. I'd never really thought about it like that. Of course, Steph would. She was a creative type. A musician who played three instruments, had strong soprano vocals, and wrote her own music. Business felt like a twenty-four/seven commitment. I never stopped to ask myself why I felt that way...and what I had been sacrificing for it.

I changed out of the dress we'd picked out and back into my work outfit.

"I'm just saying that you need to find a loophole or something," Steph said. "A way out of this box you've constructed around yourself. There has to be a third option. You can't live like this."

As I was sliding on my jacket, I froze in the dressing room. "What did you say?"

"You can't live like this, Morgan. You and Patrick are opposites, but somehow, you work together."

"No, no, not that," I said, grabbing my purse and darting out of the dressing room. "Before that."

"I don't know. You've boxed yourself in, and you need to find a loophole."

"Oh my God," I gasped.

"What?"

"I think I know what I need to do."

"About Patrick?" she asked in confusion.

"No. I have to go. Oh my God, I have work to do."

"Morgan!"

"Steph, I love you. Thank you so much for making me see more clearly. Maybe you're right, and I needed the time off to think about it. I can't wait to see you get married, but I have to go."

"What about the dress?"

"I'll pay you back!" I called as I ran for the exit.

"You owe me!"

"A million bucks!" I yelled back.

"That'd better not be an expression!"

Thirty-Two

Morgan

Today was the day.

Steph's comment at the bridal shop had triggered something and made me think in a totally different way about my problem. I had been coming at it from head-on, but I needed to go around the problem. Find the loophole. I could do that.

David stood next to me. He looked nervous. "Are you sure you're ready for this meeting?"

"Do I have a choice?"

"No. I suppose not. But you have to face the entire board."

"I'm ready," I told him.

"You're not going to tell me why you're ready?"

"Either way, the anticipation is over. I won't have to think about it anymore."

"I'm not sure I like this either-way business."

I glanced up at him. "I either convince them or I don't. That's all there is to it."

"Should I come in with you?"

"No, I'll be okay."

"You don't want anyone to have your back?"

"Jensen will be in there."

"All right," David said. "I believe in you. You're the best boss I've ever worked for."

I grinned at him. "I like to think of us as partners."

"That's exactly why you're the best."

"Keep your fingers crossed, all right?"

"I know you'll do great."

"Thanks," I told him before I walked out of the office and toward the conference room.

I knew the board was already set up in there. David was right. My fate would be decided today. I didn't want to be fired. But I felt confident, walking in there. There wasn't anything that they could throw at me that I wasn't prepared for.

I took a much-needed deep breath, and then I opened the conference room door. Everyone was already inside. But it wasn't an ambush this time. I knew what I was getting myself into. The board members who had been here earlier this week—Curt, Luke, Janice, and Jake—were in place along with Jensen, Tanner, and Bill, who had been absent at the first meeting. Unfortunately, my uncle Owen was in the room along with his sons, Jordan and Julian. For backup, I assumed. Pissed me off. I didn't get to have any backup in this fiasco.

But I put on a happy face, pushed my shoulders back, and strode into the room. I slapped my notebook down on the table and placed my hands on my hips.

I didn't wait for a greeting. I didn't pander to the stupidity of this meeting. I just got straight to the point.

"I didn't get the contract back," I announced.

Everyone shifted uncomfortably. I watched Owen's reaction and saw the smirk and self-satisfaction that I had been anticipating. He thought that he'd won. That he had this all in the bag.

I loved when people underestimated me. Then, I could put them in their place—crushed under my black stiletto heel.

"Morgan, I think we need to discuss—" Curt began.

I held up my hand to stop him. He bristled at the interruption. Zero fucks were given.

"But neither does Escoe Industrial," I informed them.

Owen sat up straighter. His beady little eyes widening in confusion.

Man, this is too good.

"No one has the contract. Our contract has elapsed with the university, and under state law, another contract must go to competitive bidding in the market place. The contract that Escoe apparently signed is not technically legal and will be thrown out. It took me several phone calls with administration as high up as I could go and a long, *long* day of legal reading to find the loophole that was somehow…missed."

"But you still don't have the contract," Janice said.

"Nope. And I think…that's okay. We'll have another shot at it in January when the university reopens. As of today, they're closed for business until after the holidays. Soon, we will be, too, and this matter will be resolved henceforth. One contract does not make or break this corporation. Would it be a loss? Of course. But I think it's preposterous to move to such extreme measures based on one contract that I still have in the works."

"I think that sounds fair," Curt spoke up.

"Thank you. You all voted me in as CEO of Wright Construction. You know that I have lived and breathed for this company. That I put in hours upon hours of work, and all I want is for it to succeed. You knew that when you voted unanimously to hire me. I don't think that this should change your mind about me. When I was ambushed by this meeting on Monday, I feared for my job. I understood where you were coming from, and I wanted to make it right. Today, I stand before you, and I've proven that I've made everything as right as possible. And, after all, what's Wright is right," I said with a broad grin as I quoted our motto.

"I'm in agreement," Luke said. "We gave her a week to fix this, a surprisingly short amount of time, and she did what she'd said she would. We didn't tell her she had to get the contract back. Just that she had to right this. I think we've acted hastily."

"I second that," Curt said. "Color me impressed, Miss Wright."

Janice shrugged. "I think we should still keep an eye on you, but termination doesn't seem to be in your future."

"Plus, it would cost a fortune," Tanner spoke up with a gruff laugh. "The severance package alone, not to mention buying out your salary. It might be worse than losing this contract."

"I think that was probably why we weren't called in for the meeting on Monday," Bill grumbled. "They didn't want a voice of reason. What do you think, Jensen?"

Jensen held his hands up. "I'm in agreement with the rest of the board."

"Morgan can do anything Jensen did," Tanner said. "Whoever said otherwise was a fool."

My eyes shifted to Owen, who looked flummoxed and speechless. Like a Scooby-Doo villain caught red-handed.

"Wonderful," I said, relishing in my victory.

Just then the door barged open, and Patrick stumbled into the conference room. "This isn't Morgan's fault!"

"Patrick, what are you doing?" I gasped.

"What is the meaning of this interruption?" Curt asked.

"I apologize for charging in like this, but there's some information that you must know about. Morgan isn't at fault behind the loss of the Tech contract. He is," Patrick said, pointing his finger at Owen.

"That's a bold accusation!" Owen said. He pushed his chair back and stood in anger.

"Morgan, who is this?" Janice asked. "And why is he here?"

"Patrick, you should just go," I whispered.

"This is Morgan's boyfriend," Owen professed. "They were having an illicit affair while he was still an employee at Wright Construction. Then, he moved into the department at Tech and convinced his boss to forfeit the Wright contract."

I laughed softly and shook my head. "Patrick and I were not together while he was still an employee. I would have never allowed that to happen. And why exactly would he convince his boss to give up that contract if we were together? Is that really the best that you can do?"

"An allegation like that is serious, Owen," Luke said. "Do you have proof that she was with an employee?"

"I...no. But I saw them together in her office."

"Not until he was already working at Tech," I corrected. "He has no proof of what he's saying because there is no proof."

"We're getting away from the real topic," Patrick said. "He wants you to get away from what I'm saying because Owen orchestrated this whole thing. He met with my boss, Bailey, who was doing the negotiating. He convinced her to give the contract to a competitor. He was doing the dirty dealings behind Morgan's back."

"Is this true, Owen?" Tanner asked.

"Of course it's not true!" Owen yelled, flustered.

"What would be his motivations for doing such a thing?" Curt jumped in.

"Because he wants to be CEO," Patrick said.

I nodded in agreement. Our eyes met, really met, for the first time. My heart skipped a beat. God, I had missed him. That crooked smile and those piercing baby-blue eyes and that subdued confidence. *Would it be wrong to mount him right here on the conference table?*

"He's been vying for my job," I agreed.

"That's ridiculous," Owen said.

"Actually," Jensen said, standing up and buttoning his suit coat, "it isn't so ridiculous."

"Of course you would stand up for your sister."

"This has nothing to do with Morgan. This has everything to do with you using the company email and Wright server to send incriminating emails back and forth with Bailey, discussing the very thing that Patrick is accusing you of doing."

"You can't go through my emails!" Owen blubbered. "That's illegal."

"Actually, it's not," Curt said, his eyes narrowed. "Company emails are for company purposes and can be checked anytime for compliance with company policies."

Owen sputtered. Both of his sons looked up at him and shook their heads. I could see them both mutter something under their breath and glance away, disgusted.

"Not to mention the fact that Bailey confessed to only doing it because you promised her a better deal when *you* were CEO in the New Year," Patrick added.

"She's not reliable. She just wanted to salvage her job. How could you believe her?" Owen asked.

"I think the emails are incriminating enough," Jensen said. He tossed a stack of papers into the center of the conference table. "You can read through them if you'd like."

"This all fits with his agenda," I continued. "He has been demeaning me, belittling me, and undermining me since the day he showed up here. His subversiveness and illegal actions give me no other choice." I stared my uncle squarely in the eye. "Owen, you're fired."

"What?" Owen cried. "You can't do that!"

"Actually, I can."

"Who the hell is going to run the Canadian branch of this fucking company?"

"I would be happy to," Jordan said, standing and squaring off with his father.

Owen looked at him as if he'd never seen his son before. As if he were looking at a traitor.

"And I'd be happy to step in under Jordan," Julian added.

"Julian," Owen said in shock.

"We thought you had changed," Jordan said. "We thought you had come here to right the wrongs of your past. To make amends with our family and bring us all back together. Instead, you were trying to tear their family apart as much as you tore ours apart."

"No wonder Mom left you," Julian punched him in the gut with.

Owen staggered back a step.

"We'll have to look at your applications, of course," I said to my cousins, "but I'd love to keep the corporation in the family."

Jordan walked a wide berth around his father and came to my side. He extended his hand, and we shook. "I'd be honored to work with you."

I smiled. Oh, yeah, I liked him a hell of a lot more than his dad already.

"Owen, you are banned from the premises. You should collect whatever things you have here and leave immediately," I said with all the authority of the CEO he wished to be.

"You can't do this, you little bitch!" he yelled as he aggressively approached me.

Patrick moved to stand in his way to stop him. He put his hand out and halted Owen in his tracks. Patrick was tall and strong and built from his hours in the gym. Owen looked like an overstuffed walrus next to him.

"Don't you ever disrespect her like that," he snarled. "Morgan has more class in her little pinkie than you have in your entire body. I would listen to what she says and get the hell out of here."

"Watch it, boy."

Everyone waited on baited breath to see what Owen would do. Patrick certainly wasn't about to back down. I took a step forward, praying it wouldn't come to blows.

"Just go," I told Owen. "There's no win for you here."

"Fuck, you sound just like your father, don't you?"

"I take that as a compliment."

"You would."

"I know that you hate my father because he sent you away to Canada, but I have no idea why you hate me so much. But, frankly, it's a little stale. You should find another shtick."

"You want to know why?" he asked, his eyes wild and manic. None of his manipulative sway held him in check. "Because I was in love with your mother from the day I met her, and your father always fucking won."

I startled back a step at his answer. "You hate me because my mom didn't love you?"

"That's why I hate him. You," he spat, jabbing his finger out at me, "you look like her, but you act just fucking like *him*. Evelyn in beauty and Ethan in brains. You are my nightmare."

"Wow," I said with a shake of my head. "That's so depressing. You are trapped in the past. You clearly deserve what you've gotten in life if you are so hung up on this that you can't even treat me like a human being because of something that happened more than thirty years ago. Get over it!"

"You'd never understand. I lost everything because of them. I even lost my wife!" He shook his head. "She left me the year Evelyn died. I was in mourning."

I swallowed at his confession and glanced at his boys. They looked pissed. And how could I blame them? They'd just found out that their mother had left him because he had been in love with another woman his entire life.

"This isn't love. It's obsession. And it's sick. You've ruined your life over something that could never be. And I

268

don't feel sorry for you. You could have had a wonderful life. You chose this instead," I told him. "Now, get out of my building. You're through with Wright Construction."

Thirty-Three

Morgan

Owen threw a few obscene words in my face before storming out of the conference room. And, just like that, it was over.

I breathed out heavily, deflating from the showdown I hadn't even anticipated having. I'd been ready for anything. I'd been prepared. But I hadn't known what Patrick and Jensen were going to bring into this meeting. I hadn't known what would come out of that. Or Owen's confession about my parents. Something I absolutely couldn't even process right now.

"Well, that was eventful," Jensen said, standing in the back of the room. "I'd say this meeting is over."

A round of grumbles came from around the table as everyone stirred from their shock at what had gone down. Each of the board members moseyed out of the room. Some gave me a sort of apologetic head tilt, others a grim smile, and at least one of them didn't even look my way.

It was only Curt who stopped and looked me in the eye. "Sorry about all this, Morgan."

"We got it cleared up and snuffed out the real culprit here."

"I wish I'd seen what Owen was up to from the start. We hired you for a reason. It was clear that my judgment was misplaced in this scenario. Accept my apology."

I nodded. "All right. Let's drop the oversight committee, and we'll call it even."

Curt laughed. "I think that sounds reasonable."

We shook hands, and then he departed. My cousins sidled up to me next. I hated the look of shock in their eyes. The realization that must have come over them at their father's statement.

"Are y'all going to be okay?" I asked Jordan and Julian.

They glanced at each other.

Jordan spoke, "I think it's time for us to get home, is all."

"We should probably talk to our mom. I think we might have been unfair to her all these years," Julian added.

Jordan sighed. "Yeah. It's not going to be pleasant."

"Well, you're both welcome back anytime. There's always a place for you here. It's kind of nice to have more family around."

They both smiled and promised to come visit again. I hoped they would. Now that I could disassociate them from Owen, I found I wanted to get to know them. I hoped it wasn't too little, too late.

Once Jordan and Julian disappeared, I turned to find Jensen leaning against the wall. I was about to open my mouth to say something when the door burst back open, and the rest of my family walked in.

"What are you all doing here?" I asked with a laugh.

Austin nudged me as he walked in. "Had to come see your big day."

"What he means is, he wanted to know if you'd gotten fired," Landon said.

"Y'all are jerks," Sutton grumbled, flopping into a seat.

"Yeah, listen to Sutton," I muttered.

I turned to my sister. She still didn't quite look like herself. Dressed in black instead of her signature pink, but her nails were done, and her hair had seen a curling iron recently, the ombré locks waving past her shoulders.

"Where's Jason?"

"I got a nanny," she admitted.

"That's great!"

"It feels ridiculous because I'm not working, but I needed to get out of the house."

"Well, if you need a job, we just fired someone," I volunteered with a laugh.

Sutton shot me an incredulous look. "Pass."

I felt more lighthearted in that moment than I had in weeks. Maybe months! *Had I really been carrying all of this stress on my shoulders for that long? Had I completely forgotten what it was like not to be stressed?*

"So, you kicked ass?" Austin asked.

"She did," Jensen agreed.

"I did," I said with a laugh. "Though Jensen and Patrick certainly helped with kicking Owen's butt out of Lubbock."

"We did what we could," Jensen said.

"Thanks," I said. "Now, hold that thought…"

Then, I turned around and found Patrick standing in the same spot where he'd stood to defend me against Owen. He hadn't said a word. Just stoically stood there as I'd dealt with all my problems. A half-smile appeared on his face, unassuming and beautiful.

"You," I said, pointing at him.

"Yeah?"

I ignored the rest of my family standing behind me, walked right up to Patrick, stood on my tiptoes, and pressed my lips against his. My hands moved to his chest, gripping his button-up. He hesitated for a split second, as if he couldn't believe we were doing this right here, right now, in front of my entire family.

Then, he relaxed, wrapping his arms tight around my waist and dragging me closer. Everything around me quieted down to that moment. I couldn't hear the catcalls behind me. Only my own heartbeat ringing in my ears. The feel of his heat pressing into my body. The taste of him on my lips.

I'd been an idiot, blaming Patrick for everything that had happened and pushing him away when I was distressed. It hadn't been fair. It wasn't even what I'd wanted. There was no reason that I couldn't work and have a love life. Jensen did it. Millions of other people had done it before me. Patrick had tried to tell me that, but I'd been too stuck in my own head to see it. Too worried about my job and not seeing clearly.

This right here was what I needed. Patrick Young's lips against my own and his body against mine and all the cares in the world dropping away.

Slowly, as if in a dream, Patrick pulled back, and I broke to the surface of the water I'd been under. His baby-blue eyes were lit up, and a cocky smile touched his lips.

"So, I guess we're back together, huh?" he asked.

"What gives you that idea?" I teased.

"Pretty sure you just made out with my face."

"I mean, if you beg, then maybe I'll consider."

"You're a hellion."

I winked. "And don't ever forget it."

Austin grumbled noisily behind us. "Is this ever going to stop? I'm getting sick to my stomach."

"Oh, give it up," Sutton muttered.

"We don't want to watch this," Austin protested.

"It's just a kiss," I told him, leaning back into Patrick's arms. "I've seen you do worse with Julia in public."

"Julia and I are totally innocent," he said with a devious look in his eye. "We're both virgins, you know? Saving ourselves for marriage and all that."

"Does anal count as losing your virginity?" Landon asked from the back of the room.

Everyone burst out laughing, and Austin just shook his head. "Dude, not cool."

"Children," Jensen said playfully.

"What did you think of Owen's confession?" I asked Jensen.

He shrugged. "I don't know what to make of it."

"What did he say?" Landon asked.

I repeated Owen's sordid story. It was particularly embarrassing for me to think that the whole reason he hated me was because I looked like his lost love. But, of course, I'd gotten my father's temperament. Minus the alcoholism, thankfully. Though the rash temper had obviously come my way. I'd lashed out at Patrick with hardly any provocation. I'd need to be mindful of that in the future. As mindful as Austin was about drinking.

"Whoa," Austin said when I finished.

"That's fucked up," Landon added.

Sutton bit her lip and looked away. It didn't help mentioning that he'd ended up divorced because he had been mourning his brother's wife. Mourning and death were not great topics around Sutton at the moment.

"I think the entire exchange was just sad," Jensen finally concluded. "Obviously, our parents weren't here to confirm or deny any of his claims. All we have is his very jaded word. What I do want to say about it is, I'm sorry."

"Sorry?" I asked. "Why?"

"You told me over and over again that Owen was treating you like shit, and I told you to deal with it. That it was just business. What I should have done is listen to you. I didn't know that he had ulterior motives. I thought he was treating you how he'd treated me when I became CEO. Pretty much like a dick."

"Well, it's okay. He had everyone under his spell. No one knew what he was doing."

"And here I thought, I looked like Mom," Sutton said sarcastically.

"Mom would never have gone blonde."

"Hey!" Sutton said, fingering her hair. "It's balayage."

"Fancy word for blonde."

"You're keeping your job. You're supposed to be happier than this and nicer to me."

I laughed. "You're right. I think I'm going to take the rest of the day off."

"What?" all of the guys said in shock at the same time.

"Yeah. I've earned it."

"I think that's a great idea," Patrick said next to me.

"Thanks. Don't you have work?"

"Well, I got the rest of the day off, too."

"Great. Let's get out of here."

"Yeah?"

I nodded, offering him my hand. He entwined our fingers together. I smiled at my family as I walked out of the conference room without them. I appreciated them being there and how much they cared for me in my moment of need. I knew that I couldn't live without them and was really lucky to have them.

But I had also fucked up something really great with a man who had never wavered in his feelings for me from the moment he made them known. While I was the one over here, who had claimed to have wanted him forever. Now, I needed to show him exactly what he had taught me was true. I could have it all.

Thirty-Four

Patrick

"I can't believe you're here," I told Morgan against her lips.

"Believe it," she said with the confidence I'd missed.

I reached up and tugged her long hair loose from its hold, so it could tumble down her back.

"I was never going to give up on you."

"I shouldn't have given up on us," she said, chewing on her bottom lip. "I didn't know what I was doing."

"It's okay," I reassured her. "We're here now."

"It's not okay. I'm sorry."

I silenced her protest with another kiss. I didn't need to hear her apologies. I'd seen them firsthand when she confronted her uncle head-on. I'd seen them when our eyes met across the room. When her uncle stormed her and I intervened.

With Morgan, I never needed many words. I'd seen in a glance that she was sorry and so happy to see me in that conference room, knowing that she didn't have to face that all alone…even though she clearly had.

That look was something I knew didn't come easy to Morgan. She wasn't one to ask for help. She never would have let someone else take the brunt of that meeting. She was the leader. She had been the one in trouble. She'd had to carry the weight. But knowing she had accepted my help, albeit without prior knowledge to what Jensen and I had planned, was apology enough.

"You're taking this all really well," she said with a shaky laugh.

"I've known you your entire life. You had to do this on your own. As much as I hated the idea of you pushing us to the side for work, I knew you had to do it for your own sanity."

"Yeah," she said, "but I hate that it hurt you. I don't want to push you away for work. There will be times when work has to come first. That's the nature of my job. But I was in over my head when I said I needed to be married to my work. I don't want to work and forget to live anymore."

"And you don't have to."

"When I was with Steph, looking at bridesmaid dresses—" she began.

"When do I get to see that?"

"At the wedding!" She shook her head at me, and I cracked a smile. "It was when I was with Steph that I was able to think clearly about the problem and find the solution. It was my downtime when my brain was able to function properly. I think that's kind of what you've been saying all along. If I work all the time, I never have any time to rest and relax. I never have *you* time. And, when I have that…I'm better and more productive for it."

"Sure, that sounds good. Also, I selfishly want you with me more."

She giggled my favorite giggle.

"God…that's my favorite laugh."

She paused and stared up at me in confusion. "I have multiple kinds of laughs that you like?"

"So many," I confirmed, pressing a kiss to her lips as I led her back to the bedroom. "You have this giggle when you're flirty or drunk and a real boisterous laugh when something really gets you. There's your sneaky laugh when you're being cheeky and a snort laugh when you're being sarcastic or don't believe the idiocy of some people. I've also learned that you have this little breathy laugh." I reached out and ran a finger across her lips. "That one is reserved for this."

I dragged her close again. Her breath hitched, and her pupils dilated as my hands ran down her body. I teased her bottom lip with my tongue. She whimpered and tried to push her way into a kiss. I grinned devilishly and then gave in to her request.

Our lips touched. A feverish frenzy that transcended coherent thought and collided right into uninhibited need.

She jumped into my arms, and we both fell onto the bed, struggling to get out of our work clothes in our haste to be together again. I ignored the buttons on her shirt and ripped it open. She laughed at my impatience and stripped out of her bra while I pulled my shirt over my head.

Her body was a road map, and I wanted to trace every route. I wanted to learn every way to bring her pleasure. And revel in the moment as we came together.

A part of me had feared that maybe things wouldn't work out. That maybe Morgan wouldn't come to her senses. Even worse, I wondered what would happen if she did lose her job. But, even in the darkest moments, I'd known that she was what I wanted. Maybe I didn't deserve her. Maybe she was *way* out of my league. But she was mine.

I threw her pants in a heap on the floor and slowly dragged her thong down her milky legs. Her eyes were heated on mine.

She hooked her finger at me. "Come here."

I slipped out of my boxers and covered her body. "You know you're all that I want," I whispered as I stared deep into her dark eyes.

"I've wanted to hear that for so long," she confided. "Actually having you is overwhelming."

"In a good way?" I asked as I slid my cock against her opening but going no further.

"Ye-yes," she gasped. She closed her eyes and shivered at the touch. That amazing breathy laugh escaped her lips.

"Ah, there it is," I said.

"I guess I do have that laugh."

"Oh, it's one of my favorites."

I moved back and forth through her slicked skin, wanting nothing more than to take her right here, right now. But seeing her ache for me, seeing the tender affection in her face, and the need for my body only made my dick harder.

Morgan had claimed me back in that conference room. Not like before when we'd been caught, and we'd both had to defend our choices. This time, it had been perfect. Her entire family there, she'd kissed me, chosen me, left with me. No more hiding—not our relationship, not my intentions, not our affection.

That time had long passed. I had been accepted into her world. It might be a world that I'd always occupied, but this was a different plane of existence altogether. This was Morgan as my girlfriend, as my lover, as my forever.

"You know what's my favorite?" she asked, gripping my hips.

"Hmm?"

"Your cock inside me."

My cock jerked in response. "Fuck, Mor."

She laughed. "I still like that nickname the best. The way it rolls off your tongue."

"You can't be Mini Wright anymore?" I teased.

"I just said I want your cock inside me. I don't think there's much mini about me."

"You're still pretty small. Maybe you can't handle it."

I pressed just the tip of my dick in her pussy. She moaned, and it took everything in me not to thrust inside her.

"I can handle anything," she ground out.

I pushed her hair out of her face and brought my lips down to meet hers. She hungrily met me, pushing every stray emotion into that kiss. I knew it was a promise. The first of many to come. Whatever had come before us was in our past. Our future lay ahead, and in this kiss, these lips, I knew that nothing and no one would ever compare to this incredible woman.

She rolled me over so that she was on top of me. Her pert tits hung in my face as she pushed down onto my cock. I moaned and then wrapped my arms around her. She bucked her hips forward and back experimentally. Then, I brought my lips to hers, and we moved together as one. Her body was supple on top of me. Her eyes locked on mine. Everything about us was aligned.

It was in that moment that I knew. With my whole heart, I knew.

I loved this woman.

I'd told Austin that was how I felt at the Christmas party. I'd said the words to her at the ribbon-cutting when she threw the words at me like a curse. I'd meant it both times, but it was different here. There was no anger. There was only acceptance. Only rightness.

The old Patrick was no more. I'd been replaced by the sap who currently took up residence in my body. And, crazy enough, I didn't even care.

How could I care when I had a woman like this?

She gasped and spread her legs wider. I could feel her about to come, so I sat up, gripped her hips in my hands, and slammed her up and down on my cock. She cried out, throwing her head back, as my ministrations took her over the edge. And, as she clenched her pussy tight around me, I seized up, releasing with her.

"Fuck," I grunted as I collapsed backward.

"Yeah," she murmured. Her eyes lidded, lips in a satisfied smirk, and face a mask of contentment.

After a moment to come down, I slid out of her and went to clean up. When I came back out, I leaned in to give her a kiss and found that she'd already fallen asleep. I laughed softly so as not to disturb her and pulled the covers around her body. She must have been really exhausted if she'd passed out that quickly. If I knew her at all, she probably hadn't slept a wink all week while she was dealing with this catastrophe. I had clearly wiped her out.

I curled myself around her naked body and pressed a kiss to her forehead. I fell asleep right there, next to her, stroking her hair and wondering how I had gotten so lucky.

I awoke before Morgan. It was already dark outside. Since it was the middle of winter, it got dark really early, but still, we'd slept through much of the day. My body must have needed it as much as hers did. And I wouldn't ever complain about having her naked figure that close to mine. I'd thought about waking her up with my dick between her legs, but I knew she needed the sleep. We'd have the entire night once she was well rested. I'd be sure to knock her out all over again.

Carefully, I eased out of bed, pulled on a pair of sweats and my Tech sweatshirt, and headed for the kitchen. We'd skipped lunch, and I couldn't even remember if I'd eaten breakfast. My stomach rumbled. I grabbed a banana to tide me over and got to work.

About a half hour later, a delirious Morgan walked out of my bedroom in an oversize T-shirt and pants that she'd left from when she was spending the night on the regular.

"Morning, sleepyhead," I said with a grin.

"What is that smell?"

I laughed. "I hope that's a good smell."

"I just realized I'm starving."

"Did you eat at all today?"

She shook her head. "I was too nervous."

"Well, everything will be ready soon. I was going to wake you up."

She stepped into the kitchen, still trying to adjust her eyes to the light. Then, she saw what was on the counter and laughed. "Are those mashed potatoes?"

I smirked at her. "Yeah. I know they're an aphrodisiac."

"Yeah, baby, mashed potatoes turn me on."

"Obviously, I know this."

"At least you've already fucked me this time, and I don't have to throw myself at you like a total embarrassment."

"To be fair, I thought I was protecting your honor."

"Never protect my honor again, okay?" she said.

She reached up on her tiptoes and kissed my cheek. I turned into her at the last minute and snagged one on my lips.

"Can't promise that. But I'll be sure to take full advantage of you from now on."

She giggled and knocked her hip against mine. "You know...I am sorry about the things I said."

"It's fine, Mor."

"No, you know what? It's not. Brushing it under the rug isn't the right solution. I know because I was trying to do that with us. And I don't *want* to do that with us. I want us to be able to communicate. On some level, Owen was right."

"About what?" I barked out in surprise.

"I am like my dad," she half-whispered. Then, she straightened her shoulders and took the good with the bad. "I'm sarcastic and a workaholic, and I have a temper. I have no idea how my mom dealt with him. And I don't want to be that for you."

"Morgan," I said, putting down the spoon I'd been stirring the pasta with and taking her by the shoulders, "I like you just the way you are. I already know those things about you. But the things you're missing are that you're strong and passionate and compassionate and determined and beautiful and loyal. So what if you are like your dad? He might not have been the best person, but it still sounds like a compliment to me. You can't take the ramblings of a deranged man stuck in the past and apply them to your life. You are your own person. You are Morgan Wright. Owen never wanted to get to know that person. He never wanted to see past the past. He can't possibly have an opinion on who you are, and you shouldn't even consider it."

"I know," she said, agreeing easily. "I'm not taking the shit he spewed at me to heart. I want you to know that I'm not perfect. I'm still just me. But I'm going to try harder and be better for you. You deserve more than me screaming at you in a parking lot."

"Well, I should have told you about Bailey. I was so worried about disrupting your already busy life that I didn't want to interfere. Maybe if I'd communicated with you better, none of this would have ever happened."

"Ugh, we don't know that," she said, reaching for the mashed potatoes.

I swatted at her hand, and she laughed.

"Not until dinner."

"You're killing me. I'm so hungry."

"Listen to me," I said, drawing her attention again. "We're a work in progress. Neither of us is perfect, and we don't have to be. As long as we're together, I don't care."

"You mean it?" she asked.

I nodded and dropped another kiss on her lips. "I'm yours, Morgan."

"I like the sound of that."

"And you're mine?"

"Of course," she said with a mischievous grin. "Now, can I have the mashed potatoes?"

I couldn't help my laugh as I passed her the entire bowl with a giant spoon. She winked at me and dug in.

I was going to spend the rest of my life with this woman. And I was damn happy about that.

Epilogue

Morgan

I stared up at the twinkling lights from the banquet hall at the Overton where Steph and Thomas had just said their vows. Patrick pulled me closer as we danced in the center of the room to a song that Steph had written. It was special. She'd written the wedding song just for Thomas. I already loved it.

And this place and the vibe and everything about it.

The wedding had been perfect. Me in my gold sequined dress, and Patrick in a tuxedo that I wanted to rip off him. Steph and Thomas had written their own vows, and a friend had played piano. Now, we were all happily getting drunk on the kegs they'd procured from a local microbrewery in town and waiting for the clock to strike midnight.

The room was full of local friends and family. Only a few people had come in from out of town on Thomas's side.

Patrick and I were in the midst of my family as they all tried to cajole me out onto the dance floor for Steph's bouquet toss. There were plenty of eligible young women, and I didn't particularly want to go. But Patrick all but shoved me, and after dragging Julia out beside me, I ended up on the dance floor with a huge group of girls.

Steph glanced over her shoulder and pointed her finger right at me.

I shook my head. "You'd better not."

She winked at me before turning back around.

The bitch. She'd better not.

"Oh, she is so aiming for you," Julia said next to me.

"Ugh!" I groaned.

Julia just laughed.

There were a million other girls who wanted that bouquet. Just because I was her only bridesmaid didn't mean that I wanted what that bouquet of flowers meant.

Still, I felt the energy all around me. I couldn't help but get swept up in it. The excitement was contagious. Even Julia raised her arms over her head and cried out with all of us. It was tradition. Us cynics couldn't even escape it.

Then, came the toss.

Steph threw the bouquet over her head. I watched it happen in slow motion. The perfect arc. The flowers in their arrangement tumbling in circles. The scream as all the girls extended their hands in earnest. And then the catch.

My mouth gaped open as Julia came down with the flowers.

"Oh my God!" I screamed.

"Oh my God!" she screamed back.

"You caught it!"

"I didn't mean to!" she yelled and then threw it to me.

I tossed it back like we were playing a round of hot potato. "You can't give that to me."

"Well, I don't want it."

She handed it back to me, and I pushed it away.

I couldn't stop myself. I burst into laughter. Here we were, arguing over who got the bouquet from the toss but in reverse. Every other girl was eyeing us like we had totally lost our minds as we both tried to get rid of the damn thing.

"You caught it, fair and square," I told her with a merciless laugh.

"I am never going to hear the end of this from Austin."

"Don't look now, but I think he's gone pale."

"Why couldn't you have just caught it?" she grumbled.

I laughed again and then pulled her into a hug. Steph ran over then and hugged us both.

"Ah...I'm so happy for you," she said. "Someone finally needs to lock down Austin."

"That's me," Julia droned. "Locking him down."

Steph kissed my cheek. "I was silently hoping it was you."

"Uh, not so subtle there, Steph."

"What can I say? I want you as a sister!"

"Let's think about that a little bit further down the road. We only just got back together."

"Eh...I don't care about that. Let me be the hopeless romantic."

"Since it's your wedding, then sure."

Steph hugged me again before being carted off to talk to more family, and I returned to my own family. Julia and Austin were talking animatedly. I could see that she was giving him a hard time and making him paler and paler. It was pretty hilarious, knowing that Julia hadn't even wanted the damn thing.

It was nice to see my whole family together like this. Jensen and Emery relaxed and happy. Heidi forcing Landon to dance to the upbeat tempos the DJ was playing. Sutton had left Jason with Emery's sister for the evening, so she could be in attendance. She and David had spent most of the night together, but when I'd asked her, she had insisted that he wasn't her date.

As the night wore on, Patrick extracted me from the rest of my family while the slow music drifted through the speakers. Finally, I could melt into Patrick's arms and forget the rest of the world. His hands on my waist. His eyes admiring me. His smile lighting up the room.

"When I agreed to be in Steph's wedding, I never imagined this would happen," I told him.

"Did you actually agree? Or did she force you to be in it?"

"Probably both."

"Well, wouldn't you rather that it turned out this way?"

I shrugged and tried to hide my teasing smile. "Eh."

"Liar."

"You already know that I want you and only you. I have since I was fifteen years old in a dumb high school cheerleading outfit, and I do now that I'm CEO. You're still the one that I want."

"I just like to hear you say it," he said, brushing his nose against mine.

"Well, it's the truth."

"You know something?"

I shook my head, dizzy with happiness. "What?"

"I love you."

"You told me that once." I smiled brilliantly up at him.

He laughed. "I did, but it was in desperation. I should have told you again."

"I think this is perfect."

"Also, I told Austin before I told you."

My eyebrows rose. "You told Austin that you loved him? Well, this explains everything."

He rolled his eyes at me. "I told him that I loved you. The night of the Christmas party, he asked me if I loved you, and I told him yes. I think it's why he calmed down."

"How did you know?"

"It was that feeling, like I couldn't live without you. I was afraid when everyone found out, but I also knew I had to step up. That I couldn't lose you."

I ducked my head under his chin and held him close. "You know something?"

He shook his head and squeezed me tighter.

"I love you, too."

"I know."

I laughed. "What are you? Han Solo?"

"Well, I do know. You screamed it at me once."

"I'm probably going to scream it a lot more," I said, pulling back to wink at him.

He snorted and twirled me further away from the crowd. We were only minutes from midnight. This was the most perfect New Year's Eve. I'd always dreamed that, one day, I would get my midnight kiss from Patrick, and this year, it would be a reality.

Steph and Thomas danced in the center of the room, looking radiant and unbelievably happy.

"One day, that's going to be us," Patrick said.

"Dancing? We're dancing right now."

"Walking down the aisle."

"Probably," I agreed. "Like at Jensen and Emery's wedding."

He groaned against me. "You're so difficult."

"You should probably get used to it."

"First, you steal all the mashed potatoes and sometimes all the covers, and now—"

"Wait, wait, wait," I said, holding a finger up. "I do not steal the covers. I wake up every morning naked."

He smirked. "Well…yeah!"

I rolled my eyes. "You're such a dude."

"You should probably get used to that."

"Throwing my own words back at me."

"What I was trying to say before I was rudely interrupted," he said.

"I'll show you rudely interrupted," I muttered under my breath.

"Is that you're being purposefully difficult when I'm trying to have a serious conversation with you."

I fluttered my eyelashes up at him. "What were you being serious about?"

"I want you to know that I'm not going anywhere. That this is real. That we're real."

"I can't wait to spend the rest of my life with you."

He grinned and tugged me closer as the crowd started counting down to midnight. I could hear their calls all around us as Patrick's gaze stayed locked on mine.

"I'm going to love you from now until forever, Morgan. I already know that one day you'll walk down that aisle toward me," he told me, his eyes shining. "I am yours, and you are mine. All the good and all the bad. From this day forward."

"I love you." My throat was tight, and tears pricked at my eyes at his words.

"I love you, too."

"Happy New Year!" the crowd cheered all around us.

Gold balloons dropped from the ceiling, and glitter was thrown in the air. We were caught up in champagne toasts and the ball drop and people jumping up and down all around us.

Then, Patrick held my jaw in his hands and pressed his lips to mine. All else slipped away, and there was just us. Sealing our promise with a kiss and toasting to a brand-new year, a brand-new us.

The End

Acknowledgments

The *Wright Secret* was a labor of love. I invested so much of myself into Morgan. My own fears and joys and reluctance about being a CEO of my own business, albeit much smaller than Wright Construction.

Thank you to all the readers who picked it up and enjoyed it. The ones who saw themselves in Morgan Wright and all her highs and lows and doubts and triumphs. I would really love if you were able to leave a review of the book on the retailer you purchased it from. I always love to hear the thoughts of my readers! Thank you for coming along for the ride.

To everyone who made this book a reality—

Diana Peterfreund and Mari Mancusi, who helped me plot this book at Disney World. You two are the best plotting buddies ever, and I'm already looking forward to our next retreat. And thank you for the original, insane idea that didn't make it into the book—for Morgan to have an evil uncle who is actually her dad. Dum, dum, dummmm. Ha! You have to start somewhere in plotting, I suppose!

Thank you for dealing with me while I wrote it. Staci Hart, who endured hours and hours of voice conversations on Facebook messenger as we stabbed the book until it became a reality. Rachel Brookes, who cheered me on every night. Rebecca Kimmerling, who knew I had it in me to write a nuanced, powerful heroine and helped me get there. Anjee Sapp, who challenged me to be better every day and believed that I could get there. Katie Miller, Polly Matthews, and Lori Francis who read this book in various stages of development and helped me see where I was going wrong. Thank you for all you do. I know it cannot be easy to deal with me writing at all hours of the night, constantly sending chapters, and being needy with feedback. You all rock my world. The best team I could ever ask for!

All the usual suspects—

Danielle Sanchez, my epic publicist who saw a vision for this series and made it a reality. I love how much you love these books. You bring them to life. Kimberly Brower, my incredible agent who sold the audio rights to this book before I even started writing it. Sarah Hansen, for the beautiful cover design. You truly are an artist. Sara Eirew, for the stunning cover image that actually brought Morgan and Patrick to life. I love that she's on top, if you know what I mean. Jovana Shirley, for her wonderful editing and formatting skills. Thank you for putting all the pieces together. Michelle New, for making it so much easier to find stunning graphic images that reflect my vision of Morgan. Alyssa Garcia, for designing said graphics and making me flail when I get a notification from you. You're the best.

Save the best for last—

> My wonderful husband, Joel. Thank you for all
> the late-night walks and plotting sessions to help
> me work out the kinks. You're my houseboat.
> Couldn't do it without you. Or the Hippo &
> Goose snuggling while I try to write at night!

About the Author

K.A. Linde is the *USA Today* bestselling author of the Avoiding Series and more than twenty other novels. She grew up as a military brat and attended the University of Georgia where she obtained a Master's in political science. She works full-time as an author and loves Disney movies, binge-watching *Supernatural*, and *Star Wars*.

She currently lives in Lubbock, Texas, with her husband and two super-adorable puppies.

Visit her online at www.kalinde.com and on Facebook, Twitter, and Instagram @authorkalinde.

Join her newsletter at www.kalinde.com/subscribe for exclusive content, free books, and giveaways every month.

CPSIA information can be obtained
at www.ICGtesting.com
Printed in the USA
FSOW01n2231010218
44095FS